CHANGING THE SPEED OF LIGHT BULBS

BOOK 4

TALES OF A FORMER SPACE JANITOR

JULIA HUNI

Cover designed by German Creative
Editing by Paula Lester at Polaris Editing

Julia Huni
Visit my website at juliahuni.com

IPH Media

For my son Douglas
Who came up with the title

ONE

Honeymoon plans shouldn't include space cruise tickets for a party of five. Unless that's your thing.

It's not mine.

Honeymoon plans should definitely not include your mother.

Unless you're me, Triana Moore, aka Annabelle Morgan, daughter of the chair of the SK'Corp board of directors. Then you get all those things.

After our fairytale wedding, and our less than fairytale "corporate reception," my new husband and I spent a night in the guest suite on Level 82 of Station Kelly-Kornienko. The reception had been a glittering affair at my mother's estate on Kaku, with guests from all the wealthiest families and companies in the galaxy.

But like most corporate affairs, it was stiff, boring, and repetitive. Using our cruise departure as an excuse, we escaped upstairs to the station before the evening dwindled to its sad close. We got to SK2 and scheduled a late morning alarm, so we'd have time for a leisurely departure.

But here's the thing—the guest suite is controlled by my mother, the Ice Dame. And she thinks sleeping in is a crime against nature.

So when the doorbell rings at seven, I'm not really surprised. I roll over groggily and flick my holo-ring sitting in the charger beside my bed. The message says breakfast is being delivered.

Making sure the door between the living room and our bedroom is closed and locked, I wave a hand through the "accept" icon and drop back to the bed, closing my eyes with a soft groan.

"Good morning, Sera O'Neill."

I open one sleepy eye. The lights in the room have risen to a faint glow, and Tiberius O'Neill y Mendoza bin Tariq e Reynolds, my shiny new husband, smiles lazily from the far side of the massive bed. At least I assume the glint of white is a grin. It's too dark to see properly.

"It's seven in the morning—there's nothing good about that." I reach out a hand, and my fingertips barely brush his arm. "And what are you doing all the way over there?"

WHEN MY ALARM goes off at a much more civilized hour, I'm alone. The glow of light through the translucent bathroom door tells me Ty is showering.

I slide my holo-ring onto my finger and check the living room. It's empty except for the very expensive stasis server that's keeping our breakfast warm. I wonder again why my mother bothered sending us food—we could have gotten whatever we want from the AutoKich'n.

But that wouldn't allow her to intrude. I'm sure she'll frame it as a sweet gesture from a caring mother, but in my opinion, it's all about showing control.

Ugh. I really don't want to be thinking about my mother on my honeymoon. I roll out of bed and head for the bathroom.

When we finally get to breakfast, it's still warm, of course. I open the stasis server, and a steamy cloud redolent of coffee, maple, sugar, and spice wafts out. The selection includes eggs, waffles, biscuits and gravy, sliced fruit, several different pastries, and a couple of dishes I don't recognize. A handwritten note from Dav, Mother's personal pastry chef, wishes us *bon appetit*.

Ty skewers a slice of fruit on his fork and raises it in salute. "Happy honeymoon, Sera O'Neill."

I clink my fork against his and stab it into a dark cake-like cube. Lifting it to my nose, I take a good sniff. Spicy, not chocolate. Still, anything Dav makes is going to be delicious. "Technically, we're Sera and Ser Morgan, now." My lips twist a little. I'd prefer to be Triana O'Neill Moore.

Or would that be Moore O'Neill? I never can get those concatenations right.

He shrugs and scoops eggs onto his plate. "It doesn't matter to me as long as we're together."

I raise my glass to him and sip.

WE ARRIVE at the gate half an hour before our timeslot. Although with a first-class ticket, they'll let us board at any time. Heck, since my mother set up the tickets—or rather, her personal assistant Hy-Mi set them up for her—they'd probably send a shuttle to let us embark after the ship departed. Or before it arrived.

Being a top-lev comes with some ridiculous perks.

A familiar redhead stands beside the door to the first-class lounge as we approach.

"Morning, love-birds." Lindsay "Vanti" Fioravanti wears her signature fitted black clothing. I know from past experience that she has dozens of hidden pockets holding everything from tiny electronics to a twenty-kilo-tonne bazooka. That might be a slight exaggeration, but Vanti is crazy prepared for anything, while looking like she's out on a casual stroll around the ninja headquarters.

"What are you doing here?" I narrow my eyes at her. "I thought you didn't work for SK'Corp anymore."

"I don't, but believe it or not, they'll let anyone book a ticket on one of these ships." Her lips tip up at the corner—Vanti's version of a full smile.

O'Neill gives her a once over. "And you're on vacation? Doesn't look like it."

"No, I'm traveling for business. I have a new job."

"That was fast. Doesn't your non-compete clause keep you from working for any other corporation's security agency for five years?"

"That only applies to corporations over a certain size." Vanti waves a hand at the door to the lounge, and it slides open. "I'm here as personal security to a well-known celebrity." She throws that last bit over her shoulder as she strides into the room.

I take O'Neill's arm as he follows, slowing his charge. "What do you think she's up to?"

He stops dead, staring. "That."

We stand in a long, narrow room. One wall is plas-glas, offering a view of the long arm that stretches away from the station on Level 40. Ships hang from five of the eight berths—three interstellar cruisers, a smaller in-system cruiser, and a private long-distance yacht. The owner of that ship is undoubtedly wealthy but lacks the connections to score a private berth at the top of the station.

Inside, thick carpet covers the deck, with a series of plush seating areas facing the windows. Several are empty, and several others have privacy shields engaged, hiding the occupants from view. As we watch, a fawning waiter takes a selfie with a smartly dressed woman sitting on the closest couch. As he backs away, she catches sight of us. "Triana! Ty! Come join us."

"Elodie?" I do a double take, then jog across the room, dragging Ty with me.

Elodie Ortega Okilo, my former roommate's mother and now net celebrity Elodie-Oh, waves again. "Hi, guys! I didn't know you were leaving today, too! Which ship are you on?"

I look at Ty, lifting my shoulders. "I'm not sure. Hy-Mi made the arrangements. How about you?"

"We're on the *Solar Reveler*." She points out the window at the private yacht. "It's that cute little one on the side. Can you believe *CelebVid* is loaning it to me? I have a corporate sponsor!"

Beside her on the couch, an enormous purse wiggles, and a huge, black, furry head pokes out the top. Apawllo's wide, flat face bears a scar from right ear to jaw, and a chunk is missing from his left ear. His golden cat eyes narrow when they fall on me. He assesses me, finds my soul wanting, and sinks back into the bag.

A man approaches the seating area. "Technically, they aren't loaning it to you." Leonidas, also known as Ervin Zhang, the caretaker from my mother's estate on Kaku, bows to us. "Nice to see you, Sera and Ser Morgan."

"Leo? What are you doing here?" I drop onto the couch near Elodie, then move a few centimeters away from the bag when it shifts again.

Leo folds his long body into a chair beside the couch. "Elodie invited me to come along. Now that I don't have to hide from my father anymore, I thought I'd do a little traveling. Hy-Mi found a new caretaker, and here I am."

I glance over the back of the couch, where O'Neill and Vanti stand, apparently ignoring each other. I know from past experience they're probably talking via audio implant. I used to get a little jealous of their relationship, but it doesn't bother me anymore.

Much.

"What's she doing here?" I jut a thumb at Vanti.

Elodie leans in close, her eyes sparkling. "She's my security."

"You need security?"

Leo stretches his legs and tries to get comfortable. "You saw what it was like on Kaku. People swarm Elodie-Oh."

The waiter arrives, bearing a couple of glasses on a tray. "Here you are Elodie-Oh! Freshly squeezed pinoa fruit juice. And a glass of firograss juice for your friend." He barely glances at Leo as he hands off the tall, green beverage. "Is there anything else I can get for you? Snacks? A blanket?" He leans closer. "Would you like me to find these people a more suitable place?" The glare he gives me on "these people" is as soul-searing as Apawllo's.

"Don't be silly, Fontaine, these are my friends." Elodie sips her drink. "And this is delicious."

"I'd like—" I start to ask for water, but Fontaine clearly isn't listening. He's getting another selfie with Elodie-Oh. Then he asks Leo to take a better picture of the two of them in front of the window.

My jaw drops. He's ignoring the Morgan heir in favor of a net celebrity? I feel like I've arrived in an alternate universe. And I'm a little embarrassed at how offended I feel. I mean, I used to crave anonymity. When did I start expecting deference and respect just because of my name?

The door swooshes open, and a woman wearing a pristine white suit strides into the room, stopping respectfully a few steps away from the couch. Her eyes light on Elodie and Fontaine by the window, but she tears her wistful gaze away and turns to me. "Sera Morgan? If you're ready, we can board you now."

Elodie waves from the window but doesn't make any effort to disengage from Fontaine's excited chatter. Leo gives me a hug, while Vanti exchanges fist bumps with O'Neill. Then my husband puts an arm around me, and we follow the white-clad woman.

"Excuse me." As we walk down the long, transparent tube to the ship, I raise my voice to get the woman's attention.

She slows her stride and turns to walk backward. "Yes?"

"What ship are we taking?"

"You don't know what ship you're traveling on?"

Her judgmental gaze burns into me. Really, what is it with people today? First Apawllo, then Fontaine, now her. I need to channel my inner Ice Dame and put these people—and animal—in their place. I lift my chin. "My assistant booked the cruise. I didn't concern myself with the details." When her face goes pale, I feel bad, but not too bad.

She slows to walk beside me. "Yes, of course. I apologize for my tone, Sera. You're on the *Solar Reveler*."

TWO

ONCE SHE'S LOGGED us in to the ship's guest system and showed us how to access all of the facilities, the woman in white departs. She sidesteps the tip O'Neill tries to pass her and whisks herself out of the compartment before we can ask more than the basic questions.

The door closes behind her, and I turn to survey the room. This yacht might belong to a mid-sized corporation, but it's a top-of-the-line ship. Larger than the yacht my mother owns, it's decked out in high-end furnishings and all the bells and whistles.

Our suite includes a small but elegant living room, a large bedroom with a huge bed and a broad external window, and a luxurious bathroom. The furniture is comfortable and attractive—not an easy combination to find, and my shoes sink into the thick carpet covering the deck. The beautiful, simulated wood cabinets in the living room hide a full entertainment system, a state-of-the-art AutoKich'n with all but the latest food maps, and easy access to the emergency escape pod required on all interstellar ships.

I turn to O'Neill. "How'd we end up on the same ship with Vanti, Leo, and Elodie on our honeymoon? I can't believe Hy-Mi did this to us!"

He turns in a full circle, taking in all of the furnishings. Then he pulls up the ShipAp on his holo-ring and sets the room to Do Not Disturb.

"Who cares? We've got everything we need here. We don't have to see any of them until we debark at Station Aldrin."

A satisfied smile stretches across my face. "Have I told you lately how much I love you?"

"No, but you can show me."

WE HIT the jump belt a couple of days out of port, as scheduled. We haven't seen anyone since we left and have carefully neglected to check the messages piling up in the ship's internal comm system. It's our honeymoon, after all! But the automated jump announcement can't be filtered out.

"Attention guests of the *Solar Reveler*. We have reached the jump belt on schedule. We will commence jump to the Armstrong system ingress belt in fifteen minutes. Please secure your belongings and engage the jump protocol in your cabin."

I flick my holo-ring. "What's the jump protocol on a ship like this?"

O'Neill's arm drops from my shoulders, and he pulls back a little to give me a surprised look. "Haven't you traveled on one of these before? I would have thought your mother's…"

I shrug. "That was a long time ago, and I don't think we followed the protocol. You know how top-levs can be." I put on a snooty tone. "It's safe, why should I take extra precautions?" I slide a hand between the seat cushion and the back of the couch. "Are there straps in here?"

He pulls up the specs on his ring. "It says the only physical restraints are in the crew lounge. The cabin systems are all synthgrav based. Your choice."

Most top-levs don't want to bother with seatbelts. They'll rely on the safety systems built into the ship. And to be fair, jump technology has evolved to the point where there are rarely any issues. I've jumped many times in my life and never experienced anything unusual. But I'm a maintenance tech at heart, and I like to prepare for the worst-case scenario.

On the other hand, it's my honeymoon, and the last reported jump error was decades ago. A ship jumping to Sally Ride reported minor turbulence on the entry. "Let's risk it for once." I settle back into the seat cushions and relax against his side.

"As you wish."

We watch a little *Ancient TēVē* while the jump clock counts down. It's one of my favorite episodes, where the starship goes through a wormhole and ends up in an alternate reality. All of the crew members have "evil" counterparts—clearly identified by their facial hair or revealing clothing, depending on gender. We chuckle at the clichés.

When the jump clock hits ten seconds, I pause the show. We count the last few seconds aloud, as if we're at a party on New Year's Eve.

When we reach zero, nothing happens. They say jump feels different to everyone. I normally feel a wave washing through the ship, bow to stern. But this time, I feel nothing. "That was weird."

"Smoothest jump I've had in ages." O'Neill flicks the show back on.

I pause it again. "That's what I mean. I didn't feel *anything*. Did you? Maybe there was a malfunction."

"No—" He sits up a little straighter and scrubs a hand through his hair. "We definitely jumped."

"How do you know?"

He doesn't respond, but his hand clamps onto my forearm, and he gestures at the cabin.

I glance at him in concern, then gaze around the small room. It's as if a filter has been laid over my vision. I still see the elegant living room with its thick carpet and comfortable couches. But I also see bare, scarred deck, plastek furniture, and a blank wall between me and the massive external windows.

"What is going on?" I blink and rub my eyes. Nope, still the same. "You see it, too?"

He shifts away from me, standing in a smooth motion to face the door. "I see a second reality. As if we've jumped halfway into another place."

"Is that even possible?" I rise slowly, rubbing my eyes again. "It's like that show we just watched."

He shakes his head sharply, then pushes me behind him, so he stands between me and the door. A weapon has appeared in his hand, but it's different from his usual mini-blaster. I can't tell at a quick glance why it looks wrong, but it does.

"Vanti isn't answering my calls." He rubs behind his ear with his free hand. "I'm not getting any indication I'm connecting to anything. See what you get."

As I flick my holo-ring and initiate a call to Leo, the visual overlay starts to fade. The elegant cabin dissolves, leaving only the utilitarian compartment. My clothing has changed as well. My cozy pajama pants and tank top have disappeared, and I wear a coverall—much like the one I wore for years as a maintenance tech. This one is gray, rather than tan, and my name is stenciled on the left side of my chest: Morgan.

Leo's call icon disappears, and I'm left with a holo showing a blank screen. Not even a login screen. "I think we're all the way in."

"All the way in what?" O'Neill moves to the bedroom door, but it's gone. This room is much smaller, as if our original suite had been partitioned into several cabins.

"The alternate reality. The other universe. Whatever we jumped into—we're one hundred percent there now."

THREE

O'NEILL TAKES my wrist and slaps the mini-blaster into my palm. "Hold on to this. I've got another one." He pats the pockets of his coverall, which matches mine, then swears under his breath. "I *had* another one. In my alternate pants." He gives me a sickly grin.

"You had two weapons on you when you were locked in your cabin with your new wife on your honeymoon?" I hold the small gun out to him. "We are going to talk about your paranoia after we get out of this."

He takes the blaster and waves it at the room around us. "Is it paranoia if they're really out to get you?"

I have to give him that one. That level of preparation is more Vanti-level paranoia—well beyond O'Neill's usual state—but I think we're going to be grateful for his forethought.

The door chimes. It's a buzzer, not a soft, musical tinkle, but the sound registers in my mind as if I've heard it a thousand times before.

O'Neill clearly recognizes it, too. He pushes me behind him and slides the muzzle of his weapon into his pocket where it will be less visible to whoever enters. We wait, but nothing happens.

The door buzzes again.

"I think we have to answer it," I whisper.

"Why are you whispering?" He flicks his holo-ring but gets the same blank interface I had. "Unless the structure of the ship has changed substantially, they can't hear us. And if they've got listening devices in here, whispering won't help."

I move around him toward the door, but he pushes between me and the portal. I smack his arm. "I wasn't going to open it. I wanted to look for an access panel."

"I can do that. You stay back." He glares until I take the four steps to the far end of the cabin. As if two meters of space is going to protect me from whatever is on the other side of that door. But I guess I'm not in line of sight from here, so that's something.

The buzzer sounds again, this time longer and more insistent.

O'Neill finally locates a panel by the door. "It's Vanti."

"Wait!"

The door slides open.

From my vantage point against the internal bulkhead, I can't see anything beyond a thin sliver of harsh white light and the gray of the passageway. A low voice murmurs.

"Vanti?" O'Neill takes a step back, but she doesn't follow him into the room. Her voice takes on a surprised tone, but I can't hear what she says. Then a tray is shoved through the opening.

O'Neill grabs the plastek-wrapped thing in his free hand. "Status update."

There's no response, and the door slides shut.

O'Neill sets the tray on the counter. His eyes meet mine, wide and worried. "She didn't respond. It was like she didn't know me."

"Did she look normal?" I step closer and put a hand on his shoulder. He and Vanti have been friends since the academy—over ten years. How could she not recognize him?

"What do you mean?" He slides the blaster into his pocket.

"No low-cut clothing or a goatee?"

He frowns at my joke. "She was wearing a coverall like ours, with her last name—her full last name—on the chest. When I said 'Vanti,' she didn't react."

"She wouldn't, would she?"

"What do you mean?"

I pick up the tray and take it to the low table beside the hard shelf that has replaced our couch. No point in wasting good food, and I'm hungry.

At least I hope it's good food.

"You know how careful she is." I sit and press a finger against the seal on the tray's plastek cover. The top peels back, revealing bread, sliced meats and cheeses, and a small pot of some kind of condiment. I lift a spoonful of the stuff to my nose. Pungent, like mustard, but sweet, too.

I look up to find O'Neill frowning and rolling his hand in a "go on" motion.

I drop the spoon back into the glop. "Obviously, we aren't in Kansas anymore. She's not going to tip her hand and let a potential enemy know she's not sure what's going on. Vanti is going to do as much investigation as possible before letting anyone into her inner circle. Even her old friend, Griz. Don't you guys have a duress word? To verify it's the real you and not evil you?"

"I like how you assume the me in this reality is evil." A little smirk twitches across his face.

I shrug one shoulder and lean forward to pick up a slice of bread and some meat. "It's canon—the alternate universe is always evil. It's how these things work. Especially given the high fashion apparel we're wearing. This looks pretty dystopian." I flick a finger at my collar, then go back to making a sandwich.

"It looks a lot like what you wore when we met." He takes the sandwich I offer and sniffs it. "I was going to say I can't believe we've been dropped into an alternate reality and you're making lunch, but I know you better than that. Of course you'd make lunch. We should test it for drugs or poisons."

"How are we going to do that?" I wrinkle my nose at the mustardy stuff. "It smells okay to me. A weird note of cilantro, but otherwise fine."

"Cilantro? You didn't put any of that on my sandwich, did you?" He peels back the top layer of bread.

"I know you, too." I spread the goop onto another slice of bread and top off my own sandwich. "We've obviously been on this ship long enough to get to a jump belt—why would they suddenly decide to poison us?" Although if that was the real Vanti, who knows what she might do.

"Good point." He sniffs the sandwich one last time, then takes a bite. "It's not bad. A little dry."

"That's what the mustardy glop is for." I take a bite and chew. "Passable. Okay, you've obviously been developing a plan while I made lunch. What is it?"

He returns to the door and opens the panel beside it again. Setting his half-eaten sandwich on the counter, he fiddles with the controls. "This opens the door and accesses the ship's operating system—in a very limited capacity. We should be able to get some information about the ship. Might be a comm system here, too."

He taps through the interface as he munches his sandwich. "The ship's name is still the *Solar Reveler*." He shoots a mocking look over his shoulder. "No, not the *Evil Solar Reveler*. The ship seems to be the same make and model, but it's a cargo ship, not passenger. I don't have access to the cargo manifest. Crew roster is here—and we're on it. You're the captain. Vanti and I are listed under crew—no titles—along with Leo—but as Ervin Zhang. You aren't going to believe this—Elodie is the mechanic. There are also a couple names that I don't recognize."

I grab a piece of fruit and cross the room. "How did you activate it?"

He shrugs. "I opened the cover, and it was on. I think it's a standard cabin access."

"But if I'm the captain, I should be able to access more." I wipe my hand on my coverall and nudge him out of the way with my shoulder. "Let me see."

Inside the panel, a lit screen glows with a list of names and assignments. I wave my hand at it, but nothing happens.

"You have to touch it." O'Neill demonstrates, tapping the line that says Annabelle Morgan. The screen flickers, and my picture replaces the text, with my name below it. "See, nothing."

I touch the panel, and the screen changes. Welcome, Captain Morgan scrolls across the top.

I choke back a laugh. "Captain Morgan? That sounds like a drunk pirate."

"I think that's because it used to be a brand of alcohol—at least in our universe." O'Neill nods at the panel. "See what else you can learn, but don't change anything. We want to make sure we know what's going on before we do anything."

"Just like Vanti would say." I tap the screen again. My holo-ring lights up and asks if I'd like to connect to the ship's system. "Cool, I'm back online." I work my way through several screens of security protocols, answering each as I would back in our world. Apparently "Evil Triana" uses the same passphrases and gestures. "I'm in."

"Excellent. Can you get me in, too?" O'Neill finishes off his sandwich and opens the small bottle of water on the tray. He pours some into a glass and takes a gulp, then spews it across the room.

"What was it? Vodka?" I settle onto the uncomfortable couch again and position holo-screens around me.

He rolls his eyes. "No. It was water—really bad water." He sips again. "There's a strong metallic taste that can't be good for us."

I let my eyes rove over him for a second, appreciating his thick dark hair, handsome face, and excellent body. Although he seems less shiny than usual, somehow. "You seem to be healthy enough. Assuming this is your regular body in this reality."

"You think we physically transitioned over here or just had our consciousnesses transferred?" He rubs his eyes. "I can't believe I asked that. This is completely surreal."

"I kinda think we physically moved to this reality. You had that blaster in your pocket, remember?"

He pulls out the weapon and stares at it. "But not this blaster. And I had a stunner, too. I don't have that now. Maybe the other me had this on him."

I nod. "Maybe these aren't our original bodies. But Evil O'Neill was probably armed."

"Let's stay away from the moral judgements. There's no reason to think the people in this reality are any different from us. I mean, you and I apparently ended up together, so we must be similar."

"Or Evil O'Neill knows a good thing when he sees it." I swipe through the OS, then zero in. "Look at this. We're a transport, owned by Morgan Corp. I'm the CEO! I wonder what happened to my mother?" My hands fall into my lap, and I stare at the data. I've always known I'd have to take over the "family business" at some point, but not for many, many years. The Ice Dame is relatively young—she's still got decades before she'll consider turning the corporation over to me. And yet, in this reality, it's mine. What would have compelled her to release control this soon? Could she be dead?

An intense wave of loss washes through me. My mother and I might butt heads more often than not, and yes, I ran away for six years, but the idea that she's no longer here suffocates me.

I force myself to suck in a painful breath and swipe some more. "I can't access anything off the ship, and there's nothing about her in this database."

"Can you get me access?" He sits beside me and puts an arm around me—he must understand how much this information has rattled me.

I flick a few icons and grant him access. "I guess Evil O'Neill doesn't use the same security protocols you do. But I've reset all that. You'll need to set up new ones."

"Thanks." He pulls his arm away and goes to work on his own interface.

I watch for a few seconds, his activity not really registering in my mind. I'm still fixated on the idea that my mother might be dead. Intense sorrow overwhelms me, but I push it back. This is not my reality. *My* mother is perfectly fine, back on SK2. I shove the grief into a dark corner of my mind and shut the door on it for a later time. I have work to do now.

"Looks like we're a merchant ship—taking small cargo contracts with whoever we can find." O'Neill bumps my shoulder with his own. "We've got a consignment of Kakuvian brandy as well as a larger delivery of silver silicon ore to deliver to Armstrong."

"Are we on the same itinerary as we were? How weird is that? Obviously, we're very different people here—I'm using my real name and our ship is kind of bare-bones. Can we assume the Morgans in this reality aren't top-levs? And yet, you and I are together."

"Our love endures across all realities." O'Neill grins as he says the words in a cheesy, voice-over tone. Then he shrugs. "Clearly, you recognized a good thing."

I smack his hard abs. "I said that about you. But my point is, based on my extensive viewing of *Ancient TēVē*, each new reality in the multi-verse is created when a decision is made. The farther back the decision, and the greater the difference in the decision, the larger the resulting differences between realities. So, why would some things be so similar"—I wave a hand to indicate the two of us—"and other things so different?"

"What is different? Aside from your mother and your name. Maybe that's the decision that created this reality—you didn't run away from home but took control of the company instead."

I gasp. "You don't think I bumped her off, do you?"

"Don't be ridiculous. You didn't kill your mother." A thoughtful expression crosses O'Neill's face. "Although, maybe this Triana did. We probably shouldn't make any assumptions at this point. Are you armed?"

I frown and pat down my pockets. I find a small tool kit—the kind I carried as a matter of habit as a maintenance tech—a thin sheaf of low-value credit notes, and a cheap chocolate bar. I look around the room again, spotting a belt with a holster hanging on a hook near the door. "Not currently."

"You sure that isn't mine?" He takes the few steps across the compartment and lifts the belt from the wall. "Nope." He turns the *lether* belt so I can see the blocky letters stenciled inside. "A. Morgan."

I take it and fasten it around my waist. It sits low on my hips, with the standard-sized blaster at the perfect location for a quick draw—at least if my childhood games are a good indication. I stand upright, letting my hand hover near the weapon's grip. Then I snap it out of the holster, aiming at the door as I step back into a half-crouch.

"Nice speed. Evil Triana has been practicing." The corner of O'Neill's mouth twitches and his eyes laugh at me.

"Makes me wonder why she needs Evil O'Neill." I put the blaster back into the holster.

"He undoubtedly has other attributes." He strikes a pose, leaning against the wall, hands behind his head, so all his glorious abs are on display. Or would be if he weren't wearing the shapeless coverall. What was Evil Triana thinking?

FOUR

The door buzzes. O'Neill and I exchange a look, and he steps between me and the opening. His hand slides into the pocket holding the mini-blaster. Peering around him, I flick an open command to the system.

When it slides aside, a man I don't recognize stands in the entry. "Captain?" He's wearing the same uniform as us, with the name Fortenoy on the chest. His strawberry blond hair is cut short, with a flat top, and a faint white scar cuts through his eyebrow. It's not huge, but in a society with widely-available nano-bot cosmetic alterations, it's noticeable. Either he likes it, or he isn't willing to spend the credits to get it repaired. Maybe both.

"Yes?" I take a half-step to the right, so I'm not hiding behind O'Neill. "What do you need?"

"We've completed the jump to Armstrong system. We'll reach our rendezvous point in four hours."

Rendezvous point? We aren't going to Station Aldrin? Who are we meeting and why? My mind spins. I want to ask questions, but until I know more about these people, I can't risk them knowing I'm not their captain. "Very good."

"And O'Neill is wanted in cargo."

"Why?" O'Neill lets his hand fall away from his pocket but not too far.

Fortenoy's brows come down. "It's your shift. Didn't you check the schedule? Stop bothering the captain and get to work." He moves into the cabin and tries to shoo O'Neill out.

"I wasn't finished briefing the captain—"

Fortenoy's eyes narrow, and his lips turn down. "You have no business briefing the captain on anything. Get out."

O'Neill ignores the intense glare. "I'll leave when the *captain* tells me to go."

Fortenoy turns to me. "I'm sorry he's bothering you, Annabelle. I'll get rid of him at Armstrong. Or maybe I can trade him to Arun when we rendezvous. I'd offer to space him, but we need the hands to unload the cargo."

What's going on here? Maybe O'Neill and I aren't in a relationship in this universe? I draw on my inner Ice Dame for a coldly impersonal tone. "It's not a problem. You don't need to get rid of him—he's doing his job, isn't he?"

Fortenoy glowers at O'Neill. "He was. But he shouldn't be in here, and he knows it."

Scrambling to keep us both out of trouble, I throw out an excuse. "I asked him to come here."

The blond moves closer, but O'Neill blocks him. Fortenoy glares at O'Neill, then his intense green eyes turn on me, burning into me like lasers. He has strong feelings about Evil Triana meeting with O'Neill in private. "Why?"

I meet his fire with ice. "I had business to discuss with him. Do you have a problem with that?"

A flicker of shock crosses his face, and he falls back a step. "No, ma'am." It has a sarcastic edge. "But they need him in cargo. Ten minutes ago."

O'Neill, still standing between me and Fortenoy, takes a step back so he can see my face without losing sight of the other man. He raises an eyebrow at me.

"You may go, O'Neill. I'll speak with you later." I let my hand drift toward the weapon strapped to my hip, trying to tell him I can look after myself.

His chocolate eyes flick to the blaster, then back to my face. "Yes, ma'am." He turns toward the door, then pauses to sweep out a hand. "After you, Ser Fortenoy."

Fortenoy looks from me to O'Neill and back. "I have my own business with the captain. You're dismissed."

O'Neill waits for my tiny nod, then leaves the compartment.

"Cargo is the other way, O'Neill!" Fortenoy calls out.

O'Neill marches past the doorway again, now headed in the direction Fortenoy indicated. The door slides shut.

"That guy is an idiot." Fortenoy takes a seat beside me on the couch, casually putting his hand on top of mine.

Are we a thing? Yikes. The guy is tall, fit, and handsome—aside from the scar. Although there is something attractive about it—like he's so self-assured he doesn't need to erase it. Or maybe the implication something dangerous caused it. If I weren't married to the sexiest man in the galaxy, I might find him attractive.

"Where'd you get the scar?" The words tumble out of my mouth before I can censor them.

His brows go up, making the white gash more noticeable. "Haven't I told you that story before?"

Zark. Ten seconds alone with the guy and I get it wrong already. "Maybe." I look away, feigning disinterest, managing to slide my hand away from his in the process. "I talk to so many people."

He laughs—a genuine chuckle, as if the idea of me talking to lots of people is ridiculous. "Right. Speaking of talking to people, what did O'Neill want?" He puts his hand on mine again. "You know I get jealous when you're alone with other men."

I straighten my spine, pulling my hand away from his. Would Evil Triana put up with this possessiveness? "Get over it. I'm the captain of this ship, and I'm going to talk with other men."

Dark color washes over his face, and his jaw tightens. He grabs my fingers again, his grip hard. "I'm trying to protect you. We don't know anything about that guy, except that he was fired by SK2 station security. He might try to take you hostage."

I give him a flat look. "Do you really think I'd let him on my ship if I thought he was a danger to me?"

Fortenoy's eyes narrow. "What's gotten into you, Annabelle? You aren't usually so… argumentative." He squeezes my hand hard enough to hurt.

An intense wave of dread washes through me—as if upsetting this man is dangerous. He doesn't like me standing up to him—Evil Triana must not push back. Maybe I should call her Pathetic Triana instead. Or just Annabelle.

I think back to my younger years—before I ran away from SK2. I was a people pleaser, always trying to make my mother happy. Until I snapped and escaped. If I had stayed—followed the path laid out for me for six more years—how would I have turned out? Would I be even more compliant? Or more rebellious? I need more information about this Annabelle so I can play the role until we can return to our own reality.

With a shrug, I pull my hand from his loosened grip and start making another sandwich. My hands tremble a little, so I keep them moving to disguise it. "There's nothing wrong with being assertive."

He sits back, crossing his arms, his expression cold. "You're sounding like your mother. She liked assertive women—until you tangled with her. Remember that? Do you really want to be like her?"

I keep my eyes on the sandwich I'm building. My heart is racing, blood pounding in my ears as this body reacts to a remembered fear. I take a deep breath, trying to calm my nerves. Fortenoy has some hold on Annabelle, and she's scared of him. Is she scared to lose him? Or scared of what he might do?

"You have nothing to worry about. I'm not turning into my mother. I was working with O'Neill on a … a little surprise. Don't ruin it." I take a peek at him out of the corner of my eye, keeping my head down.

His face softens a fraction, but he frowns again. "You know I don't like surprises."

"It wasn't anything big—I just—I don't want to ruin it." I turn to him and give my best smile, hoping he won't see the tremor of fear running through me. "I promise—it's a good surprise."

His eyes bore into mine. He seems to notice my agitation, and his lips twitch into a satisfied smirk. He likes that Annabelle is afraid.

This guy is a creep of the highest order. Calm certainty floods through me. I'm going to free Annabelle from this jerk before I leave. She deserves better than him.

Besides, if I don't, and we can't leave, I don't want to be saddled with him forever.

FIVE
LINDSAY "VANTI" FIORAVANTI

AFTER THE JUMP, I flick my holo-ring and pull up the communication app for the millionth time since we departed SK2. I haven't heard a word from Griz since then. It isn't like him to not check in when we're on the same ship.

I flick the app closed without calling. I shouldn't bother him. He's enjoying his honeymoon and doesn't need his old partner disturbing him. Besides, I need to get used to working alone. Elodie has only me for security—I'll be working without a net.

Which isn't a problem. I've been on my own for a long time. I was recruited by the Colonial Commonwealth Intelligence Agency my first year at the academy. They sought out a couple of academy cadets every year, they said—acquiring agents pre-embedded into the corporate security system. I would continue my training at the academy and get a job working for SK2 while serving the Commonwealth. A second paycheck from the CCIA sweetened the deal. Occasionally, I might be assigned a mission by them, but most of my work involved keeping the CCIA apprised of SK2 activities.

They wouldn't tell me who else from my academy class they had approached, and it was years before I got to know any other CCIA agents. I've always been a bit of a loner, so that worked for me.

But at the academy, I met Griz. We developed a professional partnership—discovering we worked well together. His meticulous planning and attention to detail complemented my intense focus and willingness to take wild risks. We became an unstoppable team.

Until we graduated. Our first assignment on SK2 made me realize I didn't want to spend my life in a tin can in space, so I transferred to the planet. The SK2 board embedded me at the Techno-Inst, to keep an eye on the runaway Morgan heir and complete other small assignments along the way. It was an uneventful few years, and I got used to working casually with the other SK2 agents.

Then Triana moved back to SK2, and I got reassigned. Griz and I were thrown back together when he came to Kaku, and our partnership fell back into place like a comfortable pair of shoes. We worked in synch for the last couple of years, until he and Triana realized I was more than an SK2 agent. Cover blown, it was time to move on.

The CCIA approved the transfer to Elodie—her current job is to travel the galaxy and get into trouble, filming it for *CelebVid*. The perfect cover for a CCIA operative—I can influence where we go whenever I need to.

I ignore the urge to contact Griz again. Doing a security check after a jump is probably pointless, but a sense of unease is making my stomach churn. I'm used to trusting my gut, so I unfasten my seat restraints and exit the empty crew lounge. This ship is operated by a captain and a single mate, and both of them are on the bridge right now. Leo and Elodie must have stayed in their cabins for the jump.

I pace through the ship, listening for anything out of the ordinary. My footsteps echo through the mostly empty cargo hold. The ship is designed for light cargo, and we have a small shipment of drones to be delivered to Station Aldrin. The stack—each unit smaller than a shoebox—sits in a corner like a forgotten pile of laundry. The tie-downs are secure, so I move on.

The crew cabins—forward of the cargo hold—sit quiet, and my intuition tells me to move on. I don't go inside. I try to respect others' privacy when I can. Up the ladder, I emerge into the passenger corridor. Two suites take up the front of the ship. Port side is assigned to Elodie, while the starboard belongs to Griz and Triana—for this first leg of the trip. I stroll past the closed doors, but no sound escapes through the excellent insulation.

Beyond the deluxe suites are the rooms assigned to me and Leo. He's on Elodie's side of the ship, while I'm next to the guest suite. Elodie has been encouraged to invite guests to join her travels, so once Griz and Triana leave the ship on Aldrin, that cabin will be available to anyone Elodie chooses. I toy with the idea of moving to the bigger cabin at that point—it would make sense for me to be closer to the woman I'm supposed to guard, and the junior suites are plush enough for most short-term guests. But I don't know what I'd do with that much space.

I pause outside my cabin. Something is bothering me, but I'm not sure what, so I reverse course and head for the bow of the ship.

As I approach the deluxe suites, the door on the left slides open. Griz's head pops through the opening, and he points at me. "Linds? Come here."

The blender in my stomach ratchets up a step. Griz never calls me by my first name—he learned back in the Academy that was a bad idea. I move closer, loitering out of arms' reach. I know I can take him, but I'd rather not have to. "What's up?"

He reaches forward, grabbing. I sidestep, snag his wrist, and twist it up behind his back, bringing him to his knees in one swift move. "You know better than that."

"Let go of me! Why are you acting so weird? Cool it! Deck hands aren't supposed to have ninja skills like that." He struggles, but I pull his wrist up, torquing his shoulder. He whimpers and goes still.

"Deck hands? What are you talking about?" With a quick pat-down, I pull the mini-blaster from his pocket. Normally he'd have more weaponry, but he's in a secure location on his honeymoon. I release his arm, giving him a shove between the shoulder blades.

He falls forward into the room. I move to the side, so the wall is between me and anyone inside the room. It's an instinctive move, born of years of practice. I know Triana is the only one inside, but I trust my training and intuition.

I take a quick look around the door jamb. Triana crouches behind the armchair, aiming a stunner at me. The range on that weapon is only five meters, so I'm on the edge of its effective reach. "What's going on, Triana?"

There's no answer. Griz scrambles to his knees and dives into the room. The door slides shut, and the access plate beside it flicks from green to red.

What the heck? I move to the far side of the passageway, putting my back against the bulkhead beside Elodie's door. There's no cover here, but the access panel's light will warn me if they open it, and I'm a better shot than Griz.

And unless she's done a lot of secret training, Triana's weapon skills are negligible.

As my heartrate slows, I slap a hand on the access plate beside me.

"Who is it?" Elodie's voice sings out.

"You know you can check the cams." I slide a little farther down the hall, in case Elodie's been infected by whatever is scrambling Griz's brain. "You feel okay? Let me in."

"I'm fine." The door slides open. "Where are you?" Elodie pokes her head into the passageway.

I motion for her to retreat, but of course she doesn't. When I get this Griz thing figured out, Elodie and I need to have a chat about my services and how this is going to work. No way I'm riding shotgun on another wild child like Triana. "Get inside!" I shoo her back into the room. "Over there!" I point across the cabin.

Wonder of wonders, she retreats to the sofa.

Keeping the opposite door in view, I slide sideways into the compartment. Then I flick the cam feeds on my holo-ring and activate the security lock on the other suite before closing our door.

I turn, putting my back to the wall. Tucking Griz's mini-blaster behind my leg, I face Elodie. "How do you feel?"

She picks up Apawllo and puts him in her lap, stroking his long fur. "I told you, I'm fine. How are you?"

"No paranoid urges? No memory loss?"

"No." She frowns at me, her hand stopping mid-caress. "I have a twinge in my neck. Probably slept on it wrong. Do you suppose I can get a new pillow?" The cat bats her hand with a paw, and she resumes petting.

"I don't know about the pillow—this is your ship, not mine. But mentally—how do you feel?"

"What is this all about? Did you drink too many mimosas at brunch yesterday?"

I refrain from rolling my eyes. "I don't drink when I'm on duty."

"You aren't really on duty—we're in transit. What are you worried about? Space pirates?" She laughs.

I give her a cold stare. "Pirates are a real concern in parts of the galaxy."

"Not near Armstrong. Or Kaku. I think we're fine. *CelebVid* wouldn't let me go anywhere I might get attacked."

Poor naive woman. "Really? You don't think 'attacked by space pirates' would go viral? That's your mission, right? To go viral?"

Her eyes go wide, and her hand stops moving. Apawllo doesn't wait more than half a second before slapping her arm again. "That's a good point. Do you think we should set up some kind of pirate defense?"

I sag against the wall. "No, I don't think we need to worry about space pirates."

"Then why did you bring them up?"

"I didn't—never mind." I push away from the wall and perch on the edge of a chair. "Griz is acting weird, and I need to know what's going on."

"How do you know? I haven't seen him or Triana since we got aboard."

I pull up the vid feed from the passageway cam and toss it to her. "Scroll back about two minutes."

While she fiddles with the vid, I try to find one for the guest cabin. The cams are there—I reviewed the security for this ship before we embarked. But they're behind a firewall I can't breach. As security chief, I should have access to that. I dash a message off to my *CelebVid* point of contact, then set a hacking program to work on the login.

It would be faster if I could get Triana to do it, but asking her to allow me video access to her suite is kind of icky. Especially since she just married my best friend. Besides, she seemed to be in league with Griz's weirdness.

"That *is* bizarre." Elodie fast-forwards through the video, watching me force Griz to his knees, then reversing so he pops upright and disengages. She giggles. "That looks like a great dance move. You'll have to teach me that."

Like I'm going to teach Elodie to put anyone into an armlock. That's a sure recipe for disaster. She'd probably use it on a security guard at a concert and get thrown in jail.

"He called me 'Linds.' And said something about deck hands. More importantly, my gut is telling me something is off." My brows draw together, and I resist the urge to bite my thumbnail. How is it those old habits never completely disappear? I thought I'd purged that one back at the academy. "He seemed less competent than usual, too. Physically."

Elodie giggles again. "Don't let Triana hear you say that."

"Please. I mean when I disarmed him. It was too easy. I'm thinking drugs."

Elodie looks up in alarm, the video rolling on unheeded. "Poison?"

I gesture to my own holo. "Personality-altering drugs of some kind. They've only eaten food from the AutoKich'n—I need to check the nutrient supplies. Unless Triana brought food aboard. Oh, who am I kidding? Of course she brought something aboard. It could have been tainted before she left the station."

I pull up the logs for the AutoKich'n supply system. Nutrient blocks are loaded through the cargo compartment and broken down by the system as required. But it's a single supply system for the whole ship, and it hasn't affected me and Elodie.

"Call Leo." I point a finger at Elodie as I continue working my way remotely through the possible points of contamination. "I need to know if he's been affected by this."

"Aye, aye, ma'am!" Elodie snaps a hand to her forehead and away.

SIX
TRIANA

I FINALLY GET RID of Fortenoy and make my way to the bridge of the ship. I *want* to find O'Neill, but I also don't want to tip our hand. I'll wait until he's finished with whatever he's doing in cargo and finds me.

The bridge hatch slides open on a small space with two seats. A woman wearing the now familiar coverall slouches in the left seat. Her curly dark hair stands around her head like a massive halo. The right is empty.

As I enter, the woman looks up, then her head pops upright like a jack-in-the-box. A wash of color floods over her dark face, and she ducks her head as she struggles to rise. "Ma'am?"

I wave her back to her seat. "Take it easy."

She subsides to the extreme edge of her seat, her back ramrod straight. Her eyes dart nervously between me and the holo-display before her. "We're on course and schedule for our rendezvous."

Dropping into the empty chair, I nod. "Perfect. What's our ETA?"

Her brows come down, and her eyes roll toward me while her face remains forward. "It's two hours and thirty-seven minutes, ma'am."

Obviously, I should have already known that. I lean back, pretending an ease I don't feel, and study the holo-display. Sure enough—there's a small countdown clock in the top corner. The main section shows a blue line—I'm guessing that's our current path. A green line comes in from the left. Both lines go from solid to dashed, then intersect at what must be the rendezvous.

I wish I knew more about astrogation. I can operate an autopilot like anyone, but anything more technical than telling the computer where to go is beyond me.

"And our… partners are en route?" I try to sound confident.

She casts another look at me. This time, she turns enough that I can catch her nametag reflected in the hologram: LaSalva. This must be the crew member listed as Carina LaSalva. "The buyer has reported they will arrive as scheduled, and that's their projected path, but you know I can't track them with their identity beacon turned off."

"Of course not." Zark. This is hard. I thought I'd be able to chat up whoever was working and find out everything I needed to know. This universe's Annabelle must be an information hoarder like my—our—mother. She's clearly got her crew locked down.

Then I remember—I *am* Annabelle. I'm the captain of this ship and can do what I want. They won't question me. I reach forward and swipe my holo-interface open.

"What are you doing?" LaSalva asks.

So much for that theory.

I give her my best Ice Dame glare. "I'm reviewing some files."

LaSalva casts a quick look over her shoulder at the closed hatch and flicks an icon. It disappears so quickly, I don't catch the title, but based on shape and color, it might have been a privacy shield. She makes a sad face. "Oh, I hoped maybe we could watch *Ancient TēVē*."

Yes! I do a mental fist pump. Alternate Annabelle might be frosty and have a creepy, controlling boyfriend, but she's got great taste in entertainment. I guess she and LaSalva are friends. Her initial reception seemed cold, but maybe it's the boyfriend's influence. Is he monitoring the bridge?

I jut my chin at the holos in front of her. "Won't he notice that?"

Her eyes narrow, and her head tilts as she considers me. Probably wondering why I don't know the answer to that question. "He shouldn't. I just turned on my spoofing program. He'll see us sitting here, not talking as we work."

I nod. "Right. Just double checking." I think for a moment. I can't do any snooping if she's right here, watching my every move. On the other hand, she seems to be on my side. Surely, she'd be in favor of jettisoning Fortenoy—I need to figure out what angle to leverage to get her assistance.

Ugh. I sound like the Ice Dame, taking advantage of friendship. Maybe I can tell her what happened to me and O'Neill and get her help in returning to my own reality.

But I have no idea how she'll respond to my revelations. Will she think I'm crazy and tell Fortenoy? Or will she believe my story and help me? I have to imagine she'll want her version of me back.

Unless she likes this me better, which let's face it, based on what I know of Alternate Annabelle, is a distinct possibility.

Better to keep the truth quiet until I'm sure where I stand with her. I go for a third option. "What do you think of that O'Neill guy?"

Her eyes light up, and she leans toward me, lowering her voice. "He's hot. I might have to get him to help me inventory the cargo." She winks, making it clear there will be no counting of product if that occurs.

A spike of possessive rage flares through me, and my fingers curl into tight fists. "No!"

She jerks back, her eyes wide. "Why? Is there something wrong with him? I heard he got fired from his last job, but you've never cared about that kind of thing. I mean look at Fortenoy—" She breaks off, looking even more alarmed. Is Alternate Annabelle touchy about the subject of her creepy boyfriend?

"Yeah." I try to keep the tone non-committal. "I mean, I heard O'Neill has a contractual partner and three kids back on SK2." I cross my fingers where she can't see them.

LaSalva's brows go up. "If he left them on the station, he can't be too serious about them, right? I might have to—" Her eyes half-close and a satisfied smirk crosses her lips. "Maybe I'll do a little *research* of my own."

I glare at her. "No. Stay away from him. Trust me on this."

"Did he turn you down?" Her tone is sharp.

"What? No—"

"You think all of the men on this ship are your property! You've got

Fortenoy—" A little shudder ripples through her shoulders as she says the name. "And you're welcome to him. But that doesn't mean you get O'Neill, too."

"No one is getting anyone. I'm just trying to warn you. He's going to say no." I make a mental note to warn O'Neill not to let LaSalva catch him in any dark corners.

Which reminds me—I need to find a dark corner where *I* can meet him. With Fortenoy around, my cabin isn't a safe place. And the bridge is out. Maybe I'd better take a tour of the ship. I've got almost three hours before our rendezvous, and O'Neill and I need to make plans.

Plus, I need to figure out how to get us back to our own universe. No pressure.

I stand. "I need to check on something."

"If it's O'Neill, don't bother. I've heard he's unavailable." LaSalva's tone is angry.

"No, I—never mind. Look, this rendezvous is making me nervous."

"Why? We've traded with this guy a dozen times." She swipes through the screens and flips a file at me.

My holo-ring pings with the incoming alert. "I don't know. I'm feeling off balance today."

LaSalva nods wisely. "That's not the rendezvous, it's the other thing. You know, the one we ant-kay alk-abow-tay."

It takes me a second to decipher her terrible pig Latin. I open my mouth and close it again. If we can't talk about it, I can't ask. Instead, I grunt and head for the door. "I'm going for a walk."

Her lips press together before she turns away. "Don't let your boyfriend catch you talking to the hot new guy."

"I'm not—" I break off, because that's exactly what I'm hoping to do.

Zark. I am in so much trouble.

SEVEN
VANTI

THE BRIDGE HATCH SLIDES ASIDE, and I slip through before it's fully open, putting my back to the bulkhead. A wide screen shows the forward view, with Armstrong's sun, Sol-489, glowing off to the right. The jump brought us in "north" of Armstrong's orbit, and a green dashed line leads from our current location to the green dot indicating the planet. Station Aldrin is too small to see at this distance. Between here and there, a number of other ships follow the same trajectory.

Captain Chowdhury Nowak sits in the left seat, her attention fixed on the navigation screens surrounding her. Thomas Fortenoy, the first mate, turns, his blond brows coming down when he sees the stunner in my hand. "May I help you, Agent Fioravanti?"

"I told you before, call me Vanti." I lower the weapon but don't put it away. "How are you feeling?"

He scowls. "Based on what I've heard about you, I'm guessing that isn't idle chit-chat. I feel normal. How are you?"

At his tone, Chowdhury turns around. Her dark hair is braided tightly to her scalp, and her dark brown skin is flawless. Her almost black eyes do a quick once-over on me, pausing on the hand now tucked behind my leg. "What's this about, Vanti?"

"Sorry to interrupt, ma'am, but Ser O'Neill seems to be under the influence of… something. Maybe a mood- or memory-altering drug. He attacked me in the passageway. Sera Morgan appeared to think his action was rational—she was covering him from inside the cabin. I've locked them in. They aren't responding to comm signals. I'd like to look at the security feeds in there. Do you have the ability to access them?"

The two pilots exchange a look. "As the designated security chief, you should have access to everything." Fortenoy pulls up a screen and swipes through a few entries, then stretches the view so I can see my name. "According to the OS, you've got everything."

Beside my login credential, the system shows access to all security data, including cameras, memory files, and cabins.

"What is that icon?" I point at a tiny yellow warning triangle blinking at the extreme edge of the visible screen.

Fortenoy frowns. "That's odd." He scrolls until the full warning is front and center, then swears as he waves his hand through it. "This says you've been locked out of that cabin. And the warning was hidden—if I hadn't stretched the view big enough for you to see it across the room, it would have stayed invisible."

"Triana." At his raised eyebrow, I go on. "I'm betting Sera Morgan hacked into the system and locked me out, then hid the evidence. She's a genius at this stuff."

"Really? I didn't know any top-levs bothered with that level of detail. Although, I guess if you're tired of being watched all the time, you might decide to learn it."

"Sera Morgan is hardly your average top-lev. Most of them would simply order me to lock the cabin cams and be done with it. She likes to take matters into her own hands." I can't really blame her. Just because you're paranoid doesn't mean they aren't watching you. "I'm going to have to go in there and subdue them. Do either of you have any combat experience?"

Chowdhury tips her head at Fortenoy. "Before he hired on with *CelebVid,* Tom did a stint with the Peacekeepers on Grissom. Not exactly combat—"

"I was a pilot, but I went through the standard Peacekeeper training.

My hand-to-hand is a little rusty, but passable." He stands, towering over me in the small bridge. "You need backup?"

I nod and turn to the hatch, waving it open. "I'm going into their cabin. They have a blaster, a stunner, and perhaps other weaponry. They were scanned on arrival, of course." We exit and head past the crew cabins to the ladder. "There were no obvious weapons in their luggage, and I know what Ser O'Neill usually carries on his person. But he's a highly-trained agent. In his situation, I would have other resources." I pause at the ladder to the upper deck.

Fortenoy scratches his head, giving me a skeptical look. "The guy is on his honeymoon, in a controlled environment on a ship that's been cleared. Why would he have any weapons? The armory is this way."

As I follow him to the end of the hall, I don't bother telling him I know exactly where the armory is. At the end of the corridor to the cargo hold, a narrow hatch on the left provides access to the engine spaces below. The one on the right reads supply. "You don't know much about Sera Morgan."

He frowns but doesn't respond. With a flick and a swipe of his holo-ring, the supply hatch opens, revealing a long, narrow room behind the port crew cabin. Cleaning supplies, including a couple of docked bots, fill the lower side shelves. A printer sits above. I recognize the model—this one can print ship components as well as clothing. These aren't normally found on a ship this small, but obviously this isn't a normal small cruiser. Screens cover the fronts of the shelves, ensuring the supplies stay in place in the event of low gravity or unexpected maneuvers.

"What kind of ship did you say this is?" I finger one of the textile blocks sitting beside the printer. This is high-end stuff.

Fortenoy grins. "We're fitted to do pretty much anything. *CelebVid* likes to throw their correspondents into… unusual circumstances and see how they make out. We needed *all* of this stuff on the last run."

"Who was on your last run?" I push my hands into my pockets so I don't chew my nail as I wait for his reply. My spine is tingling—a sure sign something is off. Could *CelebVid* have engineered Griz and Triana's bizarre behavior? I make a mental note to test the nutrition blocks. Maybe nano-bot triggered drugs?

Fortenoy unlocks the thick-doored cabinet at the end of the cabin and hands me a stunner. It's a newer model than I'm currently carrying, with several different strength settings. I log in to the interface through my holo-ring and select 'paralysis.'

"Dale Robinson el-Atrid. Have you heard of him?" At my head shake, he goes on. "No one else had at that point, either. But he's big now. It was a good run." He takes a stunner for himself, then hands me a wristband with a small box attached. "This is a force shield. It will stop whatever they shoot at you, but you have to deactivate it to fire your own stunner." He clasps one around his right arm, then slides the stunner into his holster.

With a tap, he activates the shield. There's nothing to indicate it's active. "Go ahead, hit me."

I lift the stunner. "With this?"

He nods. "You can't reach me."

With a shrug, I fire the weapon at point blank range. The beam seems to splash against an invisible, curved wall. "Cool." I lower the weapon, then dart forward and grab his arm, forcing him to his knees. "Doesn't stop a direct attack though."

He swears. "You're fast."

I smirk. "Let's go." As I move toward the hatch, I feel him shift behind me. I whirl, grapple, and shove him down again. "Don't even try."

Rubbing his arm as he gets to his feet, he shakes his head. "I'm glad you're on my side." He moves around me and heads down the hall. We climb the steep steps of the "ladder" to the passenger quarters, and he pauses before his head breaks the plane of the deck. "Check the feed—is the passageway clear?"

I show him the cam feed from that corridor. "All clear."

He continues up the steps, and I make a mental note—good recon skills. Unarmed hand-to-hand needs work.

Outside the cabin, we pause, taking positions on either side of the door. I pull up the security system and the door lock. "I'll open the door. Let me enter first—I'll take O'Neill, as he's the larger threat. Is there a way to set this shield to three-sixty, or is it unidirectional?"

"You don't trust me not to shoot you in the back?" He crosses to my side of the door, leaning close to show me the controls. "I won't take your lack of faith personally, since we haven't worked together before."

Elodie's door slides open, and we both whirl to face it, weapons up. She slowly raises her hands, her eyes tracking between the two of us. A sly smile twitches across her face. "Just me. Y'all are cute together."

I close my eyes for a brief second. "Elodie, have you met Fortenoy, the first mate?"

"Call me Tom," he says to me, then nods at Elodie. "We met at *CelebVid* headquarters on Kaku. She had to approve the crew selection. And we ran some sims together."

Elodie's head bobbles up and down. "They wanted to make sure we were compatible for a long voyage."

Leo appears behind her. "Tom. What's up?"

"Agent Fioravanti and I are going to infiltrate the guest cabin." Fortenoy—Tom—grins and jerks a thumb over his shoulder. "Apparently the lovebirds are acting suspicious. You wanna film this?"

"What? No." I slash a hand at Elodie. "I may not work for SK'Corp anymore, but Griz and Triana are still my friends. I'm not selling them out."

Elodie crosses her arms. "I agree. Any other guests are fair game, but they're our friends."

Tom shrugs. "You're the boss. But I know what HQ is looking for, and this could make for juicy ratings."

"Definitely not." Leo puts a hand on Elodie's shoulder, turning her away from the passageway. "Let's get out of range and let them do their thing."

Elodie agrees, and they retreat into her cabin. "We can watch on the cams. I know how to—" Her voice is cut off when the door slides shut.

Tom's eyes sparkle. "We have an audience."

"I was starting to like you, but I'm not so sure about this side. You seem way too into the social media aspect."

"Pilot pay rate is directly tied to the correspondent's ratings. We get a standard fee for flying, but the crew earn bonuses if Elodie's content goes viral."

Making another mental note, I nod at the door. "Take your position. I'll open the door, then go in. Aim to stun. Ready?"

He nods. "On your mark."

Making an effort not to roll my eyes at his drama—a simple head nod would do—I flick my shield to rear only so my stunner will work, and pull up the door controls. "Three, two, one, mark."

The door slides open. I duck in, crouching to the right of the internal bulkhead. In a fraction of a second, I catalogue the cabin, noting the furniture reset to provide cover and a few of Triana's red curls poking over the couch. If she's there, then Griz will be—I turn thirty degrees and aim—there. "Come on out, guys."

We wait.

Griz's head pops up exactly where I predicted, and I fire. The stunner hits him, and he collapses. I suppress a lip twitch and swivel to Triana as a stun beam hits me square in the face. My body seizes, my vision goes dark, and I topple over, unable to move my arms and legs.

"Got her!" Tom's triumphant words seep through the buzzing in my ears. "I'll secure the prisoners while you lie there and rest, Vanti."

If I could move my jaw, I'd grind my teeth. I spend the next twenty minutes sparring with Tom in my mind, throwing him to the mat over and over, in every conceivable, highly painful way.

EIGHT
TRIANA

On the way to cargo, I do a little snooping. On our ship, the crew quarters were on the lower deck, between the bridge and cargo, with the guest quarters on the upper deck. Here, the four upper cabins have been converted to six or eight smaller spaces which have apparently been assigned to crew members.

Using my OS privileges as the captain, I stop at each door and open it. The first door on each side leads to a dormitory-style room with four bunks and a small sanitary module. The rear two doors lead to the engine room—on the lowest deck—and a supply closet that also houses a small armory. I briefly consider taking a few more weapons, but based on what I can find in the OS, Fortenoy checks the inventory daily. Only he and Annabelle have access, so obviously he doesn't trust her. She really picked a winner.

There's something not quite right about the layout of the crew cabins, but I'm not sure what it is. I never visited this part of the ship in our own dimension, so I can only compare them to the specs I looked up before the jump.

Yes, I was reviewing tech specs on my honeymoon. I'm a nerd at heart.

As I loiter in the supply closet, the opposite door slides open, and a cautious head pokes out, looking both directions. The dark curls bounce as she looks up and catches me watching. She freezes, eyes wide, mouth open. Despite the smears of oil and grease, I recognize her heart-shaped face.

"Elodie?"

Her eyes go even wider, and her jaw snaps shut. She jerks back, and the door slides closed with a snap.

I swipe my controls, but the door won't open. The OS says there's a mechanical failure. I tap at the door, but no one answers. Is that the sound of retreating footsteps? I can't tell. "Elodie!"

I try an override, but the door doesn't budge. It's jammed. Or physically locked? I'll have to figure that out later. I need to speak with O'Neill, first.

Turning to face the cargo hatch, I square my shoulders and slap my hand on the access plate. The door slides open, and a wave of noise assaults my ears. Warm, damp, earthy air catches in my nose and throat. A telltale flashes in the door's access panel: "Containment required," and the door whooshes shut behind me.

I take two steps across the open metal grating of the landing and look down into the hold. In my reality, the cargo comprises this level and the one below, while the one above contains passenger spaces, including a shared living area, a small entertainment suite, and a real kitchen.

In this ship, the hold fills all three decks. Above, another landing provides access to the top deck, and open metal stairs lead down to the platform where I stand. Another set of steps—or a ladder, as ship people insist on labeling it—reaches to the lowest deck. A hatch below me probably leads to the engine room, but I can't see it.

Below my feet, a thick layer of jungle obscures everything on the bottom deck. An animal squawks, and a flash of purple catches my eye. My head snaps to the left, but whatever it was disappears into the green.

What the zark are we transporting?

I clomp down the stairs to the first landing, the green closing in over my head. My hollow-sounding footsteps disappear into a wave of squawks and squeals. Another flash of color—this time orange—and a furry animal about the size of Apawllo appears on the railing beside me. Little brown eyes sparkle, and little round ears twitch in time with its little black nose. It sits up on its back legs, back rounded and hands fisted in front of its chest.

"What are you?" I reach a hand toward the creature.

It makes a clicking sound, and the jaw drops in an adorable smile.

"You are so cute!" This must be a quockoa. The little creatures from Tereshkova were named after a mythical Earth creature. Legend says the original Earth quokka lived on an island in the southern hemisphere and liked to pose for selfies with visitors. If they were real, they went extinct long before the Exodus to the stars.

The little orange creature wraps a fist around my finger, like Kara's baby does. I reach out with my other hand to stroke between its cute little ears. The fur is thick and soft, with a faint zing—like a low level of static that doesn't dissipate. It presses its head against my fingers, and a rumbling purr vibrates my arm.

The creature grins again and then chomps its blunt teeth onto my captured finger.

"Yagh!" Pain lances through my hand. I pull away, but the creature clings, coming off the railing as I yank furiously. I shake my arm, screaming as I try to dislodge the vicious little creature. With a snap of my elbow, I fling my hand outward, and it releases, flying across the landing to clamp onto the corner of the railing. It perches there for a second, then its little arm flips back and throws.

Splat.

"Ow!" A tiny egg cracks against my cheekbone. Slimy yolk and sharp shell shards slide down my cheek and drip on my ugly coverall.

The quockoa grins and clicks out what can only be a laugh. Then it scampers down the bulkhead, using the corrugated ribs of the wall as a ladder, and disappears into the foliage.

"You little zarkhead!" I swipe at the mess on my face with my sleeve.

A male chuckle filters through the green. "Yes, they are."

Looking down, I locate O'Neill near the bottom of the steps. His hair stands on end in a way I've never seen before. Usually, it falls effortlessly into place in all circumstances. His eyes look tired, and his clothing is mottled with egg and dirt.

I hurry down the last set of steps but stop before I can throw myself into his arms. This cargo area is under cam surveillance. Plus, the rest of the crew could be hidden in the thick growth and we'd never know. "Are you okay?"

"I'm tired. We're transporting a whole zoo's worth of live animals, and I got to muck out the stalls." He shoves his fingers through his thick hair, stopping with a soft exclamation. Pulling his hand away, he shakes more eggshell shards to the loam-covered deck. "I can't believe they let the quockoa run free out here."

"I think they're hard to contain." I flick my ring and bring up a file. I was wondering why we had wildlife stories in the data files. "Yeah—this says they're escape experts, but apparently turning the cargo hold into a forest keeps them from trying to get into the rest of the ship. The cat probably helps, too. If this Elodie has a cat."

"Where are they getting the eggs? All the other creatures are in stalls, including the emui." He shoves his hand through his hair again. It doesn't fall into place like it does at home. Maybe the egg yolk?

"Those are their own eggs." I make a disgusted face, which he mirrors. "They 'lay' them in a pouch on their belly and throw them at predators so they can escape. If the egg is already hatched, they'll throw the baby instead. Then they pop out a new one. The females—and they're *all* female —have eggs in suspended development at all times."

He looks down at his coverall. "I guess it's a good thing they throw them—otherwise we'd be overrun with the little monsters. How's your hand?"

I carefully flex my throbbing finger. The creature's teeth were blunt, so it didn't break the skin, but the nail is dented and the tip is swelling. "Nothing broken, no blood. I guess I'm okay."

Movement catches my eye, and I spin, putting my back to the bulkhead. But no more egg-throwing rodents appear. Instead, it's Fortenoy and Leo. Except this Leo is even thinner than ours, and a straggly beard hangs down to his chest. A mud-colored turban covers his head, but it's tilted, and his shaved skull is visible above his right ear.

"O'Neill, stop bothering the captain," Fortenoy snarls.

"He chased off the quockoa that attacked me." I lift my hand, and the finger throbs faster, pounding in time to my increased heartrate. The way this body reacts to Fortenoy—an immediate flight response—worries me. What has he done to Alt Annabelle? Does he hit her? Why would she put up with that?

Behind Fortenoy, Leo jerks his head at O'Neill. The two of them fade into the foliage, leaving me and the first mate alone.

Fortenoy takes my hand, holding it down and away, as if he's trying to get better light to see it by. The move increases the pounding pain. I get the impression this isn't an accident. "It doesn't look too bad."

I yank my hand away and raise it to heart level where the pounding decreases. "It's fine. Maybe two minutes in the med-pod."

"Too bad we removed it when we expanded the cargo hold." Fortenoy grins. "You'll have to deal with it the old-fashioned way. There are pain killers in the supply room."

"Maybe our buyers can help me out." I watch him out of the corner of my eye as I climb the stairs.

"That's not a good idea." He keeps pace beside me, his eyes darting to me, then around the area below us. They pause for a second on the quivering branches O'Neill and Leo disappeared behind, then flick back to me. "And keep away from the new guy. He's up to something."

"This is a small ship—keeping away from a crew member is going to be virtually impossible. If you don't trust him, why did we hire him?"

He gives me a narrow-eyed look that tells me I've made a mistake. "How many times are we going to discuss this? We needed someone, and he was willing to take what I offered. I didn't realize he was going to make a move on my girl." He slides his arm around my waist, but it doesn't feel natural. More like it's something he knows he should do.

My panicked heart goes into overdrive, and I fight the urge to pull away. We gain the top of the steps, and he reaches to activate the door. I slip out of his arm and hurry through. "Don't want to let the cargo out."

His head shakes. "They can't get through the force shield. Let's go upstairs." He runs a hand down my arm. "We have a few hours before the rendezvous."

I suppress a shudder and move to the supply closet. "I'm going to get some pain killers. And maybe take a nap."

His lips press together, and his brows come down in a scowl. I wait for him to explode, meeting his eyes boldly despite the tremor of fear running through me. Our eyes lock, then he steps back. "Sure. Whatever you need. I'll wake you ten minutes before the rendezvous."

"I can set my own alarm." I back against the closet door, reaching out to activate it. He looks suspicious. "But thanks, that will be easier."

As the door whooshes open, the suspicion clears, and he gives me a smile that's probably supposed to be winning but comes across sadistic. "My pleasure. Enjoy your rest." Whistling—badly—he disappears down the corridor.

I back into the supply closet and let the door shut me in. How am I going to find a safe time and place to talk to O'Neill? Maybe I can figure out a way to connect our audio implants. The other members of the crew don't seem to have them—at least I've found no access codes in the system. And the usual access nodes—if there are any—are hidden. If I can connect mine directly to O'Neill's, it will give us a secure way to communicate.

I find the painkillers and let them dissolve on my tongue. The throbbing in my finger decreases almost immediately. I grab a pain patch—I know from past experience that doubling up on the oral and topical is safe and effective—then retreat to my cabin.

First things first—lock out Fortenoy. I'll have to come up with an excuse—maybe I can say the system is messed up. From what LaSalva said, I'm not a programmer in this universe—she's the one who spoofed the cams on the bridge.

I walk through the system, noting who has modified what and seeing no traces of my usual work. Time to remedy that. I install several back doors and a few fail-safes, then lock my cabin against everyone but me. I consider adding O'Neill, but if anyone stumbles on this code, they'll find that, too.

Then I connect my audio to the system and set up a search to identify O'Neill's. It won't connect until he enables the pairing, so I set it to run every thirty minutes, at seven minutes after the hour and the half.

That done, I delve into the files about our cargo and the buyer we're meeting. The details are sparse, with vague mentions of previous transactions but no identifying information.

The cargo is less mysterious, but highly illegal. Transporting quockoa requires licenses and safety protocol we don't have. Not to mention the other highly controlled items we've got in our hold—emui, the large flightless birds from Sarvo Six, insect-eating flowers from Gagarin, and a small herd of goat-like creatures from Impala. Where did Alternate Universe Annabelle get all of this contraband?

The answer to that lies in the address book. An actual, physical book hidden under the mattress in her cabin. It has names—only first names—and contact information, as well as the goods and services each of those contacts provides. Highly incriminating details.

I flip through the hand-written pages, wondering who wrote it. This spiky scrawl isn't mine. Finding a pen, I scribble Fortenoy's name in the back of the book, just to check. Alternate Universe Annabelle's cursive is rounder and smoother than mine—watching my own hand produce it is unnerving.

Does Alternate Universe Annabelle know...?

That name is descriptive, but way too long. "Alternate Annabelle"? No, wait. I've got it: Altabelle.

Does Altabelle know this book is here? Or did Fortenoy hide it under her mattress in case the ship is ever raided? Framing his girlfriend seems like his style.

Then a name catches my eye: Arun. Someone mentioned an Arun earlier—was it LaSalva? No, it was Fortenoy. Arun is the buyer we're rendezvousing with.

But I know that name—Arun is the nephew my father, R'ger, has mentioned many times. In our reality, he's a small trader working out of Sally Ride. Could our mysterious buyer be the same man?

NINE
VANTI

We sit in the passenger lounge at the rear of the ship. Feeling has finally returned to my fingers and toes—it took a lot longer than I expected. I haven't been stunned in a long time. I can't believe Triana got the drop on me—she must have been practicing in secret.

Griz and Triana sit on opposite ends of the couch, with room for two more people between. Tom stands beside me, his weapon in a holster on his leg. Elodie and Leo take armchairs at the end of the room, out of reach of the others. The cat lays across the back of the couch, his head rubbing against Triana's shoulder.

Which is odd. Apawllo doesn't like Triana. I file that detail away and cross my arms, tucking my tingling fingers against my sides. "What's going on with you two?"

They exchange a wary look, then turn to me. They seem oddly ill at ease, as if they barely know each other. Triana opens her mouth, then closes it again.

"What ship is this?" Griz asks.

I frown. "It's the *Solar Reveler*. Are you experiencing memory loss?"

"No. Something odd happened during the jump. We aren't where we were."

"That's what jump means." Tom smirks as he leans over the back of the chair he's supposed to be sitting in. Triana watches him with an expression I can't read.

I wish the guy would stop pacing and fidgeting.

Griz's face tightens. "I know what jump means. I've done it many times before. But this jump was different. This ship is different, now."

Triana's head snaps around, and she glares at Griz. He crosses his arms and raises his brows, then turns back to me. "We don't belong here."

Elodie scoots forward in her seat, perching on the edge as she leans toward Griz. "You're always welcome on my ship."

He gives a stiff nod, then shoves his fingers into his hair. "This is going to sound really insane—"

Triana gasps and turns a glare on him—one rivaling the Ice Dame for coldly contained fury.

Griz glares back, not cowed at all. "What? We're going to need their help to get home." He turns to me. "I think we transferred to an alternate universe during the jump. In my reality, this ship, the *Solar Reveler*, is a small transport belonging to Annabelle Morgan. Not a pleasure craft." He points at Elodie. "Where I come from, you're the mechanic, not the owner."

We all stare at Elodie in surprise.

"That's not terrifying at all," Leo mutters.

Elodie draws herself up. "Hey, I have plenty of mechanical attitude."

"Aptitude." Tom finally circles his chair and sits.

"Whatever." Elodie waves a negligent hand at him and leans toward Griz. "Tell me more."

I hold up a hand. "If this is one of your crazy jokes, Triana, it's not funny."

Triana looks around the room, then focuses on me. "Who's Triana?"

I roll my eyes and don't bother answering. "Pull the other leg. I've heard about those silly shows you watch—where the starship falls through a wormhole and ends up in an alternate timeline. That's fiction, not reality."

Griz grits his teeth and glares. Triana's eyes flick coldly over me, as if she's taking inventory and finding me wanting. I fight the urge to cower. The girl has really got her mother's technique down.

A cold trickle of doubt seeps into my mind. Triana hates her mother's Ice Dame attitude.

I initiate an audio call to Griz, but it doesn't connect. The system returns a "no such node" error code.

Triana could easily spoof that.

But would she? She likes to laugh—she's always saying or doing something silly—but a drawn-out prank like this is not in character. She doesn't have the patience for this kind of humor.

And let's face it, it's not really funny.

The most telling thing is the body language between the two of them. In normal circumstances, they can't keep their hands off each other. Now they're sitting at opposite ends of a couch, stiff and formal, barely making eye contact. Sure, they could fake it, but this feels real. And why would a couple on their honeymoon bother with such a prank?

"Did you two have a fight?" Elodie wags a finger between Triana and Griz. "I've never seen you so cold toward each other."

The pair on the couch exchange a bewildered glance. Triana turns to Elodie. "I barely know him. We don't tolerate dissension among the crew. If he argued with me, he'd be gone."

Griz nods, but his jaw is tight, as if he agrees with this statement but doesn't like it.

Elodie's brows come down, and she sits back, frowning. "Couples have disagreements."

Triana laughs, a hard, cold bark. "Couples? Me and him? Right."

At the same time, Griz says, "We are *not* a couple."

"Don't say that!" Elodie launches into a speech about love and forgiveness, muddled together with anecdotes from her own life and descriptions of the last dozen arguments between her daughter Kara and Kara's partner Erco. Triana and Griz stare at her with equally horrified expressions.

A few minutes into the monologue, the cat jumps down from the back of the couch and makes himself cozy in Triana's lap. She absently strokes the scruffy animal's rough, black fur, focusing on his back rather than Elodie.

"Hang on." I fling up a hand, then point at the woman with the cat. "What's going on with you and Apawllo?"

Triana looks up in surprise. "I'm petting him." The words come out as a verbal eye roll.

"He doesn't like you," Elodie says.

"That cat hates you," Leo says at the same moment.

"Clearly not." Triana scratches behind Apawllo's ears. Her cold voice takes on that goofy voice people use with babies and animals. "Who's a good kitty?" The cat purrs.

I turn to Griz, who's been watching our interchange with a disbelieving frown. "Tell me again what you think happened."

He opens his mouth, but I cut him off. "No, wait. Start with before that. Tell us about your ship and how you ended up on it."

Tom snaps to his feet, like a spring-loaded toy. "Vanti, a word?" He stalks to the hatch, pausing beside it.

Giving Griz a "we aren't finished" glare, I follow Tom across the large cabin but don't exit when he waves the hatch open. "I'm not leaving them alone with Leo and Elodie. We don't need a hostage situation."

He lowers his voice. "Are you trying to tell me you believe their ridiculous story?"

"We haven't really heard their story, yet, except the possibility that they've come from an alternate dimension."

"That's what I'm talking about—I've never heard anything so ridiculous! How would that have even happened?" He folds his arms across his chest, a vein in his brow pulsing.

"I don't know. Yet. But that is not the Griz and Triana I know." I point at the couch, keeping my voice low and even. "Maybe it's a drug-induced personality change, but I can't get to the bottom of it without finding out what they think happened."

Tom glares past me for a few seconds, then nods grudgingly.

I push past him and return to my chair. He follows, taking up a position behind my seat. I'm not sure if he's got my back or is planning on stunning the lot of us, but I know I can take him if necessary. But having him behind me still makes my shoulders twitch. I point at Griz. "Tell me why you're on the *Solar Reveler*."

He leans forward, elbows on knees, shoulders tight around his ears, eyes fixed on the deck, in an apologetic, cowering posture I've never seen Griz take before. "I left my previous employer and wanted to depart SK2. The *Solar Reveler* was leaving port and had a deck hand position listed on the transient boards, so I took it."

"Who did you work for on SK2?"

His gaze shifts to me then back to the deck. "Station security."

"Job title?"

"What does it matter?" His chin comes up, but at my continued scrutiny, he looks away. "I was a security agent."

"With the board?"

He laughs bitterly. "The board of directors? Hardly. I was a low-level nobody. I got framed and canned. You happy?" His eyes burn into me for a moment, then return to the deck.

I turn to Triana. "And you?"

She lifts her chin, the Ice Dame look back on her face. "I own this ship." An odd shadow crosses her features, then disappears. "My company purchased it several years ago, and I've been running a successful transport service since then. We needed an extra deck hand, so my… partner hired him."

"Your partner?" I lean forward. "Business partner?"

Her eyes dart to Tom and away. A faint flush of pink washes over her features then fades. "Yes."

"And who's your partner?"

She swallows hard, and her gaze flicks to Tom again. "It doesn't matter. What matters is this isn't my ship. Actually, it's a lot nicer than my ship. Mine has been reconfigured for cargo hauling. No fancy passenger cabins. This section"—she waves a hand around the cabin—"is part of the cargo hold."

"And where were you headed?"

Her eyes snap back to me, cold and calculating. Something inside me cowers a little under the weight of that gaze, but I don't let it change my expression. Our eyes lock for a long moment, until she finally looks away. "We were headed to Station Aldrin. We have cargo to deliver there."

I suppress a shiver and fight the urge to rub my arms. "So were we. How'd you end up here?" I ignore Tom's exasperated sigh.

Annabelle shrugs. Her attitude is so different from Triana's, I can't really think of her by that name. If this is a drug-induced personality change, it's phenomenal. This woman believes she is from another reality.

And maybe she is. I don't know enough about jump technology to know if what she's suggesting is possible.

"I suppose something went wrong with the jump drive. Maybe because the ships made the same jump at the same instant? You'd need to find a jump drive expert." Annabelle leans back in her seat, stroking the cat. She looks around the cabin, her eyes ticking from the high-end furniture, across the artwork hanging from the walls, to the Autokich'n at the end of the room. A satisfied smile slithers across her face and disappears.

"Don't worry, we will." I turn to the man—no longer identified as Griz in my mind. "Ser O'Neill, do you have any idea?"

He shrugs. "How would I know? I'm a security agent, not an engineer."

"I thought you were a deck hand?" Tom shifts behind me.

I try not to twitch at the movement. It feels like I have a target on my back.

Anti-Griz shrugs. "That was temporary. I've been through the academy. I'm a sec agent."

I make a mental note to keep an eye on him. He has training that can make him a formidable opponent, should it come to that.

I frown. I guess I've bought into their story—I'm thinking of both of them as people I don't really know. Or trust.

TEN
TRIANA

WITH A QUICK CHECK of my tracking tags—Fortenoy is in the crew lounge—I head out. I've been watching O'Neill, and after a visit to crew quarters, he headed into the engine room access corridor a few minutes ago. It's probably the safest possible place for us to meet. Engine rooms are loud and dirty, so no one wants to hang out there.

I tiptoe past the closed crew cabin hatches and open the one marked "engine." A low rumble emanates from the narrow passageway, accompanied by a puff of metallic-smelling air. I shut the door quickly, hoping no one noted the unusual sound. On a larger or more expensive ship, sound dampeners would have been installed, but like the med pod, those must have been removed to pay for something else.

I didn't buy Fortenoy's claim they'd removed the med-pod to extend the cargo hold. Medical equipment isn't that bulky—they're frequently integrated into the sanitation modules. If this ship doesn't have one, it was left out—or sold—to save credits.

Dim lights illuminate the narrow space. The dingy passageway houses a small landing and a steep stairway down. I turn around and back down the ladder, holding the metal railing tightly.

At the bottom of the ladder, another hatch stands closed. I wave a hand at the panel, but nothing happens.

"It's locked." O'Neill ducks out from behind the ladder.

I fling myself at him, melting into his embrace. After a few minutes, he steps back. His hair and uniform are clean, but Alt O'Neill isn't quite as shiny as mine. His hair is shaggy, and the coverall is creased.

"Are you okay?" we both ask in the same moment.

I hold up my finger, which has stopped throbbing. "Dented but no broken skin or bones."

He holds out his arms. "Tired, wrinkled, but alive."

"We can't spend much time here. I was able to spoof the systems—they show me in my cabin, and I've locked Fortenoy out. But if he comes looking, there's nowhere to hide."

"And he's going to wonder why I'm in the engine room entrance." He waves at the closed hatch. "I think I've met everyone aboard except Elodie. I'm not sure we have any allies here."

"Before I forget—connect your audio." I flick my holo-ring and activate the pairing. "Then we can talk safely. According to the OS, no one on this ship has an implant—except Fortenoy and LaSalva."

"Really?" He looks up from his holo-screen.

I nod. "This reality must be farther from our own than I realized. Everyone has audio implants back home."

He shakes his head. "Not everyone. Most of the people we interact with do—everyone on SK2, for example. And anyone at the Techno-Inst. But there are lots of people on Kaku and Grissom—probably the other planets, too—who can't afford one. And others who choose not to get electronics put into their heads."

My audio pings, and a call comes in tagged "O'Neill." I flick the accept icon. "Can you hear me?" I whisper.

"I thought you learned to do the subvocal thing?" He smirks.

"I did," I say through the audio, only moving my lips a little. "It's still hard, though."

"Keep practicing—you'll get it." He runs his finger lightly along my jaw, sending shivers through me.

I lose myself in the sensation, barely catching his words, until his hand lands on my shoulder, startling me back to reality.

"We need to figure out how to get home."

Biting my lip, I move closer, wrapping my arms around him again. I'm going to enjoy the few minutes we can steal together. "LaSalva might be willing to help us—she hates Fortenoy."

"Maybe we should tell Fortenoy what happened to us. He'll want his own Annabelle back, right?"

A bolt of lightning goes down my spine, and I jerk. "That is not a good idea. I don't know how I know, but I do. We need to keep him in the dark. We need to figure out what happened but tell as few people as possible. You've seen *Ancient TēVē*—the evil alternates always want to keep the good guys in their universe. For world domination or whatnot."

"That's fiction."

I give him the stink eye. "That's what we thought about moving to an alternate universe and look where we are now. No, if we have to tell anyone, it should be LaSalva. She's the pilot, so if we need to go anywhere, we can."

He laughs and pulls me close. "Believe it or not, you can fly this ship, too."

I lean back far enough to get a good look at his face without going cross-eyed. "I can?"

"Well, the other Annabelle can."

"I'm calling her Altabelle." I try to imagine swiping through the screens like LaSalva did but come up blank. I can write program loops and hack into almost any system, but I have no memory of flying anything. "She must have taken her flying skills with her." I heave a sigh. That would have been so convenient.

His shoulder shifts against my cheek as he shrugs. "Then we'll have to enlist LaSalva's help. Do you think you can trust her?"

"Like I said, she hates Fortenoy. If we can figure out a way to get rid of him, I bet she'd do anything to help."

"Altabelle might not like that when she gets home."

"If she gets home." My voice sounds morose, even to me.

"*When* she gets home." He runs his hands up and down my back. "We're going to figure this out. I'm going to see if I can get Vanti on our side, too."

"Let's call her V*al*ti—*al*ternate Vanti. She doesn't seem like our Vanti." I've only seen her twice, and both times, she was fetching and carrying. She didn't make eye contact with me either time.

"Maybe that's a cover?"

"Could be. Still, let's call her Valti, to keep things straight. I'd better go." I lean in to kiss him and promptly lose track of time.

I surface in a hurry when he pushes me away. "Someone is coming!"

Zark. I spoofed the system. If anyone checks the ship's locator, I'm still in my locked cabin. But O'Neill will show up here in the engine room entry, which is suspicious even if he's alone. I give him a wild look.

He pushes me toward the shadow under the ladder, then starts up it himself.

I duck into the dim corner, watching him climb through the open rungs. He stops about halfway up. "Oops. Hello, Ser Fortenoy."

"What are you doing down there?" Fortenoy's voice is cold, and my inclination to not trust him grows into a fully-fledged conviction. This guy is a problem.

"I was looking for Elodie."

I set my holo-ring to its lowest illumination and turn to hide the light between my body and the bulkhead. I need to modify the history so it shows O'Neill coming down here a few minutes ago instead of half an hour. My fingers fly through the loops, tweaking and adjusting as I keep half my mind on the conversation over my head.

"What do you want with the engineer? She's crazy, you know." Suspicion drips from the words.

As always, O'Neill is fast on his feet. "She's related to a friend of mine on Kaku. I promised to say hello, and this was the first chance I've had to get down here." He takes a couple more steps up the ladder. "She's not answering. I guess I'll leave her a note in the OS and forget about it. I tried."

Brighter light streams into the stairwell as the hatch above opens again. "You're a conscientious friend." Fortenoy's tone is dry and jeering.

"Like my mama taught me." The hatch clangs shut, leaving me alone in the dim, noisy space. I watch them on my tracker—they move together down the passageway and up the forward ladder. As soon as they reach the top deck, I hurry up this one and out into the corridor.

"What were you doing down there?" a familiar voice demands in a harsh tone.

I yelp and jump back against the now closed hatch, staring.

The woman before me wears the same coverall as the rest of the crew, but hers has bright colored patches sewn on the knees. A long, gauzy scarf winds around her neck and over her dark, curly hair. Huge, deep brown eyes, surrounded by a whole cosmetics counter, stare out of Elodie's familiar, heart-shaped face.

"I, uh, I was looking for you."

She looks me up and down, much like my own mother has done a million times. The dark eyes tick over my face and body as if totaling up a disappointing list of flaws. This is not the warm, welcoming woman from my reality. "You've found me. What do you want?"

I straighten my back, reminding myself Altabelle is the captain of this ship. "Just a routine check. I assume all systems are functioning nominally."

Her eyes narrow a little, and her head tilts as if she's calculating something. "If the OS is reporting all nominal, why would you question it?"

Zark. Of course Altabelle would check the OS. I channel my inner Ice Dame, but she seems to be busy inhabiting Elodie's body instead. "It's my ship. I don't answer to you. If I want to check every bolt and component, I will."

Her hand sweeps up, a stack of bracelets clashing together as they slide into her sleeve. "Please, be my guest."

Zark again. Now what? I don't have time for an inspection of the engine room. I step away from the hatch.

She waves at the access panel, and a cloud smell of metal and grease seems to puff out. She steps over the lip of the hatch, pausing halfway through to look back at me. "Are you coming?"

With a mental shrug, I turn away. One of the Ice Dame's most annoying tricks is to demand something, then blow it off when it's delivered. "No. If you say it's working fine, that's good enough for me." Pretending I don't care what she thinks of my waffling, I sweep away.

My holo-ring pings, and I swipe open a vid. It's LaSalva. "Rendezvous in ten minutes, captain. Would you like to join me on the bridge?"

She couldn't have called twenty seconds earlier? I risk a peek over my shoulder, but Elodie has disappeared, and the engine room door thuds shut, taking the noise with it. "I'm on my way."

ELEVEN
VANTI

I WATCH THE CAM FEED, but Anti-Griz and Annabelle haven't moved. They aren't talking to each other at all. I've managed to get into the net on the ship and made sure their audio implants are not connected. They don't seem to have noticed the change—maybe in their reality they don't use the comm system while aboard?

I drop back into my chair. Do I really believe their story? An alternate universe? How would they have gotten here and what happened to the real Griz and Triana? If you believe pop culture, our friends are now in this pair's reality, but is that how it really works?

More importantly, how do we get them back?

The ship is still on course for Station Aldrin. I've called ahead and have my contacts looking for a jump drive specialist as well as a toxicology expert. I'm not ruling anything out at this point.

I wish Griz were here to bat ideas around with me. Tom has returned to the bridge. He made it clear he believes we're dealing with some kind of drugs. Elodie and Leo are still in the lounge. They've decided to research by playing every alternate reality vid they can find, starting with last summer's blockbuster *Paradox Project*. Since it's a three-hour virtual reality experience, I don't expect them to be much help. Plus, it's fiction.

My audio buzzes—it's Tom. "We've been hailed by a small cargo ship out of Sally Ride, the *Ostelah Veesta*. The captain, Ser Kinduja, says he's related to Sera Morgan?"

"Zark. They're cousins, I think. Does he want to talk to her?"

"It seems like it. He asked that she return his call at her convenience, but he also sent a private message for her. It's in her queue."

I swipe through my screens and locate the comm system. I can see the log but can't open the message. If I had proper access, I'd be able to quarantine incoming communications. Gritting my teeth, I fire off another memo to Sterling at *CelebVid*, then check the hacking program that's still trying to break into the OS.

Nothing.

I resist the urge to bite my thumbnail. "Put me through to Ser Kinduja, please."

"One moment, please." Tom's voice cuts out, and an icon appears in my holo.

I swipe the green square, and a vid pops up. A young man—or at least young-looking—smiles at me from the bridge of a ship similar to this one. His face is familiar—he bears a strong resemblance to Triana's father, R'ger. Auburn hair sweeps back from a high forehead, and his face is angular, with a strong jaw and rugged, handsome features.

An eyebrow goes up, and his hazel eyes sparkle. "You must be Agent Fioravanti. How delightful to meet you. Arun Kinduja, at your service." He half-bows, as if we've been introduced at a party or business meeting. Like all top-levs, the man has charm. I think it's bred into them.

I don't waste time on small talk. "I wanted to touch base with you. Sera Morgan is on her honeymoon, as I'm sure you're aware—"

"The whole galaxy is aware," he says dryly.

I bite back a snort and nod. "True. Anyway, they've been… incommunicado since we departed SK2. I'll make sure she checks her messages before they depart the ship at Station Aldrin."

"Fair enough. I figured it was about time we met—Uncle R'ger has been telling me all about the shenanigans you all get up to—and I figured since we were in the same system, I'd give her a ring. It was a long shot. But maybe we can grab a drink on the station. It looks like we'll be arriving in the same window." He swivels in his chair and reaches off camera.

"You're headed for Aldrin, too?" An idea flickers through my mind. "Have you ever experienced any anomalies coming to this system?"

His head comes up, eyes searching. "What kind of anomalies?"

"We had a very strange arrival—smoothest jump I've ever encountered. And a few of the crew have experienced residual effects."

"Residual effects from a smooth transition? That sounds like an oxymoron."

"That's one of the reasons it's odd. But you know how jump can be. Some people have strange reactions." I struggle to keep my tone casual.

"Like what?" His eyes have narrowed, and his body has gone completely still.

"A little mental confusion." I shrug, as if it's no big deal. "I haven't jumped to this system before and was wondering if maybe there was a localized phenomenon—"

"There's nothing that I've ever experienced or even heard of. You should probably get a full workup on those crew members. How many of them were affected?"

"Only two. And they seem to have returned to normal." I mentally cross my fingers at the lie. "I'll make sure they both have full medical scans when they get home."

"Why wait? Surely that ship has a state-of-the-art med pod." At my raised brows, a faint flush crosses his cheeks. "I looked up the ship. Uncle R'ger had told me Triana would be headed this way and what ship she was traveling on. I'm kind of a nerd when it comes to spacecraft. In fact, that was really the reason I contacted you—I was hoping to get a look at your engines when you dock." He flashes a brilliant grin that would look at home on a seven-year-old who'd just found the rarest *Sachmo* card.

"You researched a random cruiser? You really are a spacecraft nerd." Maybe he can offer insight into this problem, but I don't want to mention it on the comms. They're supposed to be secure, but I have no control over the recordings on his ship. Who knows what their procedure is? I'll wait until we meet in person. "Is there something unusual about our engine?"

"It was retro-fitted with one of the new Plexoric DW-7s. There are only a few in service, and yours is the only one that's been installed in an existing ship." A faint flush stains his cheeks, and he gives me puppy dog eyes like a child hoping for a treat. "I'd love to see it."

I fight down my involuntary urge to smile back at him. "I'll see what I can set up when we get to port. See you in twenty-one hours?"

"I'll be there." He gives me another blinding smile—one that seems to warm up my whole body—and signs off.

Zarking top-levs. Their unfair advantage of years of gene tweaking and selective breeding means they're all gorgeous, charming, and super smart. My imposter syndrome rears its ugly head.

Objectively, I know I'm smarter than average. And better looking. Those are two of the reasons the Colonial Commonwealth Intelligence Agency recruited me all those years ago. Charm is definitely not my strong suit. But otherwise, I can hold my own against any top-lev. That doesn't keep me from feeling a twinge of inferiority on occasion. I'll do a double workout tonight and get my head back into the game.

Charm aside, Arun Kinduja is Triana's family. They are cousins, and the Kindujas are known for their ability to stay off the radar. Plus, if his Uncle R'ger is to be believed, he's a genius—as I said, extra smarts are bred into the top-levs. If Annabelle and Anti-Griz really are from a different reality, Arun might be exactly the kind of space nerd we need to send them back.

I need a primer on alternate reality. If we were closer to the station, I could grab data from the university, although I might not have the educational background to understand the physics.

But downloading an academic paper would take days at this distance. I'll have to take the second best option. More like the tenth best option, but it's the one I have access to right now. With a long, loud sigh, I flick my holo-ring and swipe open the *Ancient TēVē* app.

TWELVE
TRIANA

FORTENOY WORKS the controls to the rear cargo hold airlock. If we were dirtside, the tall door would rotate down to form a ramp, but out here in the vacuum of space, that would mean everything—and everyone—floating away into the unknown. Instead, he activates a force tunnel that connects to the *Ostelah Veesta's* cargo hatch, and the doors split down the center, retracting into the sides.

I stand inside the hold, watching through the window. Another force shield separates me from the animals—literally. Behind me, a whole army of quockoa hurl eggs which splat against the invisible wall. I look over my shoulder at the carnage—how can they produce so many?

And how are we going to be sure we've gotten them all off the ship? Altabelle really didn't think this cargo through.

"We're docked." The ship's OS works through the protocols, with Fortenoy narrating as it goes. "Tunnel engaged and tested. All systems green." His performance makes me think of an *Ancient TēVē* vid in which the only female crew member's job was to repeat what the computer said. I smother a snicker as he turns.

And pulls out his stunner. "Are you ready to see your cousin, Annabelle?"

I lift my nose in the air and give him a haughty look. "Do you really think you need that?"

Fortenoy lifts the weapon. "There's nothing wrong with a little backup."

I shake my head and look away. The relationship between Fortenoy and Altabelle is weird. He's controlling and a bit abusive in a gaslighty way, but he doesn't seem surprised by my more assertive responses. Of course, maybe my disdain doesn't register—how could I possibly not find him irresistible?

The doors slide apart, revealing three men. They all wear gear that looks like it came from *Handsome Rogues Catalogue*. Black *lether* jackets, tall boots, tight pants, and stunners strapped to each thigh. The guy on the right holds a blast rifle.

The tallest, standing in the center, looks like a younger version of my father—reddish hair, strong jaw, chiseled features. He has to be Arun. He smiles when he spots me and strides forward, spreading both arms wide. "Annabelle!"

"Arun." I resist the urge to hug him, presenting my cheek to be air-kissed as I've seen Mother do countless times.

He ignores the move and wraps both arms around me in a bear hug. His voice vibrates softly in my ear. "So good to see you!"

Fortenoy clears his throat and moves closer.

Arun releases me and turns to him, holding out a fist. "Nice to see you, Fortenoy." His tone says it isn't nice.

Bumping his knuckles against Arun's, Fortenoy nods. "Right on time as always, Kinduja. Do you have our payment?"

"Why are you always so anxious to get to business, Tom? Annabelle and I haven't seen each other in ages. We need to hang out. Have a beer. Gossip about the family." He slides an arm around my shoulders, ignoring the stunner in Fortenoy's hand.

Fortenoy gives up and holsters the weapon with a grumble. "I guess I'll take care of business while you two… chat." He tilts his head toward the two men still standing at the hatch. "Can they run the inventory?"

Arun waves at his crewmates. "That's why I brought 'em. Franco, Winle, make sure Annabelle's boyfriend doesn't forget anything."

Fortenoy grinds his teeth. "I didn't forget anything last time. That box was behind a—"

Arun interrupts him with a laugh. "Still so prickly, Tom? Relax. I know it was an accident." He jerks his head at the men, then turns beside me, pushing me toward the end of the airlock. "Is there a way to get around the jungle? I don't want to get egg on my jacket."

With a chuckle, I lead him past the emui stall and through another hatch. As we depart, I catch O'Neill's eye. He stands with Valti and two other crew members, ready to assist with the unloading. He ignores my look, but his voice comes through my audio implant. "Be careful."

I give a tiny nod, then we step through the internal force shield, and the hatch closes behind us.

Arun pulls on one of my red, corkscrew curls. "Do these things get curlier every time you go through the shield?"

I pull away and climb the ladder. "Why, do they look frizzy?"

"I said curly, not frizzy. The curly gene must come from your mother's side. None of us Kindujas have that much wave."

I take him to the crew lounge and get a pair of beers from the fridge. He pulls an opener from a drawer—knowing exactly where to get it—and pops the top off the bottle. Clearly, he and Altabelle have come here together many times.

He raises his bottle. "To old friends."

"Friends?" I take a sip and give him a questioning look. "We're family."

He clasps a hand to his chest. "You wound me, cousin! We're friends, too, I hope." He sips again and looks around the compartment. "Where's everyone else?"

I sit on the edge of one of the armchairs. "They're down in cargo, unloading."

"Even the lovely Carina?"

"Carina LaSalva? She's on the bridge. Who do you think flew the rendezvous?"

"You usually do it, but you were down there to greet me, so I guess I should have known. Is she going to help with the transfer?" He prowls around the room like a caged animal. Hopefully, he won't resort to throwing eggs.

"Why? Do you want to see her? She'd be thrilled to have you visit the bridge." I set my beer on the table and cross my arms. "What's going on?"

"Something feels off, today. You feel it, too, don't you? That's why you've got Carina at the ready. In case we need to—" He flicks his fingers outward.

"You think the Commonwealth have agents out here watching for contraband quockoa?" My stomach churns. O'Neill and I will never get back to our own reality if we're locked up in a Commonwealth prison.

"I don't think so," he says slowly, rolling his shoulders. "We've both paid the bri— I mean 'fees.' But something is different."

Can he tell I'm not the real Altabelle? Feigning a relaxed attitude, I sip my beer. It's good.

With a shrug, he drops onto the couch and launches into a meandering story about one of his siblings. I take note of the names—cousins I've heard about but never met—but don't worry about the details. I can use the feeling of uneasiness as a reason for not remembering later, if necessary.

He sets his empty bottle on the low table in front of the couch and leans forward. "Are you going to see your dad on Armstrong?"

I shrug. "I hadn't really decided yet."

His eyes narrow, then he smiles. "You never like to be pinned down, do you? But you're definitely going to the planet, right?"

I'd checked our flight plan earlier—we were scheduled to dock at Aldrin in two days. "I'm not sure about that either. We'll be at the station for four days, though."

"It doesn't take that long to pick up cargo." He reaches into his jacket pocket, then holds out a small, paper-wrapped parcel. "Give that to R'ger, will you? No need to mention it to Tom."

"You don't like him much, do you?" I accept the palm-sized box.

"No one does. I don't think you really like him." He leans back, shaking his head. "I don't understand why he's even on this ship. The guy is a—" He breaks off as the door slides open.

Fortenoy stands in the opening, hands on hips, brows lowered. "Isn't this cozy? But you'll have to save the reunion for later. Cargo is transferred, and we're getting out of here."

Arun raises an eyebrow at me. "I'm not in a hurry. Are you, cousin?"

I slide my hand behind me, where Fortenoy won't see the box, glancing between the two men. I definitely don't want to sit here with both of them, but I can't think of an excuse to get rid of Fortenoy. "You did say the meet was feeling off. Maybe we should—" I make the same outward motion he used earlier.

He rises, picking up his bottle. "Fair enough. We'll get together another time, Annabelle. Thanks for the beer."

As Fortenoy moves aside to let Arun through the door, I tuck the box into the pocket of my baggy coverall. Maybe this is why Altabelle has everyone wear them. You can hide a lot of stuff in these pockets. I follow my cousin down the corridor, Fortenoy bringing up the rear. He really doesn't like letting Altabelle out of his sight.

We stop at the open cargo hatch where the other two men wait. Arun gives me another hug. "Tell Uncle R'ger I said hello."

"We will." Fortenoy puts an arm around me, his hand like a vice on my shoulder. "Safe travels."

I lift a hand in farewell. Arun gives me that blinding grin again, then follows his crewmates out the airlock. They've barely pushed off into the tunnel when Fortenoy slaps a hand through the door icon. The sides of the hatch slide inward, hiding the men from view.

Fortenoy makes another angry swipe to start the disconnect process, then turns to me. "What did he want?"

The corner of the small box pokes my thigh, as if reminding me not to tell him. "Nothing. Just catching up with family." I make a mental note to deal with the lounge vid as soon as I get a free second.

"You aren't really planning on seeing *Uncle R'ger,* are you?" He sneers as he says the name.

"Why wouldn't I?"

"I don't like how proprietary he is. I know he loaned you the money to purchase this ship, but what makes him think he can tell you how to run your company?"

No, that's your job, isn't it? Bullies never like it when their victim listens to someone else's advice. This R'ger must be a lot different from my real father—he never tries to tell me what to do. Even when I ask him directly.

He's also never loaned me money, but in my reality, I haven't needed it. At least not since the Techno-Inst. "I'm sure he has my best interests at heart."

"Right." His sour tone makes it clear R'ger doesn't have Fortenoy's best interest at heart, and he knows it.

The intercom beeps, and LaSalva's voice comes through. "Attention crew. Undocking complete. We're on course for Station Aldrin. Estimated arrival, twenty hours, thirty-seven minutes."

Fortenoy swipes through commands on the control station by the door. A loud whoop sounds through the cargo hold, and I slap my hands over my ears. A tiny grin twitches across Fortenoy's face as he dials down the volume. "Sorry, darling." He doesn't sound sorry.

A red banner across the holo-screen indicates he's set the airlock to full open with a ten-minute delay. He's blowing the hatches? That will suck everything in the cargo hold into the vacuum of space.

He flicks a few more screens, activating the ship's comm system. "Cargo hold purge in ten minutes. All crew exit the hold." He slaps the system off, then turns and points toward the empty emui stables. "Let's get outta here. Gotta make sure none of those creepy little creatures are still on the ship."

"You're going to space them?" I stare at him, but he grabs my shoulder and swivels me to face the exit.

"Can't have any contraband aboard when we reach Aldrin. We cut it too close last time. I don't need to tangle with the law." He must notice the rigidity of my shoulder under his hand because he chuckles. "Don't worry, darling, we're in this together. I'll take care of you, too."

Why does that sound more like a threat than a promise?

THIRTEEN
VANTI

TWO DAYS LATER, we finally approach Station Aldrin. I've watched fifteen hours of *Ancient TēVē*—kill me now. Elodie retired to her cabin with a migraine, but Leo has worked his way through another ten hours of vid. While Captain Chowdhury brings the ship in to dock, Leo and I meet in the lounge.

"As far as I can tell, there's no consensus on how to jump between universes." Leo rubs a hand over his short hair. He's ditched the turban while aboard, and his dark bristle stands upright, like freshly-mown grass. "In some vids, it's an external force—aliens or enemy agents. In others, it's an anomaly. Sometimes it's something the crew did to try to make the ship faster. In *Galaxy Cruise: The Movie*, they cobbled together ancient alien tech!"

"*That's* what we're missing. Go find some ancient alien tech, will you, Leo?" I groan as I drop onto the couch. "If I have to watch another melodramatic, badly edited, poorly cast—"

I'm interrupted by a ping on my holo-ring. The message tells me I'm connected to the Aldrin communications network. "Finally!" I flick the icon and log into the CCIA customer service system. After confirming my registration and typing in two passcodes, I enter a secret command, which takes me to the classified agency login. There, I have to use a retina scan, an independent DNA reader, and enter two passcodes—one of which includes physical actions. Don't worry, I have Leo leave the cabin for that part. No way I'm letting anyone see me do the chicken dance.

"I'm in!" I swipe the door release to allow Leo back into the lounge. "Checking my messages…"

I slump down into the couch.

"Bad news?" Leo returns to his armchair.

"Nothing. I asked for any research the CCIA had on alternate realities, and all they've got is data on a crackpot who lives on Armstrong who claims he can see the other side." I give the last few words a spooky tone.

Leo's brows draw down. "Vanti does silly voices?"

Heat spreads through my chest, but I've trained myself not to blush. With my pale skin, embarrassment is painfully obvious. "Not normally. But I'm tired. And cranky. And if you ever tell anyone—"

"You'll kill me?" His eyes go ridiculously wide, and he wraps his hands around his throat and gags.

"No. I'll have the CCIRS audit your taxes."

"Much worse." His hands drop from his neck. "I hate to sound crazy, but maybe we should go visit the crackpot. I mean, we basically believe the same thing he does—that a person can"—he wiggles his fingers—"cross to the other side."

"The other side makes it sound like they're dead." I press my lips together, concentrating to keep my hands in my lap so I won't chew my thumbnail. "But you're right. This might be our only lead. What do we do with Annabelle and Anti-Griz in the meantime?"

He chuckles at the names. "They've got a really nice suite, with entertainment and an AutoKich'n. I say lock them in and tell the captain not to open the door. Maybe restrict their comms." As he completes this thought, his jaw drops open. He closes it and swallows. "Can this Annabelle do all the comm system juju that Triana does?"

I take a deep breath and let it out with a long sigh. "I don't know. I don't think so, but maybe she hasn't tried yet?"

"Then let's take them with us. Not that I don't trust them, but if there's one thing all those *Ancient TēVē* vids have taught me, it's 'don't trust them.'

The alternate reality characters are always evil. Although ours don't have goatees."

I give him my best steely-eyed glare, and his laughter cuts out as if I flipped a switch. *Still got it, Vanti.* Pursing my lips to hide a satisfied grin, I get to my feet. "We'll take them along. Maybe they can help us."

ELODIE HAS RECOVERED ENOUGH from her headache to pilot the shuttle to the surface. The idea that Elodie is a pilot is both incredible and terrifying. But Tom says he flew a check ride with her when they met at *CelebVid* HQ, and she's quite proficient.

A simple dirtside drop doesn't require a second pilot, so I sit in the right seat while she flies. Leo, Annabelle, and Anti-Griz ride in the small passenger compartment. A ship the size of the *Solar Reveler* can execute a planetary landing, but taking the tiny shuttle saves a lot of energy. Plus, unlike the interstellar cruiser, these things can go almost anywhere.

In this case, "almost anywhere" is the parking lot beside a Big Stuff store. Elodie sets us down so gently I don't realize we've landed until she starts the shutdown sequence. "We're here."

I squint at the holo hovering in front of her, but I can't quite read the text. With a smile, she flicks the file at me and continues swiping through the screens, flicking icons and dictating items into the logbook.

I stretch the map and enter the coordinates for our destination. A line appears, showing multiple routes, including the fastest, most scenic, and "best bars." A list of transportation options loads on the side. The closest Rent-a-Float is farther than our destination, but their app will send the vehicle to us in about twenty minutes.

"We don't need that." Elodie swipes the shut-down icon at the end of her checklist and the holo-screens go out. She jumps from her seat and climbs through the hatch to the passenger space.

Leo, Annabelle, and Anti-Griz have released their restraints and stand in the aisle between the two sets of seats. Annabelle wears an expensive pantsuit completely out of character for Triana. Hy-Mi must have packed her wardrobe. Anti-Griz looks uncomfortable in Griz's casual slacks and tunic. Leo straightens his turban and shakes out his pale green robe. The overhead lights catch on the metallic embroidery, highlighting the fantastic creatures depicted on it.

Apawllo sits upright in the seat closest to the door and yawns, as if he's tired of waiting.

I catch Elodie's sleeve. "You brought the cat?"

"No, he brought himself. Come on, Apawllo." She flicks an icon on her holo-ring, and the hatch opens, revealing steps folding down. The cat remains seated until the stairs lock into place, then he leaps to the deck and trots down the steps. At the bottom, he waits for Elodie, and the two of them head for the stern of the ship.

We're parked behind a large, boxy building. Cargo floats slide past, delivering wrapped loads to the rear of the store, where automated lifts transfer them into the building. Another in-system shuttle is parked across the way. Elodie flicks a payment to a virtual parking kiosk accessed through the planetary net.

Behind us, a green field stretches to a low fence, where another field starts. From here, it looks like the agricultural area goes on for several klicks, ending in steep hills. The tops are covered in thick clouds that rise to meet the gray overcast sky. The fields are damp, and the scents of green growing things overwhelm the faint whiff of shuttle fuel.

Stifling a groan, I close the neck of my customary black jacket against the chill and follow them. "I'm going to call the Rent-a-Float."

"I told you we don't need that." Elodie swipes and pokes, and a hatch on the back of the ship pops open. She reaches in and pulls out a hoverboard. "See, we have local transport. Who needs a rental?"

I take the first one and check out the specs. These are top-of-the-line, like everything else *CelebVid* has provided. I was skeptical at the beginning, but they seem to have done this sponsorship thing up right.

"I'm okay with hoverboards, but I don't know if the others are proficient." I raise my brows at Leo as he rounds the corner of the ship. "You can surf, so this is probably no big deal for you, right?"

"I love these things!" He takes the board I point to and activates it. The device floats about ten centimeters from the plasphalt surface, bobbing a little in the light breeze. Leo jumps on, landing lightly. The board sinks, then bounces up, and he swoops away to take a lap around the parking lot.

"No." Annabelle stands beside the ship, arms crossed. "I do not do *that*."

I hand another board to Anti-Griz before responding. "Yes, you do. It's what we've got. If you've never ridden one before, you can sit down." I flick the controls of the board, slaving it to my own, then set the altitude at one meter. "I'll tow you."

She stands there, staring me down. I refrain from rolling my eyes as I tether Anti-Griz's board to mine as well. No way I'm letting these two wander Armstrong by themselves. The real Triana is trouble, but I know her well enough to compensate. This one is an unknown quantity, and I'm not letting her out of my sight.

Movement catches my eye as Apawllo springs to the back of Elodie's board. She's got a *CelebVid* drone circling above her head, filming as she trails behind Leo around the lot. "Wheee! This is awesome!" The board tilts into a corner, and Elodie's arms windmill, but she doesn't fall. The cat looks bored.

I check on Annabelle. She's still standing beside the floating board, her eyes focused beyond the ship. I increase my altitude to look, but there's nothing interesting. She's just using the Ice Dame's trick of staring off into space to make everyone else feel ignored and inferior.

I shake off a twinge of annoyance and flick the board interface. The unoccupied board drops a little lower. "Morgan." When she finally turns, I point at her, then the board, and give her the steely-eyed glare that cowed Leo earlier. "Sit."

Her lip curls, then she turns away to lower her butt onto the gently bobbing surface. It drops a few centimeters as her weight settles, and she hitches herself a little more securely onto it, sitting sidesaddle, her ramrod straight back to me. I raise the board so her feet won't hit anything, but she doesn't react.

With a shrug, I set it to travel a meter in front of and to the right of my own, with Anti-Griz's in the same position on the left. "Ready?"

"I can ride this thing," Anti-Griz grumbles. "I don't need the tether."

"I want to make sure we stay together." I set the destination into the system and flick to engage icon.

"You mean you want to make sure I have no control. It's not like I'm going to wander off." He glares over his shoulder at me.

"I don't know that. For all I know, you're a wanted man in your own reality, and you've decided to stay here instead of going back."

Did his shoulders tense in response to that remark? I peer at Annabelle, but she's still ignoring me, riding the board like an ancient queen on her high-tech litter.

But that raises a question. Do they want to go back to their own reality? Here, Annabelle is the pampered heir to the Morgan mega-fortune and Anti-Griz is her new husband. From the little they've told us, in their reality, she owns a small cargo ship and not much else. He seems to be a newly fired security agent she employed as a deck hand. Neither of them have mentioned family or friends—they seem to have little to go back to.

In the *Ancient TēVē* vids, the evil alternates always want to stay and plunder the new reality.

I grit my teeth. I can't believe I'm making decisions based on *Ancient TēVē*.

But keeping an eye on these two is second nature to me. I'm known for being suspicious and careful, and I'm going to stick to my image to the letter on this adventure.

We exit the parking lot and move into a lightly populated street. Leo and Elodie catch up, then slow to match my cautious pace. Hoverboards, float panels, and a few enclosed vehicles share one side of the broad road, all traveling in the same direction. The other is reserved for pedestrians. It's late afternoon, and a lot of people are out and about, strolling, shopping, and chatting.

The buildings on either side rise four or five stories. Businesses and shops occupy the ground level, and the upper floors appear to be homes. Flowering plants hang from balconies, hiding chairs and tables. Laundry flutters from lines strung across the side streets.

Nearly everyone we pass points at and comments on the cat. Heads turn and voices exclaim. Has no one here ever seen a feline on a hoverboard?

Elodie waves and responds to the comments as if she's part of a parade. The drone continues to circle overhead, catching all of it and probably broadcasting it across the galaxy.

I make a mental note to ask Elodie about that. We don't want our current situation reported. Anything related to the Morgan family needs to be kept under wraps.

It suddenly occurs to me that I no longer work for SK'Corp and protecting the Morgan name is not my concern. It was always secondary to my real mission for the CCIA, but maintaining their privacy was essential to preserving my cover. Now that I—ostensibly—work for Elodie, I don't have to care about the Morgans.

Except upsetting the status quo could draw attention to me. Not to mention Annabelle and Anti-Griz shouldn't be out here without their regular security contingent, and that's my fault.

They didn't travel with security because SK'Corp has agents on Station Aldrin waiting to protect them as soon as they leave the ship. But we didn't follow the planned itinerary, and the security team doesn't know we've taken a little jaunt dirtside.

Ice water pours through my veins. I've become so convinced they aren't the real Griz and Triana that I've circumvented their security. I've done this countless times before—but always in service of my CCIA mission. This time, I've dragged them into potential danger on an unfamiliar planet for no good reason.

Except I believe they're completely different people. Maybe I'm the crazy one. *Okay, Vanti, time to regroup.* No one knows who we are. I've been watching for potential dangers because that's second nature to me, so I'm not worried about opportunistic thugs getting the drop on us. After a quick mental weapons inventory, I relax a tiny fraction.

But the attention the cat is getting makes me nervous. Maybe I should send Elodie on a side trip.

We leave the little shopping district, and the buildings on either side decrease in height. We pass fewer pedestrians, and they all move with more purpose, as if they have a destination in mind. Most of the heads still turn to watch Apawllo as we pass, but we get fewer comments called out. Elodie sends the drone back to the ship without me asking.

I initiate a call to her. "Why'd you do that?"

"What?" She turns to look at me and almost loses her balance. The cat meows loudly, leaning to the side to counterbalance her weight. The board jitters, then steadies.

"Careful! I don't want to have to peel you off the street. Why'd you send the drone away?"

She casts another tiny grin over her shoulder, only wobbling a little this time. Apawllo bats her leg in reprimand, and she straightens up. "We don't want this broadcast all over the galaxy. No one needs to know about the alternate reality thing."

I stare at her in disbelief. "Did you get shifted from an alternate reality, too? The Elodie I know is all about the publicity."

Her hoverboard drops back until we're side by side, and she turns a wounded look on me. "I would never throw my friends under the shuttle! I may be frivolous and careless, and I know I got this job because I seem to be a little bit wild, but I love Triana and Ty, and I'd *never* sell them out." Tears pool in her eyes.

I think about all the times Elodie has misbehaved in my presence, and she's right. She's always protected Triana. "I'm sorry. That was uncalled for. I know you wouldn't betray a friend."

She wipes away the tears that trickled down her cheek and smiles, all forgiven. She might be a pain in the neck, but she doesn't hold a grudge. With a watery smile, she bounces the board a little, earning an angry hiss from the cat. "Sorry, Apawllo." She bends to stroke the cat's head—somehow maintaining perfect balance—then straightens and looks at me. "Where are we going, anyway?"

FOURTEEN
TRIANA

I SLOUCH in the right seat as we approach the enormous sphere of Station Aldrin. I've never been here before, and it looks a lot like the evil empire's planet-killer from *Ancient TēVē*. Carina LaSalva gave me a funny look when I told her to dock, making me think Altabelle doesn't usually let her do it. But after a long, thoughtful pause, she nodded and initiated the docking procedures. Which is a good thing, since I have no idea how to do any of it.

Note to self: learn to pilot a ship.

Before we can open the hatch, the station demands payment. I wave a hand through the QuikPay icon. My access to the ship's OS has connected me seamlessly to the station's systems, and the charge goes through to Altabelle's account. The telltale stays red for a long moment.

I should probably check how much credit she has in there. What if she's overdrawn?

Then it flips to green, and the open icon appears on the hatch panel.

"What are you waiting for?" Fortenoy leans past me to tap the screen. "I have an appointment."

I look at him in surprise. I thought I'd have to give him the slip, but he's going to just walk away? Perfect. "I didn't realize you had anything planned."

He flushes a little and coughs. "Not really a plan. I have to see someone about our next cargo."

"Should I come, too?" I mentally cross my fingers, hoping he doesn't want me along. I wish I had one of Vanti's bugs so I could find out what he's up to, but I'm more interested in getting rid of him than knowing.

"No, I've got it covered. Take your spa day—I'll deal with the business." Without waiting for a reply, he strides away.

His condescending tone sets my teeth on edge—even though Carina and I *do* have appointments at the Relaxed Spacer Sauna and Massage Center. I force my shoulders away from my ears and exit the airlock, the rest of the crew on my heels. When the last person exits, I lock the ship and set a few extra security precautions in place. With a tiny nod to O'Neill, I follow LaSalva toward the spa.

The Relaxed Spacer is a low-end spa with automated facilities which is perfect for my needs. Carina disappears into a changing cubicle with a "see you in a couple of hours, boss."

I step into the tiny room and wave at the program panel. It lights up with a range of spa services, including a few I've never heard of. Hot chocolate wrap? It's meant to be decadent, but it seems like a terrible waste of chocolate. Although it's probably a chocolate scented fake.

I link my holo-ring to the panel and hack into the system. A few quick tweaks sets a remote lock on my cubicle door and logs a full spectrum of services for the occupant.

When I'm done, I peek out into the hall. No one is in sight, and I've spoofed the cams. I slip out of the facility, then remotely lock the room and slink into the crowd on the concourse outside.

Aldrin has been renovated many times over the centuries—in fact, according to social media, it's constantly under construction. But this is my first time here, and I'm impressed. Sleek brushed metal and matte black plastek give a modern vibe to the ancient station. The padded decks put a little bounce in my step—or maybe that's the lower-than-standard gravity.

I stride past the typical spacer bars and dance halls, all hidden behind genteel facades, and head for the dirtside shuttles. At one time, our ship had a shuttle capable of dropping to the planet, but Altabelle must have sold it to make room for more cargo—or pay off some bills.

O'Neill lurks behind a tall potted plant in the departure lounge. I don't bother suppressing a grin when I spot him, and he smirks back at me.

Which is when I notice his face.

"What is that?"

His hand creeps to his chin, fingering the rough bristle around his mouth. Pink washes over his cheeks, but he lifts his chin. "I'm growing a goatee. Alt-O'Neill should have one, don't you think?"

I close my eyes, biting my lip. Of course he looks just as shiny with facial hair... Except he doesn't. My eyes pop open so I can double check.

Nope. For whatever reason, in this reality, O'Neill isn't his usual, shiny self. Clearly Alt-O'Neill has led a rougher life, and it's reflected in his less than perfect skin and the hair that refuses to fall into place at all times.

But I still love him.

After a quick look to make sure no one who might know us is watching, I lean in for a kiss. His arms slide around me, and I lose myself in a blissfu—

"Ahem."

We jump apart, swinging around to confront the intrusion.

Valti stands before us, eyes narrowed, hands on hips. "What is going on here?" Unlike O'Neill, the multi-universe has granted Lindsay Fioravanti perfect hair and skin in both realities. Her mousy attitude has vanished, and the resemblance to our Vanti is unsettling.

Heart thumping at double speed, I straighten my shoulders and stiffen my spine. "Nothing that concerns you."

One brow goes up. "My employer might not agree."

"I'm your employer."

O'Neill takes a half-step forward, shielding me from her glare. His voice lowers to a menacing growl. "Who is your real employer?"

Her eyes flick over his face and body, cataloging the threat, then slide to me as if he's of no concern. But she angles herself in a way that makes it clear she's wary of both of us. She jerks her chin at the shuttle gate. "I need to speak with you in a neutral location. On the shuttle would be acceptable. I assume you're dropping?"

"We might be." I move a half-step to the right, so O'Neill's shoulder doesn't block her face, but stay back. I might have discounted this version of Lindsay Fioravanti when we first arrived, but she's shed her cowed deck hand persona and appears to be as capable as our Vanti. Maybe more.

She nods once and strolls to the ticket kiosk.

O'Neill gives me a quick look and follows. I hang back, giving him room to do his thing if she becomes an active threat. Something about this reality makes me more cautious. I make a mental note to brag about my prudence later.

He waits until Valti moves away from the kiosk, then turns so he can watch my back while I purchase fares. I wave a hand through the interface, selecting two seats in economy and charging them to Altabelle's account. I hold my breath until the icon flicks to green and the tickets appear in my virtual wallet.

We wait in the lounge, not speaking. I keep Valti in my peripheral vision while watching the entrance to the lounge. Hopefully I gave Fortenoy enough time to get wherever he's going, but since I'm not tracking him, I have no idea where that might be. He could decide to take a shuttle to the planet.

Finally, the boarding sign changes to green and my holo-ring vibrates with the boarding message. O'Neill and I join the queue of passengers, but Vanti hangs back. My ring vibrates again as we cross the threshold, marking us as present. We walk down the opaque gangway tunnel and enter the shuttle.

A narrow aisle stretches the length of the craft, with fifteen rows of three seats on either side. I step into the second vacant row and take the seat by the windowless wall. O'Neill settles in beside me, leaving the aisle seat empty.

As the hatch clangs shut, Valti appears and slips into the empty seat on the aisle. The shuttle isn't full—the rows in front of and behind us are magically empty, as are the seats across the aisle.

"How'd you manage that?" I nod across the aisle.

"Trade secret." Valti fastens her seat restrains and closes her eyes. "Wait until we launch."

I raise my eyebrows at O'Neill, and he shrugs in response. My audio implant pings with a local call, and I accept.

"I'm betting she's CCIA here, too." His voice is warm and comforting in my ear.

"That would be a good thing, right?" I murmur.

"Depends on what her mission is. But generally, the CCIA are the good guys." His head waggles side to side a bit, as if he's reconsidering that comment. "Mostly. Sometimes."

Wow, I feel so much better. But I get where he's coming from. Vanti has always been a bit fast and loose with my security, thanks to her secret CCIA missions. I lean back in my seat and take a few deep breaths.

The intercom pings, and a voice welcomes us to the shuttle. "The system reports all passengers and crew are strapped in. We're pushing back from the dock right now. Once we clear the arm, we'll boost away from the station, then begin our descent. We'll arrive at the Collinsville space field in about twenty-three minutes. Prepare for acceleration."

We lose gravity, and my butt drifts away from the seat, but the five-point harness keeps me in place. Nothing seems to happen for a while—without windows, there's no way to know how far we've moved. Then we're shoved back into our seats as the engines kick in. Despite shielding built into the craft, the rumble of the engines rises.

"The empty seats weren't my doing," Valti admits, her voice barely audible over the burn. "That was luck. Engine noise is sufficient, as long as we keep our voices down. Do you two have audio?" She taps her jaw under her ear.

O'Neill raises his brows at me, then turns to Valti. "I wouldn't give my private ID code to a stranger if I did."

"Stranger?" Her lips press together, then she nods. "Fair enough." She flicks her holo-ring, and mine vibrates with an incoming introduction file.

I tap my ring and pull up the file. A blue frame flashes around the data, indicating it's been cleared and confirmed by the station OS, even though we're no longer connected to the station. Either she's very good at faking government credentials, or the ID is accurate. It lists Lindsay Fioravanti as a CCIA operative.

O'Neill makes a tiny shrug and speaks through our audio link. "Looks legit to me."

"Looks legit in our reality," I mutter under my breath. "I can't double check it here until we reach the planet."

"Vanti always tells me to trust my gut, so I'm going to see what she has to say." He waits for my grunt of approval, then flicks his ring.

My audio pings. "Incoming call from Lindsay Fioravanti. Add to call?" O'Neill approves the connection to our joint call, and an icon appears on my holo showing a third participant. I accept and swipe the interface away.

"As you can see from the ID, I'm a CCIA operative." Valti's voice is low and clear in my ear. "I was assigned to infiltrate your ship and monitor the activities of one Thomas Fortenoy."

"Why are you telling us this? Sera Morgan is in a relationship with Fortenoy, and I just joined the crew."

A faint snort comes through the system. "That was true a few days ago. But something happened during our jump, didn't it?"

My eyes fly open, and I lean forward to look at Valti. She relaxes in her chair, eyes closed, face blank. One eyelid cracks to give me a piercing glare, then closes again. "Sit back, Morgan."

"Why do you think something happened during jump?" O'Neill asks.

Another snort, this one a little louder. "You mean aside from Morgan confirming it with her reaction?" She doesn't wait for a response. "You stopped communicating with me. And when I tried to check in, you called me Vanti."

"Why would I do that?" O'Neill tries to keep his voice as emotionless as hers, but I can hear the excitement in it.

"Exactly. You would never attempt to communicate with me in front of a target. That made me suspicious. Then I noticed you taking risks to speak with Morgan. You didn't respond to my attempts to communicate. She's started standing up to Fortenoy, when before she did whatever he demanded. And now you're sneaking off to the planet together. I want to know what happened."

FIFTEEN
VANTI

I HOLD up a fist to indicate a halt, but Elodie skims past me. She reaches the far side of a neatly paved courtyard, then spins her hoverboard on its tail to look back. She's become surprisingly proficient during our little jaunt. "Are we stopping?"

The cat hisses, his claws gripping the plastek surface.

"That's what this means." I raise my hand higher and wave it a little.

"Sorry, I didn't study military hand signals." She floats back toward me, as if bobbing down a lazy river.

"I didn't either, but even I know that one." Annabelle slides off her board, jumping the few centimeters to the ground.

Anti-Griz stays aboard, his knees slightly flexed, poised to leap off at a moment's notice. He's a trained sec agent—even if he was fired—so his alert stance is second nature. "Why are we here?" He waves a hand at a sign that reads "Department of Experiential Physics."

We've stopped in a courtyard at the University of Armstrong, Collinsville. Tall buildings soar on all six sides of the space. Narrow alleys between the buildings provide glimpses of the rest of the campus. Hoverboards and float chairs zip across broad, green quads, and students play rev-ball in the distance.

But this courtyard is quiet. Blank windows, some covered by broken blinds and tattered curtains, stare down at us. The buildings cast a heavy shadow on most of the paved hexagon—we've stopped in a narrow stripe of sunlight.

"We're here to see Professor Wilmer van Lieugen y Ongkowijaya." I clear my throat, the words I'm about to say balking on the way out. "He claims he can see across the multiverse."

The others don't say a word. I expected ridicule, but I guess they're as invested in this idea as I am.

Hopping off my board, I flick the controls to land Anti-Griz's and Annabelle's next to my own. "We can leave these here." I tilt my board against the brick wall of the nearest building, putting it at the best angle to allow the solar surface to recharge in the sun. The others lean their boards beside mine. Once they're all lined up, I engage the mag lock. It essentially attaches the boards to the building so no one can walk away with them.

We troop into the building and up one flight of wide stone steps. The code slip on my holo-ring makes it vibrate in a way that feels like someone pulling my hand forward. I follow the haptic directions down a wide hall and turn at a narrower one. Near the middle of a long, dark hallway, the sensations stop by a plain synth-wood door. The placard on the door indicates our quarry is inside.

Or at least this is his office. I slide my hand over the panel, but it doesn't light up. Trying again produces the same non-result. With a mental shrug, I knock.

A muffled response comes through the door. Assuming the speakers tied to the non-responsive panel are inactive, I turn the archaic knob and push the door ajar. "Professor van Lieugen?"

A hand snaps out and latches onto my wrist. Instinct kicks in immediately, and I swing my arm around, twisting against my attacker's thumb. He drops my arm with an exclamation. In the same instant, I lock onto his wrist and rotate, spinning him around until his hand is pinned behind his back.

"Hey!" An elderly man with gray hair and a wrinkled face twists his neck to peer at me over his rumpled shoulder. A beret-style hat slips across his bald pate, and he grabs it with his free hand, holding it in place.

He shifts, trying to get me in view, and I pull his arm upward, wrenching his shoulder back.

Ignoring his gasp of pain, I instantly catalogue the room. A heavy desk sits in front of a narrow window that looks out into a courtyard so small it's probably better classified as a ventilation shaft. Stacks of old-style books and papers litter every horizontal surface, seeming to defy gravity as they lean crazily against one another. Cryptic equations and text in tiny, cramped writing cover the side walls. No one else is in the room—there's no space for anyone else.

I release the man's arm. "Are you Professor van Lieugen?"

He scrambles away, rubbing his shoulder, then turns to face me from behind the desk. "Get in here and shut the door!"

That was not the response I expected. The five of us shuffle into the room, the cat slinking around our feet. Leo pulls his broad shoulders back, sucking in his abs to swing the door closed. We all face the short, rumpled man.

"Lock it!" He points at the door.

Leo raises his brows at me, and I nod in response. A locked door is not going to stop me from leaving this room if that becomes necessary. I've already evaluated my potential escape routes. I can easily break the lock or squeeze through the window. I could probably put a foot through the wall, but that gets messy, and sometimes these old buildings are sturdier than they look.

Leo twists the lever on the door, then raises both hands, as if to disavow responsibility. He tries to back away from the door but runs into a chair hidden beneath a meter-high stack of paper. Elodie reaches out to steady the swaying tower before it crashes to the floor.

The click of the antique deadbolt seems to reassure van Lieugen. His shoulders sag, and he drops into an ancient, squeaking chair. "Have a seat."

We look around the stuffed room but don't bother pointing out the impossibility of accepting that invitation. I scoot around the end of the desk where I can face the little man and still see both exits.

He pulls the beret from his head, and a bit of metallic interior catches the light before he drops it on one of the shorter piles of books perched on his desk. Peering between the stacks, he gazes at the five of us. "Who are you?"

I shuffle forward the few centimeters the cluttered room allows, holding out a fist to bump. "I'm Lindsay. I contacted you to ask about alternate universes?"

His eyes light up, and he jumps from the protesting chair. "Yes, of course!" A quick hop over one of the shorter piles puts him within millimeters of Annabelle who hastily scrambles as far as she can get from the little man. The professor taps the wall beside a dense scrawl above his shoulder. "You can see here the theoretical possibilities of—"

I let my hand fall to my side as I cut him off. "I'm not really interested in the theory, Professor. I want to talk about real-world application."

His brows come down, and his wizened face goes still. "Did you read the sign on the building? This is the theoretical physics department. The-o-ret-i-cal. That means theory, not application."

Elodie lifts a hand, as if she's hoping the teacher will call on her. When he doesn't, she blurts out, "Actually, the sign said Experiential Physics."

"Experiential physics? That isn't a real thing!" His arms cross over his chest, and his eyes narrow to slits. "Did those undergrad students deface the sign again?"

I try to bring him back to the topic at hand. "I don't really care what department we're in. I've heard you can see other universes. That's what I want to talk about."

He waves both hands like he's fighting off a swarm of gnats. "That's crazy talk. No one can see outside our reality. By definition, each universe contains everything you can see, detect, or probe. If other universes exist, they are unobservable."

"But I was told you have seen the other side." I resort to the phrasing Leo used earlier. The reports I read said this guy was a crackpot—maybe the fantastical phrasing would resonate with him.

His face goes dark, and he points at the door. "Get out."

"But Professor—"

"Get. Out!" He thrusts his hand at the door again. "And fix that sign when you leave!"

Leo unlocks the door, and we shuffle out. As we pick our way between the stacks of books and papers, Apawllo looks up from his position beside Elodie. He watches us depart, his yellow eyes narrowing to slits.

Elodie pauses by the door. "Apawllo, let's go."

The cat stands and stretches, pushing his backside toward the professor. He straightens and gives the glaring old man another unreadable look, then stalks toward the door. Just before he crosses the threshold, a paw snaps out, hitting the closest pile a few centimeters above the floor. The tower teeters, the top-most pages fluttering to the ground. For a second, it seems to reach a new equilibrium, then it tumbles, hitting the next stack.

The professor shrieks as the precarious towers lean, slip, and fall, each one setting off the next, like a careful arrangement of dominoes. The cat pauses long enough to lick a satisfied paw, then swaggers out the door.

I herd the group toward the stairs. Muffled swearing follows us down the hall. Elodie huffs out an exasperated sigh. "Why did I send the vid drone back to the ship?"

SIXTEEN
TRIANA

I LEAN FORWARD to peer down the row of seats at Valti. She opens that accusing eye again, and I shrink back. The rumble of the shuttle's engine creates a cocoon of noise around us.

"Are you saying I'm part of the CCIA?" O'Neill's voice sounds strained through the audio implant.

"I'm neither confirming nor denying anything. But why wouldn't you know the answer to that question?" She sounds exactly like our Vanti.

I should have known the Vanti in any universe would be more than a meek deck hand.

"Because I'm not the Tiberius O'Neill you know."

I suck in a breath at O'Neill's admission. We'd agreed not to tell anyone about our unbelievable transference until we were sure they could be both trusted and helpful. I'm not sure Valti meets either of those criteria.

"Are you saying you've been replaced? By a clone or android? Because you look and sound exactly like the Ty O'Neill I know."

He sucks in a surprised breath, his ribs expanding abruptly against my arm. Our Vanti never calls him Ty.

"Replaced isn't the right word. But we've been swapped in some way." He goes on to explain our theory about the jump.

"Huh. That makes sense."

"It does?" My surprised exclamation breaks through the engine noise. The others dart glares in my direction while pretending not to notice me.

"Well, the only thing I could think of was personality-altering drugs, but I couldn't find any evidence such precise drugs exist. Neither of you appears to be paranoid or hallucinating, and you have a consistent understanding of reality between you, right? I suppose you could be victims of a group hallucination, but why isn't it affecting anyone else? And I found no evidence of any drugs in the ship. Believe me, I've been looking. But I'd like to have a med pod evaluation when we get to the planet."

"I wonder if that's why Fortenoy got rid of the med pod." I say.

From behind O'Neill, I catch a glimpse of Valti's surprised jerk. I smile a little—it isn't often I outthink her.

"It's possible, but he seems to be getting a negative effect rather than positive." Vanti sounds thoughtful. "I mean, you've been standing up to him, which he isn't used to and doesn't like. In fact, you probably need to be careful about that. He's suspicious by nature, and he's going to start wondering why you're not your usual, compliant self."

"Yeah, explain that to me." I cross my arms, feeling defensive. "How does a strong independent woman like Annabelle Morgan end up under the thumb of a guy like him?"

"That's a good question, but let's get back to the matter at hand. You two seem to know each other better than you should."

O'Neill has obviously decided to trust her, so I may as well jump aboard. "Our reality is different. We don't know Fortenoy there. He's the co-pilot of our version of that ship. But we hadn't met—we were passengers, not the owners." I glance at O'Neill, trying to judge how much to tell her. "And in our universe, we got married last week."

Valti leans forward to peer around him at me. Her face is a mask, but her voice sounds incredulous. "Married? As in life-time commitment? I thought only rubes from Grissom did that?"

"Hey—"

I cut O'Neill off. "He's from Grissom, but I wouldn't call his family rubes."

"You've met his family?" She drops back in her seat.

"I told you—we got married. That usually implies meeting the family. Why? Have you met them?"

"Yeah, of course." Her voice is tight.

"Of course? I thought you two were work partners. Why would you meet his family?" This time, I lean around O'Neill to look at her. He turns, too.

Valti's face goes pink which is strange because our Vanti is so controlled. I don't think I've ever seen her blush—which is unusual for someone that pale. Her eyes dart to O'Neill, then to me and away again. She flicks a finger at him. "Because here, *we* are two years into a five-year non-procreational contract."

Zark. My heart contracts so hard it hurts. I try—but fail—to keep my voice even. "You're contracted to my husband?"

She gives me a cool look. "Technically, you think you married my partner. We've been together longer."

O'Neill lets out a shaky breath. "This is awkward."

I poke his arm. "You told me you and Vanti would never—"

He lifts both arms, waving off my emotions. "We wouldn't. She and I don't—there's nothing between us. We're not even work partners anymore." He turns to her. "And no offense, but I can't imagine—"

"Let's not discuss it. Obviously, you think you're a different person, and we need to get to the bottom of this. I'd like to have my partner back." Valti's voice trembles faintly at the end, and she presses her lips together.

He touches her arm, and she flinches back.

"I'm not cheating on you. Because I'm not him." He glances back at me with a "help me" look.

I take a deep breath and lean forward to peer around him at Valti. "This will be easier all the way around if you believe our story. We aren't the Ty and Triana you know. I'm guessing the ones you know are in our universe, and I'm sure he's staying faithful. Because he's that kind of guy, isn't he?" I put my hand on my husband's arm. "My O'Neill is."

"Yes, he is. At least I think so." Her eyes flick to my hand, and I pull it back.

"He is. Trust me. Better yet, trust him. The other him. This him is mine."

She looks away for a long moment, then turns back to me. "Why did you call yourself Triana?"

That explanation takes the rest of the flight. As we touch down on the shuttle pad, Valti holds up a hand, cutting off our joint explanation. "I think I believe you. How else would you have the same backstory so perfectly rehearsed?"

We sit quietly as the seats ahead of us empty, then follow the rest of the passengers out of the craft. We shuffle through the open airlock and down the short flight of steps to the plasphalt. The shuttle sits amid a grid of other shuttles. Hover panels pull up to the rear of our ship, and robotic arms begin unloading cargo. The passengers stream away from the ship in a straggling line toward the terminal.

An overcast sky hangs low over our heads, giving the landscape a gloomy appearance. A wide, green verge separates the shuttle port's plasphalt from the ring of surrounding buildings. A row of public bubbles waits by the exit, offering transportation to the city of Collinsville.

After a short wait in line, we get a bubble. I sit in the front, feeling bereft when O'Neill takes a seat in the rear. Valti leaves the seat beside him empty and sits on the left. It's as if we've all decided to stay physically distant when we're together. Keeping my hands to myself is going to be a challenge.

I feed the location I pulled from the *Solar Reveler*'s database into the bubble, and it trundles away from the port. The streets here look a lot like those on Kaku or Sally Ride, with bubbles maneuvering around each other in the center and raised pedestrian areas. Our bubble zig-zags through a couple of intersections, then veers off to the right through an oval opening in the sloping ground. External lights illuminate, and the bubble picks up speed, but the featureless gray walls make judging our velocity impossible.

I swivel my chair to face the others.

Valti pulls a device from her pocket and flicks a few commands, then sets it on her knee. "We can talk now. Where are we headed?"

"Arun gave me a package to deliver to my father, so I'm doing that." I glance at O'Neill.

He nods. "Then we need to find someone who can help us figure out how to get home. Someone with expertise in jump drive technology."

Valti grimaces. "I'm supposed to be following Fortenoy, but he'll have to wait until we get this sorted out." She flicks a hand from O'Neill to me.

I gape at her. The Vanti I know would never let personal concerns interfere with her mission. But if she's contracted to Alt-O'Neill, maybe she's softened a bit.

A sudden thought flashes into my brain, and my heart seizes again. What if this isn't an alternate reality? What if Valti's version of the world is right, and I've somehow convinced myself O'Neill is married to me instead of her? Which reality makes more sense? That I'm the pampered daughter of an ultra-wealthy woman, or that I'm a sad ship owner who's let herself be controlled by her creepy boyfriend and is now mooning over a new employee?

Occam's razor sucks.

As if he can hear my brain spinning into the vortex, O'Neill leans forward and taps my knee. His eyes lock onto mine, and he raises one eyebrow—a feat he knows I've always envied. The simple gesture reminds me if I'm crazy, he's right here with me. And always will be.

O'Neill turns back to Valti. "You think this professor will be able to help us?"

Professor? What did I miss while wallowing in self-pity?

Valti flips a file at me, and my holo-ring buzzes in response. I open the folder. Professor Francois van Lieugen y Ongkowijaya is a discredited physics professor from the University of Armstrong. He's been drummed out of the Academy of Physics and the Grand Order of Physics Experts—which bears the well-thought-out acronym GROPE—and now lives in a remote part of Armstrong.

"How's this wacko supposed to help us?" O'Neill asks Valti.

Her eyes narrow and her brows go up. "Wacko? You're the one claiming to be from another universe. Believe me, if I thought there was anyone else we could ask—"

We travel in silence while O'Neill and I study the disgraced professor's file. He was discredited and forced to retire after he reported being able to see other dimensions. Now he sells Other Dimension Detectors on the net to fund his research.

"He really should have picked a different product name—this screams scam." O'Neill stretches the holo to get a better look at the small black box. Lights flash and a shadowy vid shows ghostly figures moving around a gray landscape.

I lean forward. "What is that supposed to be?"

"Those are the ghosts who live between dimensions," Valti says in a sing-songy voice.

My eyes snap to her. Our Vanti doesn't make jokes like that. Her face is blank, but the faint wash of pink gives her cheeks a hint of color.

She has a tell. Excellent. In our world, Vanti is impossible to read.

We continue to speed through the tunnel, only the readings on the holo-screen giving any indication of our speed. Other bubbles may be ahead of or behind us, but we're isolated. I take advantage of the net connections to research my father and the rest of my family.

In this universe, like ours, the Kindujas are reclusive, so data is scarce. I'm able to find a few images but little more than the names of the eldest family members and a rough estimate of their net worth from twenty-five years ago. If I hacked into the government systems, I could find tax details, but that's more risk than it's worth.

Arun is also difficult to find online. He's a junior member of the family, and I find one reference indicating he emigrated to Sally Ride ten years ago, just as R'ger once told me. Details from that world are scarce, and there's no indication he's involved in anything shady.

Of course, there's nothing suggesting Altabelle is dealing under the table, either. Let's face it—if anyone knew, they'd be shut down. But Arun said something about paying the appropriate fees, so maybe we've bribed our way to safety.

A tiny jerk catches my attention, and I look outside. The featureless tunnel wall has been replaced by a patchy white stripe which slowly resolves into words as our speed decreases. The name of the exit becomes readable—Everet—then we pop out into the overcast afternoon.

The bubble darkens around us, then lightens as our eyes adjust to the muted glare. Water glints on one side, and a series of colorful buildings front the street on the other. Pedestrians saunter along the boardwalk, wandering in and out of businesses. Most of them carry food or beverages —a wide selection ranging from ice cream cones to candy to foam-topped mugs that might contain beer or soup. They all wear summer clothing and translucent sunscreens or hats.

The bubble rounds a corner, heading inland. Three intersections later, it stops in front of a modest-looking white house with a neat front yard and dark windows. The bubble's holo-screen flashes, and a receipt for the trip pings on my holo-ring.

"I guess we're here." I press the button to open the door, waiting for the steps to unfold before climbing out.

Valti and O'Neill follow me, both of them watching our surroundings in a way that looks casual but suspicious—shoulders tense, arms hanging loose by their sides, eyes darting, heads turning slowly from side to side. I try not to giggle as Valti slowly shifts until she's back-to-back with O'Neill.

He notices my expression and raises his brows. "Unfamiliar area, unknown contact. It pays to be cautious."

"He's not unknown." I turn my back on them and pick my way across the unevenly set flag stones leading to the front door. "He's my dad."

O'Neill grabs my shoulder and puts himself between me and the front stoop. "We don't know him."

Valti stops behind me. "She knows him—he funded her company. But you and I have never met him."

I push past O'Neill. "See, nothing to worry about. He and Altabelle are friendly." I wave my holo-ring at the welcome panel, and it lights up.

"Coming!" a voice calls out—not through the speaker in the panel or our audio implants, but a man actually yells through the open window. The door shakes as multiple locks tumble, then it swings wide. "Annabelle! Come in! Who are your friends?"

My father stands inside the building, arms open in a welcoming gesture. He looks like the R'ger I know, with fading auburn hair brushed back from his high forehead and the beginnings of a paunch above his belt. He wraps his arms around me in a warm hug, then holds me away to get a good look. "You look tired, dear."

I step back, letting his hands fall from my shoulders. "Let me introduce my friends. This is Lindsay and Ty." I don't identify R'ger—I'm not sure what Altabelle calls him.

The three exchange fist-bumps, everyone measuring up the others in a silent, intense once-over.

I do a mental eye-roll and reach into my pocket. Before we came down, I considered opening the package Arun entrusted to me, but I have no way of knowing if he's placed a failsafe on it—maybe it will explode if opened improperly. Or at least tell R'ger if I tampered with it. "I have something from a friend."

R'ger takes the box without looking at it and places it on a shelf behind him. Half a dozen identical boxes already sit on the shelf.

"Aren't you going to open it?"

He blinks at me, then his eyes narrow. "Why would I do that?"

"Because—never mind." I drag my eyes away from the stack and bring them back to his face.

R'ger stares at me a long moment, then offers us beverages. Valti and O'Neill decline. I shake my head, too, and smile apologetically. "We can't stay. We have another meeting."

My father gives me another suspicious glare. "If that's from *a friend*, where's yours?" His eyes remain fixed on my face.

I glance at the boxes on the shelf. What could be in them? Does Arun know he doesn't open them? Or does he wait until Annabelle leaves to see what's inside? Maybe the other boxes are empty?

Why didn't I look inside before I brought it down?

"Uh, I'll bring it next time." I nod jerkily.

R'ger stares me down for a bit, then nods in reply. "Next time."

"Right." I make a face at O'Neill. "I guess we'll be going."

R'ger follows us to the stoop, the smile back on his face. "I'm so glad you came! It's too bad you can't stay longer. Maybe next time."

"Uh, sure." I lean in to give him a kiss on the cheek.

He wraps his arms around me and squeezes tight. Too tight. His voice growls low in my ear. "You might have protection this time, but don't forget my payment. I expect it before you leave the planet."

SEVENTEEN
VANTI

"Now what?" Elodie sits cross-legged on her hoverboard, staring at the sign that now reads "Experiential Pigeons" as she strokes the cat.

Leo leans back on his elbows, face turned toward the sun. "Did we get the wrong professor?"

"No. It was definitely Dr. van Lieugen." I flick my holo-ring and pull up the files. "This guy is supposed to be an expert in—wait! Ugh. It's the right name—kind of. What are the odds of there being two of them?"

Anti-Griz scoots a little closer, leaning over my shoulder to stare at the files. I give him the stink eye and shift a few centimeters away. His face drops, then goes blank. What's his problem?

Leo sits up. "Two of them?"

Annabelle, sitting on a shaded bench by the building, glances up, then looks away, pretending disinterest. I can feel her watching, though. I flick the files to Leo. "There's another Professor van Lieugen y Ongkowijaya. This one is named Francois, though, and I think he's the one we want."

Elodie jumps off her board to peer over Leo's shoulder, reading choice bits from the file aloud. "Disgraced experimental physicist? Retired to a mental health facility? Ooh—get this: 'believes he can see other realities.' This sounds like our guy."

The cat glares at Elodie for a moment, then curls up on the board, looking away. The resemblance between Apawllo and Annabelle is remarkable.

Anti-Griz gets up and stretches. "What are we waiting for then? The sooner I can get home, the better." He gives me a dirty look.

"What?" I try to keep the surly tone out of my question, but I'm not very successful.

"You're not the woman I know."

This guy is not nearly as smart as Griz.

"I thought we established that." I flick the controls of my hoverboard and enter the disgraced professor's address. The screen flashes red, then blinks blue for a few seconds, then a map appears. "We need to head back to the ship. This is well out of our boards' range."

AT THE SHIP, Elodie enters the new coordinates. "Looks like there's plenty of room to land there—this guy lives in the back of nowhere." She works her way through the launch sequence, then we lift off.

In a single smooth motion, we reach a cruising altitude, then the ship eases forward, increasing speed so slowly it's barely noticeable. I watch the city flow away beneath us, and we skim across a wide swath of green fields. The agricultural land gives way to low mountains, then we reach a vast, brown plain. The ship banks to the right, and we land at the mouth of a narrow canyon.

The map shifts on my holo-ring, zooming in to an area marked Edorra Plains. "We'll have to ride the hoverboards from here. It's about two klicks to the professor's reported location, but the canyon is too narrow to land in." I turn to Elodie. "Do we have any survival gear?"

"Survival gear? Why would we need that?" Elodie rises from the pilot's seat and stretches.

I unbuckle my seat restraints and get up. "We're going into an uncivilized location too far from the ship. We aren't familiar with the weather or terrain. We take survival gear if we've got it."

"Yes, ma'am!" She flips a jaunty salute, then moves to the rear of the ship, behind the passenger seating. Using her holo-ring, she unlocks a compartment at the back of the small cargo hold. The door pops open, revealing a neat arrangement of long, flat boxes. They all bear the *CelebVid* logo. "They showed me all this stuff at HQ. These are supposed to have food and water for three days. Plus, we can take an Insta-Up shelter." She opens another compartment, revealing a white meter-high cube.

Leo leans in to read the tiny print on the top. "Does this thing have a built-in hover capability? How cool is that?" He taps his holo-ring and waves it at the cube. "It won't pair."

"I think it only works for me." Elodie swipes her ring at the box, and lights flash on the side. "Yeah!" She pumps an arm in the air. "Oh, I should be filming this!"

Annabelle and Anti-Griz both make aborted protests. Interesting.

"If you can film without revealing our location or including the rest of us, that would be acceptable." I take one of the smaller rectangles down and pull out the straps. "These are backpacks, folks. Everyone grab one. You can wear them or strap 'em to your board. You don't want to get caught in the wild without supplies."

"Armstrong is a heavily colonized planet." Elodie activates the hover on the cube, then presses a finger on top, making it bob a little. "We don't really need this stuff here, do we?"

Annabelle grabs a backpack and slings it over her shoulder. "The cities are civilized. There's a lot of 'not city' out here. They only settled in the easy-to-build areas. Places with good weather, low incidence of natural disasters, easy access to resources. The rest of the planet, they left empty —because they had four other planets to colonize. Then more, as they discovered them and developed jump tech. Parts of Armstrong are still dangerous, and the Edorra Plains is one of them."

"You've been out here before?" I hand a backpack to Anti-Griz and another to Leo.

Annabelle's eyes flick away, then back to me, like she's calculating what information will help me the least. "Once." She's so little like our Triana it's stunning. I guess those years at the Techno-Inst were formative.

I finish doling out the survival gear and get Elodie to slave the survival cube to my hoverboard. Then I point at Apawllo, sleeping on a nearby seat. "The cat stays here."

Elodie pouts, but a peek out the window convinces her this desert is no place for her pet. She grabs his face in both hands and puts her nose against his. "Be a good wittle kitty while I'm gone."

Apawllo pulls his head free and looks away, bored. I suppress an eye roll and push everyone out and lock the ship.

The sun beats down, even in the narrow canyon which lines up almost perfectly at this time of year. Slivers of shade can be found at the southern side, but they are small and disappear quickly. This part of the planet is much warmer and drier than Collinsville was.

Dusty hills rise on both sides, with equally dusty weeds clinging to the steep sides. A trickle of rocks cascades down, startling us, but there's no one in sight. Probably dislodged by wildlife high above us. A sharp but dusty scent fills the dry air, making my sinuses tighten.

I flick through the app attached to the survival pack and find a control that extends a sunscreen from its top over my head and body. The bubble darkens in response to the commands, giving me a patch of mobile shade. I consider increasing the filter which should help raise the humidity inside my portable dome, but it will also increase the temperature, so I leave it alone. A few flicks sends the instructions to the others, and we continue into the valley, cooler and more alert.

Ahead, the late-afternoon sun reflects against a steep rocky wall where the canyon seems to end. According to the map, the professor should be right here. My shoulders tighten—have we come on a fool's errand? As we get closer, I realize the canyon doesn't end here—it turns sharply to the right.

I raise my fist in the—hopefully now recognized—command for "stop." A quick look over my shoulder reveals my followers *can* be taught. I hop off my board and leave it hovering in place. Pressing my finger against my lips, I open an audio call to Leo and Elodie. After a second's thought, I add Triana and Griz to the call. Apparently the two people with us are still physically our Triana and Griz because the call goes through.

"What?" Annabelle snaps. Her face maintains its still, bored expression

—clearly she's worked harder at invisible and inaudible communication than Triana ever did.

"There's a turn ahead. I'm going to scout it before we all blunder into whatever might be waiting."

Anti-Griz jumps off his board. "I'll come with you."

I swing around and point at him, then the ground. "You stay here."

"You know I'm good at this kind of reconnaissance, Linds."

I glare at him. "I don't know that. I know nothing about you. And don't call me Linds."

His mouth opens, then snaps shut, and he looks away, a defeated expression on his face. What's going on with him? He must have a different relationship with the me from his reality. I push aside a twinge of curiosity and focus on the task at hand. I can explore interpersonal relationships later. When I know we're safe.

In other words, never.

Giving Anti-Griz another stern look, I creep away, approaching the corner on foot. The sides of the canyon are almost vertical here, so I flatten myself against one and dart a look around the corner.

"Hey, I got this!" Elodie sings out through the audio.

What now? I shake my head vehemently. "No, it's all good. I've got experience in this—"

One of the tiny drones zips past me, whirring softly around the corner. I bite back a reprimand, taking a deep breath and letting out my annoyance. She's trying to help. And our target isn't a hostile enemy agent—he's a retired physics professor.

"There's a little house! It's so cute!" Elodie sends the video to our holo-rings.

I pull up the picture. A small wooden cabin sits in front of a western-facing cliff-face. A tiny cascade splashes down the rock nearby, and a small patch of green grows around the cabin. The last rays of the setting sun glint against the windows—

—and off the nose of the tiny missile that slams into the drone, taking out our vid.

"Eep!" Elodie jumps back and falls off her hoverboard, stumbling into Leo.

Let me amend my evaluation: *crazy* retired physics professor. Or at least protective of his privacy. Actually, I'll probably have a similar system to safeguard my retirement home. But maybe lasers instead of projectile weapons.

I risk a peek around the corner, then duck back as a laser fries the fringe of weeds hanging over my head. "Anyone got a plan B?"

EIGHTEEN
TRIANA

"THAT WAS WEIRD, RIGHT?" Another bubble speeds along another featureless black tunnel. I lean my head against the headrest, wondering what Altabelle has gotten us into. From what I've pieced together, her father funded her business and is demanding payment. It sounded like he was ready to do her physical damage if she didn't come up with whatever he deemed appropriate. He is nothing like the R'ger I know. "And kinda scary."

And what was in that box Arun had me deliver?

"I can't believe you didn't open the box." Valti plays with the little black jamming device sitting on her leg. "If I'd known you were going to deliver a package, I would have checked it."

O'Neill gives me a sheepish smile and turns to Valti. "It's okay, I did."

I sit upright. "You did?" I sag back. "Of course you did."

Valti scowls at me. "You wouldn't last a day in my line of work."

"Good thing I'm not in your line of work," I snap back. Although Altabelle is probably much more wily than me since she's survived this long in what appears to be a dangerous mob-like life. I turn to O'Neill. "What was in the box?"

"Cash. Seventy-five thousand credits in plastek bills. With a receipt that had no identifying information."

"Why doesn't he open the boxes if they're full of cash? And what's the point of a receipt with no other information?"

O'Neill's brows come down. "Why do you think he doesn't open them?"

"There was a stack of boxes in his house—he put mine on the shelf. Didn't you notice?" I rub my forehead. Maybe I'm going crazy?

Valti shrugs. "Those were probably empty. Maybe he keeps them to freak you out. Or he likes how they look. It doesn't really matter. What matters is we know Arun is paying R'ger in regular installments, and you —" She lifts a hand when O'Neill jerks in her direction. "Sorry. The other Annabelle is supposed to be paying him as well. Maybe you were supposed to bring a payment of your own today and screwed up."

"There were no little boxes of cash in Altabelle's cabin."

O'Neill's lips twitch at the name, but he doesn't say anything.

"And we had to purchase tickets to come down here—there was no indication she'd planned to see him." I cross my arms and lean back in the chair. "In fact, based on the spa reservation, I'd guess she intended to skip the visit and maybe keep Arun's money, too."

"You think you've never faked a spa visit before?" Valti looks away in disgust. "Annabelle visits that spa every time they arrive at Aldrin. And my information says she slips away and comes down here at least half the time. I've never had the chance to follow her before—I've always been on Fortenoy's trail. Which was one of the reasons you joined me." She nods at O'Neill. "We were supposed to split up and follow both of them."

"Sorry." He doesn't look sorry. "If you've followed him before, you must know where he goes."

She flushes. "He's always given me the slip. You were going to try this time, and I was going to follow her." She jerks her head at me.

"So now what?" I squint out the window, but the unrelenting black continues.

"Now we see Professor Crazy Head, then return to the ship. It's all we have time for." Valti fiddles with the jammer again, turning it ninety degrees and setting it back on her knee over and over.

It's so weird to see Vanti fidgeting. In our world, she's unrufflable. Of course, in our world, she's not in love with my husband.

I don't think.

In the past, I've been suspicious of Vanti's motives toward O'Neill. But over time, I've realized they don't have that kind of relationship. They're work partners. And she dated his brother, for a while. Which I suppose could be a consolation prize kind of thing, but I never got that impression. And now she's moving to a new job that will take her out of our lives most of the time.

But the faint suspicion remains. And now it's been fanned to a flame.

In this universe. Vanti and Valti seem to be very different women. Our Vanti is completely controlled and contained. Cunning and a bit cold. This Valti has a human side that must have made her more attractive to this universe's O'Neill.

I dart a glance at my husband. Surely only *this universe's* O'Neill? He's watching me, as if he knows what thoughts are swirling through my mind, and he gives me that heart-stopping smile. Even in this less-than-shiny iteration, his smile makes me feel like the only woman in existence.

"Does the professor know we're coming?" O'Neill asks, still gazing at me.

When she doesn't respond, we both turn. Her killer glare is trained on me, and it's every bit as devastating as Vanti's. More, because I know the real Vanti likes me. At least I think she does. This one would have been happy to leave me in creepy R'ger's seaside resort of doom. And probably help him dismember me.

The bubble jinks to the right and an uneven white line appears again. We slow, and the line becomes the word "Samag" repeated over and over. Another small bump, and we emerge into a brilliant sunset.

The bubble darkens on the west side as it grinds to a halt in the middle of a dusty square, The door opens. Hills crowd close behind us, with a desert stretching out ahead to a distant mountain range. The sun seems to teeter on the top of one of the peaks. Red, yellow, pink, and purple streak the sky beyond. Buildings stand on either side of the square—blocky and unattractive. A few people wander from one to another, while a small family climbs into another bubble which disappears into the transit chute.

"Looks like a lovely place to live." I suck in a lungful of hot, dry, dusty air and cough.

Valti produces a water pac from thin air and hands it to me. I give it a suspicious look as I raise it to my lips—should I worry about her trying to poison me? She said she was supposed to track me, not kill me, so I should be fine. I take a swig and hand it to O'Neill, keeping one eye on Valti. She doesn't flinch.

I let out a breath.

A sly smile quirks across her lips and disappears. Great, she knows she's got me freaked out. "Professor van Lieugen lives a few klicks from here, but we'll have to go on foot. Or hoverboard."

I raise my hand. "I vote hoverboard."

"Do you have one?" She smirks again but doesn't wait for my answer. Since I obviously don't. "There's an outback gear store over there." She starts across the dusty square.

Parekh Outfitters is the largest of the buildings on this side of the square. The others are a small grocery and two liquor stores. I look back —across the plaza are an almost identical assortment of stores, but the outfitter looks less prosperous. They probably have better prices, but I'm not going to fight with Valti over this. Annabelle can afford a couple of top-of-the-line hoverboards. I checked her account. And the secret one she's apparently hiding from the government. Or maybe Fortenoy. Or both.

Anyway, she's got enough credit to cover what we need without making a huge dent. But now that I think about it, there was a scheduled withdrawal from that account for fifty thousand credits. That must be R'ger's payment—and it will leave her almost broke. If I don't want Altabelle in trouble, I'd better leave her enough credits to pay that off.

Inside, only half the lights seem to be on. As we enter, the rest brighten, bathing the selection of gear in a golden glow. Holograms of animated spokespeople appear as we stroll past displays of artfully arranged gear. A woman with long green hair extols the virtues of the Corbat-20 climbing system. A few steps later, a young, attractive man with impressive muscles recounts his experience in the Forwalt Flyer.

Valti strides through an image of an older woman loading crates onto a sled while yapping creatures stalk around her, their harnesses reflecting the snowy landscape, and stops by a hoversled. "I need one of these."

A virtual assistant pops out of the floor. The avatar's blonde hair is pulled back in a high tail, and blindingly white teeth fill her smile. "An excellent choice, friend. The Thorbalt 23-K is a top of—"

"Can it." Valti crooks her fingers at me as the holographic woman smiles in happy acquiescence. "You're the one with cash—pay the woman."

I pause by a display of lower-priced15-Rs. "Are you sure this—"

"This one." Valti points at the 23-K. "It comes with the survival pod, and I'm not heading across the Armstrong desert without it."

I hitch a shoulder and access Altabelle's account. If we don't buy much else, she'll have enough to cover the debt to Creepy R'ger. Barely. I flick the "accept charge" button and the digits roll downward on my dashboard. "Anything else?"

"We're going next door for supplies, too."

I trail her out the door while O'Neill arranges pickup of the sled. "How far away is this place?"

"It's not far—a couple of hours by sled. If the *Solar Reveler* had a shuttle, we could have landed much closer. But there's no public transport beyond here. We could have *rented* a sled, but the rentals in places like this are usually poorly maintained, and that's a risk I don't want to take out here."

I bite my lip and do some financial calculations. "We aren't talking about a week-long trip, right? It's a quick out and back. We shouldn't need a lot of supplies."

"We can resell whatever's left when we return. Think of all this stuff as an insurance policy."

"I'm not sure Altabelle can afford insurance." I flick through the numbers again and explain about the regular withdrawal. "If we spend too much, she won't be able to pay off R'ger."

Valti shrugs. "Do you care? I don't. I want my partner back." She strides into the grocery store.

I follow. I haven't been in a grocery store since I left the Techno-Inst. Usually I ate on campus, but occasionally we'd venture out into the city and pick up treats. Those stores were huge buildings with shelves full of thousands of products.

This store is different. I push through the door and nearly crash into Valti—the interior is tiny. She stands in the middle of the three-meter cube, holograms swirling around her. She waves products aside with impatient gestures, paging through the large catalog of food.

"Where's all the stuff?" I peer over her shoulder as she pushes a pile of lemons aside.

"This is an auto-mart. You pick the items you want, and they deliver." She pushes away a display of delicious looking CheweyBars, and pulls out a NutriEats ad instead, selecting ChocoDream and Sweet-n-Salty. She swipes again, and a counter appears, ticking up to ten of each. Then she pushes that aside and selects another product.

While she continues to work, I squint through the holograms. The flat black walls provide an excellent backdrop for the colorful displays. A door at the back of the room slides aside, and a cart trundles in carrying two plain white boxes. Their contents are listed on the outside—the recently ordered NutriEats. I pop the top on the first box to find ten bars individually wrapped in shiny white plastek with the flavor printed across the length in block letters.

I wave one at Valti. "These don't look very yummy."

She continues flicking and swiping, not sparing me a glance.

I slide one of the ChocoDreams into my pocket, and red text flashes across the front of the cart. "Payment required!" I put the bar back, and the red fades to blue.

"I'm done." Valti pushes the last holo aside, and the overhead lights brighten. Two more carts have appeared behind the first one, each bearing institutional-looking boxes. "Pay the bill." She grabs a box and turns to leave.

I flick the payment icon and authorize the deductions from Altabelle's account. Valti's purchases make a big dent in the total—I hope we can get back to our own reality before R'ger discovers she doesn't have enough cash. If we're lucky, maybe we can get enough for the sled to cover the deficit when we get back. I wonder what the mark-down is on used survival gear.

I snag one of the ChocoDreams again, then heft the two boxes. They weigh a ton, considering it's only twenty bars. Well, nineteen now.

As I carry the food out to the sled, I wonder about the flavors. They sound good, but I've been burned by Vanti's protein bars in the past. Hopefully, her alter ego has better taste.

NINETEEN
VANTI

ELODIE HAS A PLAN B, but I'm not convinced. We've retreated a few hundred meters up the canyon and huddled under a rocky ledge at the sheer cliff wall. Hopefully the professor thinks we've left.

I pace along the shadowed edge of our refuge and scowl at her. "If you send in another drone, he's going to fry it like the first one. You don't have an unlimited supply of those things."

"Actually, I can order more as soon as I can connect to the net. *CelebVid* said there's no limit on the number of drones—they want footage."

"And the riskier the better, right?" Leo shoves his hands into his baggy pants and scowls.

Elodie's eyes twinkle. "Gotta go viral!" She turns to me. "I'm going to send in two. One making a frontal assault, and the other dropping down from above. We'll get a look at how robust his security really is. If I get one through, we can use it to speak with him."

We all stare at the woman.

"What? Do I have something on my face?" She flicks through her holo screens and turns the drone on herself to use it as a mirror.

"Did you just use the words 'robust security'?" I turn to the others. "Are we sure Elodie wasn't swapped from a different reality, too?"

Elodie rolls her eyes, but a strange shadow seems to pass through them.

I reach out to grab her shoulder. "Is there something you aren't telling us?"

She smiles, and the shadow vanishes as the drones rise. "Don't be silly. I've been watching a lot of crime shows lately. They always talk about credentials and security and things being robust. I must have used it right." She shrugs off my hand and sends the drones into action.

With the holos stretched wide, we all watch the tiny crafts' progress. One streaks upward, the canyon wall blurring as it rises. It tops the steep ascent and crosses a scrubby ridge. The other zips forward, then pauses at the canyon's tight corner.

"Going in three, two, now." Elodie swipes a command with each hand, and the scenes shift as the drones react. The one on the right lifts a bit more, then the ground drops away as it moves toward the roof now visible below, maintaining its altitude.

On the left, the rocky cliff disappears as the drone rounds the corner. It immediately begins jerking in random directions as it moves closer to the little house, presumably avoiding invisible defenses.

I lean closer, trying to read the tiny print scrolling across the bottom. "Do these things have an evasive maneuvers setting?"

"Cool ain't it?" Elodie flips a file to me, making my holo-ring buzz. "They're designed to defeat anti-paparazzi measures."

"Anti-anti-paparazzi? That's a thing?" I need to do some research when this emergency is over. If I'm going to stay with Elodie, these capabilities could come in handy.

"Oh, yeah. All of the celebrities have protection against drones." Elodie's tongue sticks out of the corner of her mouth as she focuses on the screens.

I frown at Anti-Griz and start to ask why we weren't aware of this tech when I remember this isn't my Griz. Who knows what his universe has?

"Hey, professor! We need to talk to you!" Elodie's voice rings out of the holos and echoes back to us from around the cliff. "We come in peace! I brought snacks!" She shakes a bag of Gooey Bars, as if he can see her.

Leo shoots me a grin that says, "There's the Elodie we know," and jumps from his hoverboard to pick up the snacks.

The screen on the left flares bright enough to leave shadows on my retinas. "One down."

"I can send these in all day, professor." Elodie grins like a maniac as she sweeps away the dead screen and flicks the commands to launch another drone. How many does she have?

On the right screen, the view shifts as the second drone descends. The cabin roof grows larger, then we drop below the roofline and peer through the windows. A small man who bears a startling resemblance to Wilmer van Lieugen y Ongkowijaya comes into view. But this man's white hair stands around his head in a wild halo, and his rumpled clothing hangs off his bony frame.

"Francois?" Elodie's voice is so soft this time we don't get the echo. "Can we please come talk to you? We have people from another dimension with us. They want your help to get home."

The little man's glare drops away, leaving a curious expression. "Really? You aren't just saying that to make fun of me?"

"No. We need your help. Can we come talk to you?"

"Did you say you brought snacks?"

Elodie casts a triumphant grin at me and Leo. "I did. I hope you like Gooey Bars."

"I prefer Sticky Yums."

"I have some of those, too." She pulls a couple of small packets out of her pocket. "But only two of them."

The man's eyes narrow, as if he's calculating advanced mathematical equations. "How many of you are there?"

"Five, but only two are from another dimension."

"Universe," he snaps. "They're from another universe. Alternate dimensions are science fiction."

"Sorry. Two from another universe, plus me, Vanti, and Leo. Will you turn off the lasers?"

He nods. "But I'm not sharing the Sticky Yums."

Elodie chuckles. "A man after my own heart."

I reach out to flick the mute icon. "I don't trust him."

"You don't trust anyone," someone mutters through the audio implant, but we're all still on the call, and I don't recognize the voice. Probably Anti-Griz .

"That's right, I don't. That's what keeps us alive." I pull the holo screen closer. "Can I take over the controls?"

"Sure, it's all yours." Elodie flicks through a couple of commands, and the two drone dashboards re-pair to my holo-ring. I turn off the anti-paparazzi evasion system—I refuse to call it APES—and fly the newer drone to the cabin. Nothing happens.

Then the front door opens, and Francois steps onto the front porch. "What's taking so long? I want those Sticky Yums!"

With a nod from me, Elodie zips away on her hoverboard, with Leo close behind. Anti-Griz shoots me a pointed look, reminding me his board is tethered to mine. I power mine on again and send us forward. Annabelle ignores me.

As we round the corner, I watch for potential threats, but nothing happens. We drop to the dirt in front of the cabin, and everyone jumps off their boards.

Francois points to the far end of the covered porch. "Leave your stuff there. I don't want anyone spotting it from above. No need to encourage any other visitors."

We stack our boards under a bench by the wall where the roof hides them from the drone still hovering overhead. I set the drones to watch for external threats, and we troop inside.

Functional furniture sits around the perimeter of the room—a couch and two plastek chairs. A worn rug hides the wood floor between these seats and a wooden rocking chair with a thick cushion. On the right, a fire burns behind the grate of a stove. The back of the room holds a small old-fashioned kitchen under a window and a door. A steaming mug and a pad of paper lie on the tiny table beside the rocker.

"I've set an exception for your two drones, but don't launch any new ones or my system will shoot them down." Francois stands guard in front of the rocker. He points at the couch beneath the front window. "Sit."

Leo and Annabelle take opposite ends of the couch. Anti-Griz casts a look at the window and moves to the side of the room near the wood stove where he can put his back to the wall and watch the doors. It's the spot I'd already identified as the most secure, so I grimace and move to the second-best place, beneath the stairs leading to the open loft. My neck itches, knowing someone could be up there, but I rely on my excellent senses to warn me.

Francois glares at Anti-Griz, then at me. With an exasperated sigh, he picks up a remote and clicks a button. The windows grow opaque, turning to a flat beige surface that doesn't match the surrounding walls at all. "Happy?"

"Not really." I flick my holo-ring and bring up the drone cams again. "At least when it was clear we could see what was out there. I don't like being blind."

He flings a hand at me. "You aren't blind, so suck it up, buttercup."

Elodie clears her throat and holds out the candy in both hands, moving slowly toward the professor. "Here you are! This one is a little smushed, but it will still taste good."

He snatches the food from her and backs toward the table. Casting a glare at me and Anti-Griz, he flips his now-full hands at the couch. "Sit."

Elodie sits between Leo and Annabelle, crossing one leg and leaning back. She waves a hand at Anti-Griz. "They're security people. They can't sit. Tell us about the universe."

TWENTY
TRIANA

THE SLED ZIPS across the desert, then into a narrow canyon. We've been riding for an hour, and sun beats down on my head. O'Neill and I sit on the sled atop the crates of supplies while Valti clings to the little platform in the rear. A force shield casts a shadow over her bright copper hair.

I'm pretty sure the shelter could be extended to our part of the sled, but she didn't offer. And I didn't ask.

"Why did she buy the sled?" I mutter to O'Neill. "Three grav belts and a crate lifter would have been cheaper."

His lips twitch. "I think she's taking advantage of the extra resources. I'm not sure her operation is very well funded."

"I guess she doesn't care what happens to Altabelle and No'Neill when we get them back here."

"No'Neill." He chuckles. "I get the impression she cares very much what happens to No'Neill. Altabelle—not so much. Or anyone else."

"Do *we* care?" I squint against the sun reflecting off something metallic. I glance at O'Neill, then my eyes snap back to the glint. "What is that?"

"Bogie, eleven o'clock." O'Neill looks over his shoulder. "Does this guy have defenses? Is he expecting us?"

Valti's eyes narrow. "I messaged him, and he replied. He does have surveillance."

O'Neill pulls something from his pocket and glares at Valti. "That doesn't look like surveillance. It's coming toward us."

"Could be a drone."

"You think? It could be armed." He lifts a small, black device.

"Where'd you get that?" Valti's voice is sharp.

"A little something I picked up on the ship." O'Neill hands the box to me. "If I say now, press the button."

The flat rectangle weighs more than I expect. It has a matte-black finish and two buttons that are flush with the surface. There are no markings. "Which button?"

"That one." He points at one and flicks his holo-ring. "I need to see what kind of signals this thing is emitting."

"*Where* on the ship did you get that?" Valti awkwardly pats down her invisible pockets, keeping one hand on the sled's controls.

O'Neill shrugs. "Might have been your bunk." He swipes through screens of data. "That thing is locking on to us. Triana, now."

The sled hits a bump, and I fumble the box. "Zark!" I catch it before it falls to the ground speeding by beneath us and hold it out to O'Neill. "Which button?"

His eyes are locked on the data streaming across his palm. "The one I showed you! Push it. Now!"

I peer at the buttons. "Why are there no markings? What kind of crazy person builds a device with two identical buttons and no labels?"

"Gimme that!" Valti swipes at me, trying to grab the box. The sled seems to hit another bump—she's doing it on purpose! I duck away, knocking into O'Neill. The sled jerks to the left as Valti tries again.

"Which button?" I shove the device at him.

He looks up, eyes wide. "Too late!" He throws himself at me, taking both of us off the side.

We slam into the ground, tumbling together across the dusty, rocky surface. Sharp things jab into my back, head, legs—every part of me that isn't pressed against O'Neill. The force of our landing shoves the air from my lungs.

As we rattle to a stop, rolling into a brittle, prickly bush, something explodes. Light stabs my eyes, and I slam them shut as the roar splits my eardrums. A wave of dirt and small rocks pummel us, and a flash of heat sears my exposed skin then is gone.

I'm crushed on my back in the dust, gasping for breath. O'Neill is slumped over me, his shoulder pressed into my face. Roaring fills my ears, and smoke burns my nose and throat.

O'Neill jerks and pushes up, removing his jacket from my face. His voice is barely audible. "You okay?"

I take a moment to test out my limbs. "I think so." My whole body throbs, each part at a different tempo, and my skin tingles, as if it's been singed, but everything still seems to work. I take the hand O'Neill offers and let him pull me to a seated position.

A fire rages beyond O'Neill in the direction we had been going. The flames dance and shift in a breeze that blows down the canyon. I lift a shaky finger and point. "Is that the sled?"

He crouches beside me, his head turning back and forth, assessing the current danger level. It must be low because he glances at me and nods. "Used to be. Come on, let's move. Close to the cliff wall."

I crawl beside him to the side of the steep canyon. "What happened to Valti?"

We reach the meager shelter of an outcropping of rock, and he pushes me into a narrow cleft between it and the canyon wall. Swallowing hard, he slowly rises to his feet. "No one could have survived that blast."

I climb to my feet, using the solid rock behind me to lever myself up. My joints and muscles scream. I put a hand on his bicep. "If anyone could, it's her."

"Look at that thing!" His voice is an anguished whisper. He stands in front of me, facing the debris. "There's no walking away."

"We did. Well, we fell and rolled away. But we're walking now." I take a step to demonstrate, and my left ankle collapses under me. I smother a cry and clamp onto O'Neill's arm to stop my fall.

He reaches out to catch me, then his face goes slack. "Vanti?"

"Don't call me that! You call me Linds." She's as battered and bruised as we are, and smoke drifts from her shoulders and hair. Which still looks perfect.

O'Neill stares at her. "How'd you—?" He waves an arm at the wreckage.

She shrugs, then winces. "I had help." She pulls her jacket open, revealing a grav belt. "I always have an emergency jump sequence programmed. Several of them, actually. Which you'd know if you were the real Bear."

"Bear?" I ask, stepping between them. I don't like the way she's looking at my husband.

"That's what I call him." She looks away. "The other him. It's short for Tiberius." She says it "tie-BEAR-ee-us."

My jaw drops, and I turn to O'Neill. "Is that why she—why our Vanti—calls you Griz?"

His face goes a little pink, and he waggles his head side to side. "Maybe."

I narrow my eyes and give him my best "you'd better fess up now or you're sleeping on the sofa" look. I'm not very good at it yet, but I understand it's an important part of every married woman's arsenal. Or so *Ancient TēVē* and O'Neill's great grandma Angie would have me believe.

He relents. "Yes, that's why. She used to say I was too soft to be an agent—more like a teddy bear. I always told her a grizzly looks cuddly, but you shouldn't try to take it home." He pushes me back into the narrow cleft formed by the stone. Heat radiates from the canyon wall, and sheltered from the steady breeze, the temperature rises quickly. "But right now, we need to figure out what happened."

He steps between me and Valti—and the open canyon. "Where's the threat coming from, and how do we circumvent it?"

"Circumvent? I'm going to neutralize it! They destroyed my sled!"

I glare over O'Neill's shoulder at her. "*Your* sled?"

The eyeroll is so subtle I almost don't see it. "Annabelle's sled."

O'Neill raises a hand. "Doesn't matter. Who is attacking us? Is it this professor?"

"I don't know why he would. He's not the violent type." Her eyelid twitches.

"What aren't you telling us?" O'Neill takes a step closer to Valti and grabs her arm. "You're withholding something. What do you know about this guy?"

She looks at O'Neill's hand on her arm, then up at his face. Her lips part, and she leans a little closer to him. "I wouldn't lie to you, Bear."

O'Neill scowls, and he drops her arm, stepping back, almost on my toes. I put out a hand to stop him, and he jerks around in surprise. His face softens, and he puts his arm around my shoulders, turning back to Valti. "I'm not Bear, and you know it. Tell us what's going on, or we'll—"

She straightens her spine and a little smirk twitches across her lips. "Or you'll what, Ser O'Neill? You need my help, so don't try to threaten me."

"It goes both ways, *Linds*. You need our help because you want your partner back. So, come clean. What's going on with this professor?"

TWENTY-ONE
VANTI

My eyes start glazing over as soon as the professor starts talking. I let the words wash over me, trusting that someone else—anyone else—is paying attention. I'm not a physicist or an engineer, so it's like listening to a Gagarian speaking Leweian with a Tereshkovan accent.

Instead, I watch the security feeds and listen for intruders. The drones should catch them first, but I don't trust technology one hundred percent. After a while, I catch Anti-Griz 's eye and jerk my head toward the door. He gives a minute nod, so I slink outside.

It's dark out here. Really dark. Armstrong's three small moons haven't risen, and the stars, while spectacular, provide little illumination. The automatic windows have no chinks, and only a tiny line leaks out under the door. I wait on the porch for my eyes to adjust, then move out to check the perimeter.

My footsteps sound loud in my ears, and a dry herbal scent rises with each footfall. The local insects creak and crackle, their song undeterred by my passage. According to my research, the local criquettes are wary of humans, but they don't seem to mind me.

And yes, before you ask, I am human. But I get that question a lot.

I keep my blaster handy and hope the light from my holo-ring will scare off any nocturnal predators. The creatures are said to be fierce hunters, but their sensitive eyes mean they're easily warded off by bright lights. My holo-ring flares and dims as it checks in with each of the professor's security checkpoints.

When he finally gave me access to the system, I made a few adjustments to ensure we didn't have any unexpected visitors or "accidental" drone launches. I may not be a programming genius like Triana, but I can run almost any security system out there. And I know how to install a backdoor so I can get in again.

The criquettes go silent, and I freeze. Did I tread too loudly, or is something else out here? Dialing up the lumens on my holo-ring, I raise my hand to shine it across the yard. Light splashes against the canyon wall, illuminating the rough stone and dusty ground. I turn slowly, eyes raking over every centimeter, ears on high alert.

Then I see the eyes. Three glowing, red eyes.

A chill passes through me, and adrenaline hits my bloodstream. My heart pounds, but my hand is steady as I swing it, slicing the beam of light across the darkness. I catch a blur of dark fur, long legs, and big teeth. A creature yips—in surprise, not fear. I freeze, but the eyes disappear. Light footsteps gallop away.

I continue my patrol, heart beating faster, ears even more alert. The blaster doesn't leave my palm, and I keep the holo-ring on high power. I'll need to give it a supplemental charge soon, but I'm not risking darkness with those things around.

When I return to the cabin, Francois is still droning on. A holo-projector shines, filling the room with detailed engineering diagrams. The professor stands beside one, making tidy notations and adding data to a file on his holo-ring while explaining it to Elodie. Leo snoozes on the couch, with the cat draped over him. Anti-Griz watches from his chosen location, his eyes flicking to me as I enter.

I cross the room, ducking through a bunch of diagrams and equations, stopping beside Anti-Griz. "Where's Annabelle?"

"Sanitary facilities." He nods at the closed door, then glances at his chrono. "She's been in there a while."

"Think I should check on her?" I'm not the "let's go to the bathroom together" type, but her absence makes me nervous. The hoverboards are locked—I made sure no one could wander off alone before we left town. But my intuition is prickling, and I always trust my gut.

Suppressing a shudder—math is my kryptonite—I push through the equations and head to the internal door. My fingers graze the knob but it rotates out of my grasp.

Annabelle stares at me from the now-open doorway. "What? Don't you trust me?" She's daring me to pretend I was simply headed for the facilities myself.

But I'm not playing games. "No, I don't. You aren't the Annabelle Morgan I know, so you haven't earned my trust yet."

Her face goes blank, and she blinks in surprise. "Oh. You're one of those 'say what you think' people. I'm not used to brutal honesty. People tend to tread lightly around top-levs. Or former top-levs." Her expression darkens a bit.

I shrug and step back, waving for her to enter the room. "Get over it." She passes in front of me, leaving the door open. Probably a power move to make me feel like a servant. Her mistake. I've been closing doors for top-levs for years.

Catching Anti-Griz 's eye again, I jerk my head toward the other room. Time to investigate. His eyes flit to Annabelle, and he nods. I'm not sure why I trust *him*, except he feels more like Griz than not. And he clearly wants to get home, so we've got a common goal.

The other room is a lab or workshop. Engineering schematics and rough drawings cover the walls. Heavy equipment fills the room. Wires and electronics cover most of the horizontal surfaces. The scent of grease and oil lingers, with an underlying whiff of metallic burn.

A door in the rear wall leads to a functional sanitation room, so I make use of the facilities while I have the chance. I pause in the doorway to give the lab one more quick look. Nothing obviously amiss sticks out at me, so I return to the front room.

"That should do it!" Elodie lunges across the room to grab Anti-Griz's arm. "Come look at this—I think it will work."

Anti-Griz pulls back, holding up both hands. "I don't know anything about physics or engineering. If you want to assess a threat, I'm your guy, but building a cross-dimensional transporter? Nope."

Francois frowns. "Trans-universal transference device. I told you, alternate dimensions are science fiction."

Anti-Griz ignores him.

I frown. "When did you become a physicist, Elodie?"

She shrugs. "I don't have a lot of training, but I'm good at synthesizing and seeing the connections in the bigger picture."

Leo sits up, roused by the conversation. "There's a big picture?" He waves at the dozens of files floating around the room. "You can't just look at this stuff and understand it. Unless you're some kind of genius or savant." His eyes narrow as he looks more closely at her. "Are you?"

She shrugs, then points at a file. "I've dabbled in quantum wave duality and entanglement. My professor said I had a knack for it, but you can make more money styling hair, so I became an aesthetician." She stretches the file bigger as the rest of us stare, open-mouthed. "But this piece here is really elegant." She turns to Francois. "He's the genius."

Francois preens.

"Say, genius." I fold my arms across my chest as I stare him down. "Any idea how these two got dumped into our world in the first place?"

TWENTY-TWO
TRIANA

VALTI GRITS her teeth and glares at O'Neill. He stares back, his shoulders tense. The sun blazes, baking the life out of the canyon and everything in it. A hot breeze blows, swirling dust at our feet.

I lean against the warm stone, waiting for the staring contest to end. Nearby, the fire that consumed our sled crackles merrily, sucking even more moisture out of the air. A winged creature cries out overhead, and I almost expect to hear a wooden flute in the distance, like in the old *westirns* on *Ancient TēVē*.

Crack!

Valti and O'Neill's heads snap around, both facing the potential threat. The flames expand, then contract, and the burning hulk collapses on itself.

O'Neill turns to me. "Let's start walking. There's a small town a few klicks that way." He juts a thumb toward the sunset.

"Don't be stupid. You'll never get there before dark, and the Edorra Plains are not safe at night." Valti holds up a hand when O'Neill starts to protest. "Your stunner won't be enough. There are big nocturnal predators."

O'Neill crosses his arms and glares again.

"Please, don't start another stare-off." I turn to the redhead. "We're on the same side. We want to go home, and you want your Bear back. Tell us about this professor. Can he really help us? What do you know that you're not sharing?"

Valti's lips press together, and she gives me a once-over. Then she heaves a sigh and sags back against the warm stone of the canyon wall beside me. "I ran into Professor Francois van Lieugen y Ongkowijaya when I first started this assignment."

Her eyes drift away from me, ranging over the dry landscape as she tells the story. "As I told you, I'm investigating Thomas Fortenoy's black-market activity. The cargo you just unloaded would be enough to shut down both him and Arun Kinduja—if I worked for Customs and Tariffs. Frankly, the CCIA doesn't care about small time gray trading like Annabelle does. But we've been watching Fortenoy for a while—he's doing something different. When he moved in on Annabelle's operation, I joined the ship. I don't know what he's up to, yet, but on their last trip to Aldrin, he met with the professor."

"I thought you said he gave you the slip." O'Neill's jaw tightens.

"He did—*after* he met with the professor. They talked for a while—they must have had a jammer because my bugs weren't able to get a decent feed. After that, before they left Station Aldrin, Fortenoy had new equipment installed in *Solar Reveler*—that's when he removed the med-pod. He told Annabelle it was security gear, and she seemed to accept that. Of course, she believes everything he says." She shakes her head. "It's not like her."

"How well do you know Annabelle?" I ask.

"I worked on SK2 for several years. I didn't interact directly with her, but I got a feel for who she is. About three years ago, she cut ties with Dame Morgan and borrowed money from R'ger to start her own company. Dame Morgan disowned her—I believe one of her half-siblings has been named heir."

Relief washes over me—my mother isn't dead. Then I snap my jaw shut. "My mother disowned me?"

"Not you." O'Neill's arm tightens around my shoulders, and he gives me a little shake. "Altabelle, not you."

I nod. "Right. So, Fortenoy is in league with this professor?"

"That's my assessment of the situation. I suspect the equipment Fortenoy installed on the ship is what caused your… transition. It's interesting that only you two were impacted."

"Are we sure that's true?" O'Neill's arm drops from my shoulders, and he leans against the rocky outcropping that shelters us from whatever is at the other end of this canyon. "For all we know, some of the others transferred too. We didn't tell anyone—maybe they didn't either."

"You two were the only ones acting weird." She swings her index finger from O'Neill to me. "I think we—*I* would have noticed anyone else. I've been flying with this crew for a while."

"Yes, but you noticed because you know *Bear* very well." O'Neill grimaces as he says the nickname. "You realized he—I was acting strange. As a deck hand, you wouldn't have much opportunity to interact with Annabelle."

"No, but I was watching her. Why do you think I came to her cabin? She summoned Bear before we jumped, and I wanted to know why. I figured I'd get the details from him later, but I'm not a patient woman."

A grin flits across O'Neill's face, as if he's remembering other times when Vanti wasn't patient.

I clear my throat. "I thought you said you contacted this professor guy."

"I did." Valti tears her eyes away from O'Neill with an almost audible snap. "He was expecting us. He told me he had security, but that he'd let us in."

"Why did he change his mind? You don't think Fortenoy is there, do you? Maybe that's where he went?" I wish again that I'd put that tracker on him. Which makes me wonder why Valti didn't. "Aren't you tracking him?"

She shakes her head, her copper hair shimmering. "No—well, yes. I put a tracker on him—several, in fact. He's got to be using some kind of burner to kill them. Probably part of standard pirate operating procedure. The trackers always die before he leaves the station. I've followed him to the surface, but he gives me the slip." Her cheeks go pink again—this failure clearly weighs on her.

"If Fortenoy is there, we need better weapons." O'Neill pats the pocket where his stunner resides.

Valti glares at the smoldering pile of wreckage. "I had some in the sled."

"You don't have any on you?" I find that impossible to believe.

"Only the usual." She pulls a small stunner from a hidden pocket. Like our Vanti, she seems to conjure things from thin air—there are no bulges or wrinkles in her skin-tight outfit. "Stunner, mini-blaster, tranq pin, holo-burner, retractable garrote, knife—" She removes, brandishes, and returns each item as she names it. "Captio injector, truth dart, secondary mini-blaster." She lifts her feet one at a time and taps her ankles. "Stiletto." She waves a decorative metal hairpin, then swiftly twists her hair in a sleek roll, using the weapon to secure it. Then she glances at her now empty hands and holds them palms out. "And these, of course."

O'Neill bites back a smile. "Can I use one of your mini-blasters? Bear is not so well-loaded. He only left me a stunner."

She lifts the cuff of her drainpipe pants, revealing an ankle holster that should have created a bulge in her pant leg. Going down on the other knee, she unstraps it and hands the weapon and holder to O'Neill.

"What about me? Can I have your tranq pin?" I put out a hand. "Your alter ego has trained me to use them."

Her lips purse, then she reaches into her waistband pocket as she stands. She holds the ring between her thumb and index finger, giving it a long, considering look. "This is non-lethal, but it will put a victim under for about twelve hours. You wouldn't want to use it on anyone out here on the plains—that would be a death sentence, at least after dark." She nods at the brilliant sunset now painting the desert sky behind us.

"I promise not to abandon anyone in a dangerous location—unless they really deserve it."

"Works for me." She drops the ring into my outstretched palm and turns to O'Neill. "Let's come up with a plan."

"Quiet." He's staring around the sheltering rocky outcropping. "Someone is coming to investigate the wreckage."

I crowd close to him, peering over his shoulder, but I don't see anyone. "We should have brushed out our footprints."

He turns his head slightly, and his new beard rasps across my lips. "Brush out our footprints? You've been watching too much *Ancient TēVē.*"

"Always." I breath in his warm scent and press a kiss against his scruffy cheek. "But still—"

"The wind probably covered our tracks." Valti's harsh whisper through my audio implant grates against my nerves. "Either way, it's too late now."

An elderly man with a wild white halo of hair steps down from a hoverboard beside the sled debris. He stumbles a bit on the dismount, catching himself with his cane. After a slow circuit of the wreckage, during which he stops several times to poke the smoldering ruins, his head comes up. His eyes travel slowly across the barren dirt, pausing on several rough outcroppings in the canyon wall on either side. His gaze catches on our hiding place, then continues on. Then he turns and step onto the hoverboard again.

A voice booms behind us. "Well, what are you waiting for?"

TWENTY-THREE
VANTI

PROFESSOR VAN LIEUGEN stands in the center of his living room, stock still, his eyes darting between us like a pinball. I glare, trying to intimidate him, and his gaze jumps away like a frightened criquette.

"You can tell us." Elodie takes a half step toward the man.

"Don't!" He waves his cane to keep her back.

"Don't what?" She reaches out and grabs the cane as it swings by, nearly toppling him. "What are you afraid of? Tell us how they got here."

"I can't."

"Can't? Or won't?" She pulls the cane, hand over hand, until she's standing next to the little old man. "Based on what you've shown me, someone had to have installed equipment on our ship. Who was it?"

Francois' jaw hinges open and closed, but nothing comes out. Elodie presses him gently into his rocking chair and kneels beside it. She hands him the still-steaming mug and encourages him to sip.

She sits back on her heels. "Feel better now?"

He drops the mug on the table with a loud crack. "No, I don't feel better! I need a drink! A real drink!"

Elodie looks around the room, her eyes locking on a cabinet built into the wall beside the fireplace. Several bottles are visible through the gray glass.

As she rises, I grab her arm. "I don't think giving him alcohol is a good idea. We need him clear-headed for his calculations and engineer-y stuff."

She shakes me off and opens the cabinet, pulling out the bottles one by one. As she reads the labels, my audio implant pings with a call from her. "I'm going to give him enough to loosen him up. Once we know what's going on, I'll slip him some BuzzKill."

I should have thought of that.

My heart stutters. When did Elodie become so logical? Maybe *I've* been sent to an alternate dimension in which everyone else is smarter than me. The thought dances across my brain, and I banish it. I'm exactly where I'm supposed to be, and I need to get my head in the game and bring my friends home. "Good idea."

She smiles and takes two of the bottles back to the professor. "You've got some good stuff here. Let me grab a glass."

"Don't bother." He grabs the shorter bottle, pulls off the lid, and chugs some of the clear liquid. "Gah! That stuff is vile." He tips the bottle back again.

When his hand drops, Elodie snags the bottle and puts it on the floor out of easy reach. "Do you feel better now?"

"It'll take a second to kick in." He leans back and closes his eyes, breathing deeply.

"Don't let him fall asleep," Leo hisses.

The professor's eyes pop open, and he glares at Leo. "I'm not a lightweight. I just needed to take the edge off." He turns back to Elodie. "What were you asking, dear lady?"

Elodie flutters her eyelashes. "You were going to tell us how Annabelle and Ty got transferred from their universe to ours." The old man opens his mouth, but she cuts in before he starts speaking. "Not the theory, but the nuts and bolts."

"And the culprits." I lean against the wall, my arms folded, staring at him. "Who put that equipment on the ship and why?"

"To be honest, I only know part of the story." He looks at the items on the side table, then at the liquor cabinet and back to Elodie. "Where did the Alturian FireWater go?"

She pats his hand, then hands him the mug. "You've had enough of that for now. Try the tea instead. You can have more firewater when you've told us everything."

He glares and sips from the mug. After a long stare down with Elodie, he finally sets the mug down and leans forward. "I was approached by a venture capitalist firm a few months ago. They heard I'd been looking for backers to fund a field test of my system." He glances at Annabelle. "I've burned my bridges in the academic world. When they threw me out of GROPE, I lost any chance at support for my experiments. So I've been soliciting private donors. These people said they would install my equipment on a ship and attempt a multi-verse translation." His eyes wander to Anti-Griz, then back to Annabelle, who both watch him closely. "They were supposed to have carefully vetted volunteers for the mission. You—" His voice cracks, and he tries again. "You didn't volunteer?"

"Do I look like I volunteer for experiments?" Annabelle sits on one of the uncomfortable plastek chairs, her back ramrod straight, her eyes narrowed to slits. I've spent enough time with the Ice Dame to recognize the glare, and I would not want to be the target.

A chill goes down my spine. She looks and sounds nothing like the Triana Moore I've become friends with. Her curly red hair is pulled back in a severe braid. She wears Triana's clothing—the fancier stuff our Triana has no interest in—but the expression and attitude give her a completely different appearance.

Elodie and Leo gaze at Annabelle with wary expressions.

But the old guy doesn't know any better. Or maybe he's too drunk to care. "I dunno you—maybe you volunteer for rishky things all the time! I bet the payout was good."

"Payout?" The word is soft and deadly.

Van Lieugen doesn't answer. He stares at his hands, turning and wiggling them as if he's not sure what they're used for. Elodie snaps her fingers in front of his face, but he doesn't flinch.

I grimace and turn back to Annabelle. "Galactic law requires all study participants be adequately paid for their risk. Usually there's a survivor's benefits plan, too."

"What kind of government thinks it's okay to do dangerous experiments on people if you pay their heirs enough credit?" Anti-Griz demands.

Every head in the room swings to face him and variations on the same answer come from all of us. "All of them."

Annabelle shakes her head in disgust at his naiveite and turns back to the professor. "Who got paid?"

The force of her glare seems to catch his attention. He shrugs. "I did. And the inveshtors were supposed to pay the vict—I mean the shubjects. They shet up the whole thing. I builted th'equipment. But if only two of you got translated, then shomething went wrong." He waves his arms. "The whole ship was supposhed to jump. And come back, too."

"If you look at the equipment, do you think you could figure out how to fix it?" Elodie waves at the equations still floating in every corner of the room. "The theory looks sound to me, but can you correct the machinery?"

His face wrinkles as he frowns at the files then hiccups. "I can try."

"Excellent." Elodie rolls to her feet in one smooth movement. "Let's—"

A klaxon rings through the room. I sweep up my connection to van Lieugen's security system. "We've got incoming. A small sled at the mouth of the canyon." I flick the file open, then swipe the vid to the large projector.

The drones have excellent night-vision capability. Although their cams can't pick out color, the security system analyzes the materials and calculates pigments and hues. The enhanced projection makes it look like it was filmed in bright daylight.

A sleek craft arrows down the canyon. The matte black exterior with bright red pinstripes along the sides screams credits—lots of credits. It moves fast, starlight glimmering off the plastek windscreen. The silhouette of a single occupant is visible through the windows.

"Who's the rich guy?" I nod at the display.

Francois squints. "Looks like my inveshtor. Isn't it a shweet ride?"

I catch Elodie's gaze. "Dose him."

She nods and slaps a patch onto Francois's neck.

His eyes close, then pop open. "Why'd you do that?" His words come out crisp and clear, the drunken slur gone.

I point at the display again. "Your investor is coming. You need to be sober to talk to him." The sled has slowed to negotiate the tight corner, so I turn to face the door.

"You need to hide. He can't know I told you what's happening! I signed an NDA!" Van Lieugen leaps to his feet, and Elodie catches him before he tumbles over. She shoves his cane into his hand. The old man shifts his grip on the support, steadies his stance, then starts waving the cane through the holograms which pop and disappear like bubbles. "Get upstairs. Hurry!"

Leo springs up, grabbing the various cups and napkins that have been scattered around the room while the professor worked. He dumps them all into the sink and drapes a towel over the whole thing.

Elodie shoves the bottle back into the cabinet, and Anti-Griz pushes us toward the steps. We hurry up to a wide-open room with a bed tucked under the sloped roof and a broad dresser under the single window. I push everyone toward the back where we won't be visible through the open railing.

Elodie and Leo drop onto the bed while Anti-Griz and I crouch in the shadows near the stairs, all our attention focused on the front door barely visible below.

When a hand falls on my arm, I almost jump out of my skin. I glare at Anti-Griz. "What?"

"Where's Annabelle?"

TWENTY-FOUR

TRIANA

We spin to face the voice, O'Neill and Valti dropping into defensive crouches. I stagger and catch myself with a hand to the rocky outcropping we're hidden behind.

There's no one here.

"It's a drone." O'Neill nods at the tiny speck hovering three meters above the scrubby dirt.

Valti whips out a scanning program and waves her hand at the device. A holo report pops up, and she reads it. "Audio and vid. Registered to Francois van Lieugen y Ongkowijaya."

"Who is currently getting tired of waiting for you." The voice assaults us on a decibel setting probably outlawed by most governments due to the potential for hearing loss. It's loud and quavery and extremely cranky.

"Did you attack us?" O'Neill asks. "We aren't coming out there to get fried."

A coughing throat clearing rumbles from the drone. "That wasn't on purpose. Darn thing misfired. I wanted to see when you'd get here."

The three of us exchange a look. O'Neill raises a brow, optimistic but alert. Valti presses her lips together—skeptical but sure she can handle anything. I roll my eyes because that's my default response.

That pretty much sums up the three of us in any given situation.

"We're coming." Valti waves the drone ahead. "But you stay in front of us, where we can see you. You and your drone." She waits for the drone to buzz away, then peeks around the outcropping. "I see him. If he has accomplices hidden up the canyon, we'll be walking into an ambush."

"Do you believe it was an accident?" O'Neill leans out to do his own assessment. "I thought this guy was supposed to be some kind of genius."

"*Some kind* is a good description." Valti flicks a few commands on her holo-ring, and her protective bubble forms over her head. It stretches, extending a meter on either side and down in front of her face and chest. "Get under my force shield. We'll have to stay close together, but it should stop any incoming laser or blaster fire."

She waits until O'Neill and I have crowded close on either side, then we walk together into the main part of the canyon. Our Vanti is prickly about personal space, so I try to stay close enough to be protected without actually touching her. It's an awkward shuffle, like trying to share a small umbrella with someone you don't like.

I peer behind her at O'Neill. They walk shoulder to shoulder, their steps in perfect synch.

As usual when they're on assignment. This is why I have those twinges of jealousy and suspicion. They're too perfect together. But I suppress them because O'Neill and Vanti have proven their faithfulness many times.

Valti, on the other hand, has done nothing to earn my trust. And she's admitted to being in a relationship with No'Neill.

"What did you mean about the professor?" I skip a little, trying to match my stride to theirs. "Some kind of genius?"

She chuckles a little. "He's a genius at physics. But like many super smart people, he doesn't do real life that well. It would be totally in character for him to blow up a friendly by accident."

"Hey!" The cranky voice issues from the drone a few meters ahead of us. "That's not nice."

"Is it incorrect?" Valti asks.

The drone doesn't answer.

Beyond the drone, near the end of the canyon, the old man waits. He sits on his hoverboard, drawing in the dust with the cane. As we approach, the drone zips away to the right, around a blind corner. The hoverboard rises, with the old man still sitting on top, and slides away in the drone's wake.

When we reach the turn, I look at the dirt. A complex math equation covers the open space, much of it already blown away by the constant breeze. There's also a drawing of a cat's head on a buff, shirtless man's body, one hand holding an ice cream cone.

He's definitely an odd guy.

A few meters beyond the abrupt corner, the canyon turns left, resuming its original East-West direction, then ends in a sheer wall. The splashing of water is audible over the constant murmur of the wind. The cliff behind us casts long shadows over the space, but lights glow from the windows of a small cabin, illuminating the area.

The small structure sits in the center of the rectangular space. Green plants grow around the home, some neatly regimented in a fenced area on the south side, others crowding and climbing the posts holding up a deep porch roof. The building is tiny—probably two rooms on the ground floor with a loft above. It's an ugly, prefabricated design, but the greenery softens the harsh lines, giving the space an almost fairytale charm.

The professor stands on the porch, his hoverboard under one arm, cane in the opposite hand. Light shines from the doorway behind him, creating a bright aura around him and making his features difficult to see.

Valti stops at the two steps leading to the porch. She holds up both hands, palms facing the professor. "May we come in?"

He grunts and steps backward through the door. Valti follows a few steps behind, knees flexed, hands out, as if expecting an attack.

She's always expecting an attack.

O'Neill gives the place a once over, runs a scan on his holo-ring, then nods for me to precede him onto the porch and into the house.

A hard-looking couch sits under the large front windows, with two cracked chairs that might have come from the University's trash heap. The threadbare rug's leafy pattern has faded almost completely to a mottled gray. A small fire burns in the woodstove built into the right side wall, and a beautiful bent-wood chair with a thick, red-patterned seat cushion rocks gently beside it.

Beyond the rocker, a stove, sink, and several cupboards stand under another window. In the shadowy corner, there's a narrow door that must lead outside. A stairway against the internal wall on the left leads to an open loft and shelters another door that probably provides access to the second room.

The professor stabs at his holo-ring, and the automated windows darken, hiding the yard. He slams the door shut and turns the deadbolt, then throws a hologram into the center of the room. It shows views of the outside and a dashboard of alerts above.

"Sit." He points at the couch and slumps over his cane. "My security system should catch anyone else coming in, but you being here is dangerous to me. Your sled explosion might have alerted my enemies to your visit."

"Whose fault is that?" Valti puts her back against the wall where she can see all of the entrances. At least I assume that's why she's standing beside the fire. If it were anyone else, I'd think they were cold, but this is Valti. Plus, we're in the desert.

O'Neill's eyes flicker to Valti, then to me, and he jerks his head at one of the nasty chairs. As I take a seat, he moves to a position against the other side wall, near the steps.

"If you hadn't been here, there wouldn't have been anything to explode." The old man drops into his rocker, then leans forward to swipe through the holo screen hovering between us. He flips a few icons from red to green and waves the display down to a meter-high cube. Then he pins a glare on Valti. "What do you want?"

"Do you recognize my friend?" She nods at me.

Are we friends? Probably just a figure of speech.

The professor peers at me. "Red hair, blue eyes, brown skin—she looks like that girl my partner was targeting."

I stare. "Targeting?"

Van Lieugen's bushy brows come down and his nose wrinkles. "I guess that's not the right word. More like using."

"Thanks, I feel much better."

"He said you had a ship he could use." The old man takes a sip from the steaming mug on his side-table. "You want something to drink? Help yourself." He waves at the kitchen.

With a quick look at O'Neill to make sure I'm not endangering us all by crossing the room, I get up and refill the kettle on the stove. Mugs hang from hooks under the upper cabinets, and a box of homemade tea sachets, each neatly labeled, nestle in a basket beneath. After perusing the selections, I select a peppermint for me and a green tea for O'Neill. "Va—Linds? Any tea?"

She shakes her head, and her perfect twist comes undone, the pin clattering to the floor. She bends to scoop it up and returns to standing in a single, graceful movement. "I want to hear the rest of the professor's story. How was he going to use Annabelle's ship?"

"He installed my experimental equipment to see if we could open the door between universes." In a sudden, jerky movement, he spins around to stare at me. "Did it w—"

Before he can finish the question, Valti is beside him, her stiletto knife pressed against his throat. "Don't move."

"Vanti!" O'Neill takes a step away from the wall but freezes at something he sees in Valti's expression. His hands come up, palms out, in a placating gesture. "Linds. He was going to tell us more. Please, let the man talk."

Valti's gaze darts to O'Neill and back to van Lieugen, then her hand drops, and she steps back. "Sorry. You moved so suddenly." She gathers her hair into one hand and sweeps it back up, the sheathed knife disappearing into the smooth, copper roll.

Van Lieugen rubs his throat, although there's no mark. He casts a dirty look at Valti, then turns to O'Neill. "Keep her under control, young man."

Like anyone can do that.

O'Neill seems to hear my thought—his lips twitch, and he darts a quick look at me. At his nod, I cross the room, leaving his tea on the chair nearest him. Then I take my seat and turn back to the professor.

"Your equipment seems to have worked. When the ship jumped to this system from Kaku, Ser O'Neill and I ended up in this new reality." I nod at Valti. "We know her in our own universe, but she's different. The ship we flew on belongs to a company called *CelebVid* rather than me, and the other people we were traveling with aren't here. Well, not all of them."

Valti's eyes flick to me, then back to the professor. "Who's missing?"

"Our friend Leo is on the ship but doesn't seem to know us well. In our universe, Elodie is a *CelebVid* star. Tom Fortenoy was listed as the co-pilot, but we hadn't met him before the jump. The ship's pilot was a woman named Chowdhury Nowak."

Valti shakes her head, but her eyes don't leave the professor. "Never heard of her. Elodie keeps the engines running. She's a bit of a flake, but good at her job. A genius, even, according to *our* Annabelle."

Van Lieugen vibrates on the front edge of the rocking chair, his hands shaking. "You really translated from another universe! I succeeded! I'm not a washed-up has-been! Take that, Wilmer, you pompous *verdigo*!" The excitement in his voice is palpable.

A quick holo-ring search translates *verdigo* to "spider monkey." I try and fail to imagine a pompous monkey. "Who's Wilmer?"

"My brother. He's the one who got me thrown out of GROPE. Suck it, Wilmer! I'm going to be famous!"

I consider asking what GROPE is, but I have more important questions. "If you brought us here, can you send us home?"

Van Lieugen stops bouncing. "I—yeah, I should be able to send you back. After—"

"After what?"

"Well, I need to write my paper. And I'll need your statements to do that. This is big! We'll do the rounds of all the science conferences. Not only physics, but astrophysics, astromechanics, maybe even philosophy! And the engineers will want to talk to us. And they'll induct me into the GROPE Venue of Heroes! You can't miss that! And then—"

"No." O'Neill's curt voice cuts through the professor's babble. "We aren't doing any of that. We are going home. The other us—"

"Altabelle and No'Niell," I throw in.

O'Neill's eyes roll—just a little—but he continues, a tiny hint of humor threading through his voice. "Yes, Altabelle and No'Neill can give you their statements and do the press junket."

"But they're from here!" van Lieugen cries.

"And they have been there." I point across the room, as if that's where the alternate reality lives.

"But that won't have the same impact!" Forgetting Valti, he jumps up to pace across the floor.

Valti jerks, then stills. Her shoulders bunch, like an attack dog held on a tight leash. Her teeth clench and her eyes burn. Then she takes a deep breath, and the calm façade snaps into place. "I want my partner back. Now. Make it happen."

TWENTY-FIVE
VANTI

I LEAN OVER THE BANISTER, peering down into the living room. Annabelle stands next to the professor, facing the door. She holds a mini-blaster pointed very obviously at van Lieugen.

Before I can say anything, the front door opens. Tom Fortenoy stands on the porch.

Fortenoy is the investor? How can the co-pilot of a ship owned by a social media company have enough credit to invest in a massive, universe-spanning physics experiment?

Or maybe there was no credit involved? Annabelle and Anti-Griz didn't get paid. Maybe van Lieugen was so happy to have a ship, he *gave* the equipment to Fortenoy. Let's face it, the financial details of the deal don't matter. We know who's pulling the strings now.

The smile falls from Fortenoy's face when he sees Annabelle holding the physicist hostage. "What's going on here?"

She grabs the professor's arm and pulls him away from the door, giving Fortenoy room to enter. "How about you tell me, Tom."

Fortenoy casts a questioning look at her and steps into the room, hands raised. "Have we met?"

Annabelle snorts a little. "Not in this reality."

The old man huffs. "I told you—"

Annabelle shakes his arm. "I don't care. I'm calling it what I want. You two did an experiment that brought me from another reality to this one when we jumped from Kaku to Armstrong. I want to know why."

Slowly, I ease away from the railing and into the shadowy loft. I'll let Annabelle find out what's going on but be ready to jump in if she needs backup. Just like old times.

"We wanted to see if it worked." The professor's voice is excited. "And it does, Tom! This woman is from a different universe!"

I crouch low and lean forward so I can see them. Annabelle stands with her back to me, with van Lieugen to her right. Fortenoy's face is the only one I can see. His eyes sparkle. "Did the transmission work?"

"What transmission?" Annabelle demands.

The professor shakes his head. "Didn't come through."

"How do you know the translation worked, then?"

"They told me." The old man points at Annabelle. "She said she and the man translated."

"What transmission?" Annabelle shakes the man's arm.

"We rigged a drone—"

Fortenoy cuts him off. "She doesn't need to know. What man?"

Van Lieugen's bushy brows snap down. "Man?"

"You said she and the man translated. What man? Where is he? And who else is here?" Fortenoy's eyes swing up and across the loft.

I freeze, but he doesn't seem to notice me in the shadows of the railing.

Annabelle shakes the professor's arm, but he answers anyway. "The man. O'Neill. He's upstairs with the others."

Busted. With a mental shrug, I stand and lean casually against the railing. "Ser Fortenoy. I take it you are more than simply the co-pilot of the *Solar Reveler*." I signal the others to stay out of sight.

His head snaps up, and his eyes zero in on me, cold and assessing. "Ah, Agent Fioravanti. When I heard you were accompanying Elodie-Oh, I was afraid you might get in the way of our… experiment."

I stroll down the stairs, my stunner held where it's quite visible. "I guess I missed a step. But it never occurred to me that I needed to look for experimental multi-verse translation equipment. Would you care to share what your intention was?"

Elodie, Leo, and Anti-Griz follow me down the steps. So much for my signals. Amateurs.

Fortenoy smiles, but the expression doesn't reach his eyes. "No."

Behind me, Elodie chuckles. "Isn't the villain supposed to do a monologue on his evil plan?"

Surprise crosses Fortenoy's face and disappears so fast I almost miss it. "You think I'm a villain? I'm just a guy trying to make his company more profitable."

"What company would that be?" I pause on the bottom step, keeping plenty of distance from everyone in the room.

Unfortunately, Elodie doesn't follow my lead—she's breathing down my neck from the step right behind me. "You're the CEO of *CelebVid,* aren't you?"

Fortenoy's eyes widen and his jaw drops. "How'd you know?"

Elodie shifts behind me. "I looked you up. I'm pretty handy with a search engine."

A file slides over my shoulder and settles to the center of the room, expanding to fill the space. Fortenoy's face appears, stretching to a meter-high image, accompanied by an article about his ascension to the top spot at the entertainment corporation.

"*CelebVid* is voracious—they're constantly looking for new content to feed their viewers. If he could get vid from another universe, that would be a jackpot. And sending a well-known vid star there would be even better." She flicks her fingers over my shoulder, and the holo dissipates. "Right, Ser CEO?"

Fortenoy lifts his shoulders and raises his hands. "What can I say? You got me. Too bad the drone transmission didn't come through."

"You sent a drone along to feed the video across?" I ask.

"Of course. There was no guarantee anyone we sent would bring vid back, so we had to get it ourselves." Fortenoy leans against the wall, looking bored. "But that part didn't work, so we're back to square one."

"Unless you interview the vic—participants!" Van Lieugen bounces on his toes, his hands clasped in front of his body. "I can explain what we did, and you can interview Ser O'Neill and Sera Morgan—"

"No." Anti-Griz pushes past me and gets into van Lieugen's face. "You're sending us back. Now."

"I'm not sure I can do that." Van Lieugen waves, and the data he and Elodie were working on appears, floating around the room like holographic clouds.

Elodie slinks by on my other side.

I mentally throw up my hands in disgust. How am I supposed to protect people when they won't follow simple hand signals?

"We can do it." Elodie pushes a cloud of data closer. "This bit right here—we need to tweak these configurations and re-run the trigger event."

"What does that mean?" Annabelle still holds the professor's other arm, and now she shakes it to get his attention. "In words a non-physicist can understand? How, exactly, would you make this happen?"

Van Lieugen exchanges a look with Elodie, then turns to Annabelle, staring pointedly at the weapon. The guy has more guts than I expected.

Annabelle puts her mini-blaster back into her pocket and takes a step back, lifting both hands, palms out in a pacifying gesture. "Please, explain."

"We'll go to the ship and reset the equipment. The existing framework is correct, but we need to adjust these variables for continuity."

Annabelle's lips press together, and she clears her throat.

Elodie giggles. "Everyone gets back on the ship, and we make a jump back to Kaku. The jump will trigger equipment with the new settings, and you and Ser O'Neill will translate back."

"But we were jumping at the same time," Anti-Griz says. "How will you get the ship in our reality—" He intercepts a glare from van Lieugen and holds up both hands. "How will you get the ship in our universe to jump at the same time? How did you do it the first time?"

"Our two universes are very closely linked." The old man's voice takes on a lecturing tone, making it easy to imagine him teaching at a university. "So closely linked that they will be trying to do the same thing we are. Time is flexible, so as long as they're jumping at about the same time, it should link up."

"How do you know?" I ask.

They all turn to stare at me—as if they'd forgotten I existed. "What?" van Lieugen asks.

"How do you know what's going on in that other universe? You said your drones don't work. Maybe you got lucky last time, and they just happened to be jumping at the right time and place."

"That's not how the universes work." The professor pushes the data cloud away and starts writing mathematical equations. Numbers appear as he writes, hanging in the air. "Each new universe is created as we make decisions. Each decision drives the new universes farther apart. The one you came from was identical to ours until a recent event—"

"That's not true." Annabelle crosses her arms. "This universe is very different from mine. The Annabelle here is still her mother's heir. She married him." She points at Anti-Griz. "The other him. In my universe, I only met him a week ago, and I haven't spoken to my mother in years."

Van Lieugen gulps so loudly we all hear it. "That's not good."

"Why do you say that?" Anti-Griz asks.

"Because the more different the universes are, the farther apart they are. Not physical distance, of course, but let's use distance as a means of explaining it more simply." He raises both hands, the palms close together, then pulls them apart as he speaks. "The farther apart they are, the faster they drift." His hands slide, one moving closer to his face and the other away from his body as he pulls them so they separate in a diagonal. "My equipment can only bridge a small gap. If they get too far apart, we won't be able to send you back."

TWENTY-SIX
TRIANA

PROFESSOR VAN LIEUGEN paces across the floor, throwing data files around the room. Soon, the living room is fogged with clouds of numbers, symbols, and drawings. I leave the genius to it and search the kitchen for food. The professor blew up our supplies, and I'm starving.

I find a jar of something that looks like soup in the fridge. A quick sniff confirms, so I use my holo-ring to look up instructions on reheating soup using ancient technology. The stove turns out to be surprisingly easy to use, and soon I have a pot simmering on the heat circle.

Van Lieugen absently accepts a bowl of soup. "Hey, this is pretty good."

I chuckle. "It came from your fridge."

He nods but doesn't reply. After scooping up a few spoonsful, he sets the bowl on a side table and resumes his pacing. "I need to get to the ship. I think I can adjust the continuity variables and re-trigger the event. But we need to do it soon."

"Soon?" Valti looks up from her bowl. "Why?"

"Our universe is currently in alignment with that one. The longer we wait, the farther out of alignment they become. It takes more power to make the jump. Your ship has a finite power source." He gives me a piercing look. "I assume."

I lift my hands. "It could hardly have an infinite one."

"Exactly." He stabs a finger at me. "The sooner we make the jump, the better."

"Let's go, then." Valti jumps up, leaving her half-eaten soup on a side table.

I take her bowl and the professor's into the kitchen, speaking over my shoulder as I go. "We have a little problem. What about Fortenoy?"

Valti shrugs. "What about him?"

"He's going to wonder why we're jumping back to Kaku so soon." I dump the soup and stack the dishes in the dish cleaning machine.

Van Lieugen grabs a spoon from me and starts reorganizing the bowls. "You're not doing it right."

"It's your ship." Valti pins me with a steely glare. "You can do whatever you want."

"You think? That's not the impression I got." I cross my arms. "It looks to me like he controls Altabelle and her ship."

"What do you care? Dump him. She'll be lucky to be rid of him."

I chew on my lip. I definitely got the impression Carina LaSalva felt that way. In fact, the only one who seemed to be happy to have Fortenoy aboard was Fortenoy. And possibly R'ger. I nod. "Fine. Let's do that. We'll take the professor back to the ship and get away before Fortenoy returns from wherever he's gone."

"Won't that interfere with your mission?" O'Neill asks Valti. "You were supposed to be busting his operation."

Her nose wrinkles. "Yeah. But getting my partner back is more important than the mission."

A wistful shadow crosses O'Neill's face and disappears. Is he wishing our Vanti was willing to put relationships ahead of the mission? The ugly green monster twinges inside my chest again.

O'Neill catches my eye and shakes his head slightly, an understanding smirk twitching at the corners of his mouth. How does he always know what I'm thinking?

Van Lieugen finishes playing with the dirty dishes and closes the washer. A green dot lights up, and the machine starts humming softly. "Let me grab my gear, and we can go."

Van Lieugen disappears into the other room. A few minutes later, he guides a sturdy grav sled through the door. It's weighed down by a haphazard stack of metal, plastek, cables, and wires. "I'm ready."

"What is all this stuff?" I run a finger along one of the cables.

"My prototype, with a few new features." Van Lieugen pats the stacked sled. "The equipment already installed should work, but if anything needs to be repaired, I want to have what I need. And, as I said, there are a few little extras that should make the reverse translation easier."

O'Neill stretches the surveillance vid larger and checks the perimeter. Or something like that. I trust him to keep us safe. He and Valti hold a quiet conversation in the corner, then they turn back to us.

"We're going up instead of out through the canyon." O'Neill traces a path on the surveillance vid and a line appears in bright red going up the face of the box canyon and over the top. "It's the long way around, but we don't want to run into opposition."

"Opposition?" I glance at Valti, but her face is blank. I turn to the professor. "Do you expect Fortenoy to come here?"

He shakes his head violently. "No. He knows better than that! We never meet here. Our contract was handled by a confidential intermediary, and I shipped the equipment via their recommended agent. The only time we met was on Aldrin. He doesn't even know this cabin exists."

"I sincerely doubt that." Valti leans over the sled, checking the cargo locks. "I'm sure he knows everything about you, including where you live."

Van Lieugen's hair waves around his face as he jerks in alarm. "How?"

Valti finishes checking the sled, then straightens. "I've been after this guy for months. He's thorough. I'm sure he hired a team to research you before agreeing to the deal. It's what I would have done."

A klaxon blares, and the surveillance holo flashes red. A mechanical voice announces, "Incoming."

Valti smiles coldly. "See?"

O'Neill swipes through the vids, throwing various angles up around him. "That isn't Fortenoy. Or if it is, he's brought reinforcements. There's a whole team coming down the sides of the canyon."

Valti whips out her weapons as she reviews the holos O'Neill has arrayed in a semi-sphere around his head. They conduct a swift and indecipherable consultation using phrases like "target discrimination" and "charlie foxtrot." When she catches us watching, Valti stops mid-word. Her eyes take on that slightly unfocused appearance associated with initiating a private call.

O'Neill casts a look at her, then jerks his head at me. "They need to know what we're planning, too."

Without acknowledging his statement, she turns and slips out the door.

"What's going on?" van Lieugen asks.

"We have a large team coming in from all sides." O'Neill points at the red images overlaid on the videos. Ghostly figures—probably wearing grav belts—drop down the steep walls of the canyon. Another group approaches through the narrow valley. "We can't sneak away—the equipment is too bulky and you two aren't exactly stealthy."

"Hey!" I react instinctively, then my shoulders drop. "You're right."

He gives me a quick smile. "Linds is going to sneak out—she'll be our ace in the hole if we need help later. Right now, we need a cover story. Why are we here? We don't want Fortenoy to think we're onto his plot."

"You trust her?"

He shrugs one shoulder. "We don't have much choice. And we have a common goal, so I doubt she'll sell us out."

"What possible reason could we have for being here that doesn't involve the whole alternate universe thing?" I wave wildly at the pile of equipment on the sled.

"Maybe the professor contacted us?" O'Neill continues swiping between holos as he muses.

Van Lieugen straightens, hands on hips. "Are you throwing me under the shuttle?"

"Believe it or not, I feel no loyalty to you." O'Neill swings around to pin a glare on the old man. "You dragged us out of our honeymoon and into your reality without permission or even a warning. We were thrust into what appears to be a black-market shipping company, flying with crewmates we can't trust. We owe an undetermined number of credits to a man who has made it very clear he's not above using violence to get his due. I think pinning the blame on you is quite reasonable." Although his voice is low and even, I can feel the anger burning through O'Neill's words.

Unfortunately, so can van Lieugen. His eyes grow wild, and he clutches the sled. "But you need me! I'm the only one who can send you back!"

"Can you?" O'Neill advances on the older man. "Can you send us back? You didn't seem one hundred percent sure of that. I need to assume we might be stuck here, and I want to make sure Triana and I are in the best possible situation. If that means—" He breaks off, his gaze focusing on a holo. "Too late now."

Someone pounds three times on the front door. We all exchange a wide-eyed look, then O'Neill swipes surveillance holos away. When the pounding resumes, he jerks his head at van Lieugen. "Answer it."

The professor casts a quick look toward the front windows, then darts into the adjoining room, slamming the door behind him.

"Ugh." I stomp across the room and fling the front door open. "What?"

A quartet of men dressed in black combat gear and holding plas-rifles and blasters stand on the front porch. The two in front consult their holos, then sidestep to either side, revealing an older man with fading auburn hair.

R'ger's cold eyes assess me over an obviously fake smile. "Why, Annabelle. Whatever are you doing here?"

TWENTY-SEVEN
VANTI

THIS TIME, it's Anti-Griz who grabs the professor's arm. "You need to send us back. Now."

Fortenoy lifts both hands in a placating gesture. "Please, calm down. We'll send you back. That will give us another shot at the drones. I suggest we return to the ship and begin."

Van Lieugen heads toward the interior door. "I need to get some equipment first. Give me a hand, will you?" He throws the request over his shoulder, not waiting to see who responds. With a dissatisfied grunt, Anti-Griz follows him from the room.

"Is there room for all of us on your sled?" I ask. "I saw the creatures who prowl out there—no way I'm walking."

"You'd be safe with your grav belt." Fortenoy's eyes drop to my waist, then slide back up, taking long enough to make me want to punch him.

I suppress the feeling. I'm not giving him the pleasure of seeing my discomfort. I seriously misjudged this guy—he's not the harmless, pleasant pilot I thought. "The others don't have grav belts. Just hoverboards."

Fortenoy slouches against the wall beside the door. "Hoverboards from my shuttle, I assume. They can maintain enough altitude to provide safety. But I wouldn't dawdle."

"Fine. Annabelle, Elodie, Leo, we're heading back now. Anti-Gr—I mean, O'Neill and the professor can ride with Fortenoy. We'll meet you back at the ship."

"I think I'll pass." Annabelle settles onto the uncomfortable couch as if it's a throne.

"You wanna ride with Fortenoy?"

"No. I'm not going back to the ship. I have no intention of 'translating' back to my universe." She pulls out her mini-blaster and lays it across her lap, her hand hovering nearby. "This world is a much nicer place for Annabelle Morgan. I plan to stay."

We stare at her.

"You can't stay." I stab a finger at her. "We want Triana and Griz back."

Annabelle shrugs. "Tough. I'm not going back. I'm going to stay here." Her hand drops closer to the mini-blaster.

"Zark." Elodie drops onto the other end of the sofa.

Annabelle rises, holding the blaster as if she isn't afraid to use it, and urges me toward the door. If this were Triana, I could disarm her easily, but Annabelle handles the weapon like a pro. If I try to get the jump on her in such close quarters, someone is likely to get hurt.

"Go on, go back to the ship. I'll take care of myself. Maybe a luxury cruise back to Kaku to see how dear old Mum is doing." She retreats to the kitchen, the weapon now swiveling in an arc to cover all of us.

Elodie stands. "If you want luxury, you should come back to our ship. It's much nicer than a cruiser."

Annabelle's eyelids lower, as if she's considering Elodie's suggestion. "It *is* a nice ship. And if it belonged to the Annabelle from this universe, I'd take it. But it's his, so it's not worth the risk." She nods at Fortenoy. "I don't trust him. But he can't translate me if I'm not on board."

"I'm going home." Anti-Griz stands in the doorway, his own blaster in hand. "You can't stop me."

"Why would I?" Annabelle leans her butt against the kitchen counter. "You can do whatever you want. But count me out."

Zark. If Griz comes back but Triana stays in the other universe, I'll never hear the end of it. I calculate the odds of disarming Annabelle without injuring anyone else, but they still look bad. Better to let her think she's won. I can track her when she leaves here and scoop her up when she's least expecting it.

"Come on, then, let's go." I jerk my head toward the door.

"You want us to leave her here?" Leo demands. "What about Triana? We need to swap her back."

"You heard what she said." I turn my head enough that Leo can see my slight wink but Annabelle can't. "She won't go back. We'll have to figure out another way to get Triana home."

Annabelle stiffens, and the blaster swings back to me. "On second thought, none of you are going. You think I'm going to let you ambush me later and drag me back to the ship?"

Fortenoy straightens from his slouch by the door. "I assume you won't object to *me* leaving? I have no skin in this game, but I have business to attend to."

Annabelle purses her lips for a moment. "You can go. And him." She jerks her head at Anti-Griz. "Not them. They might do something stupid to get their friend back. I'll pay you handsomely to never take these three on board again. You know I'm good for it." A self-satisfied smirk slides across her face.

Fortenoy's gaze ticks over Leo, Elodie, and me, calculating. "It will have to be substantial. Elodie-Oh is a gold mine. I'm not giving that up to make you feel comfy."

"Hey!" Elodie jerks as if someone poked her. "I'm standing right here! I'm not a commodity to be negotiated." She rubs her temple as she speaks. Her face is gray, and a crease has appeared between her brows.

Leo puts a hand on her arm. "Are you feeling okay?"

"Sure, why wouldn't I be? I like being held at gun point and haggled over like *terkfiske* at a Leweian market!"

"Enough. You *are* a commodity to be negotiated." Fortenoy turns and opens the door, ignoring all of the weaponry pointing in various directions. "Your current popularity is the only reason you're using my ship. I expect a return on my investment. If I can't recoup that from you, Annabelle will have to make it worth my while." He swings back around and pins a stare on Annabelle. "How much?"

While they haggle, I catch Leo's eye and tilt my head at the door. He and Elodie shuffle toward it and the negotiations break off.

"Stop." Annabelle swings the blaster at Leo. "I said you aren't going anywhere."

This is getting old. Annabelle is out of reach, but Fortenoy is close. In one swift movement, I jump behind him and get an arm around his neck, my blaster pointed at his head. "We're leaving. Now."

"No, you aren't." Annabelle's blaster points at my human shield. "I'll shoot him."

"Go ahead. I don't know how it is in your universe, but here, even Annabelle Morgan can't blast random people without consequences. Especially with the Ice Dame for a mother. You want a cushy upper-lev life, you need to stay on the right side of the law." I dart a look at the others. "You can bet Ser *CelebVid* has a drone filming all of this. Unless you want a comfy cell in Attica Prison on Sally Ride?" I wait a second, and her blaster droops. "That's what I thought. Everyone, out. Now. Get on the hoverboards and get aloft."

"Do you really need to strangle me?" Fortenoy's voice is barely audible.

I loosen my arm barely enough to let him breathe, but not enough that he can slither free. This isn't my first rodeo.

Annabelle still leans against the kitchen counter, but every muscle is tense and her frustration simmers, practically shooting steam out her ears. I can't help but admire her control—this version of Annabelle Morgan and I have a lot in common.

Except her look-out-for-number-one attitude.

Once everyone is out, including the professor and his unwieldy grav sled full of electronics and gizmos, I back toward the door, taking Fortenoy with me.

He stumbles a little as we shuffle across the small rug by the door. "Seriously, she isn't going to shoot. You don't need to hold me hostage."

"I have no doubt she'd shoot *me* in a heartbeat. You're too well-known a target. But I'm a rogue security agent. The Ice Dame already doesn't like me—Annabelle could probably convince her I was a threat. So I'm going to continue to use you as a shield. No offense." I pull him through the door. "Close it."

The door clicks shut. I turn my head a few degrees to address the others. "Lock it, professor."

The lock clicks. I release my hold on Fortenoy and step back.

"You could have used a stunner shield. I gave you one back on the *Solar Reveler*." Fortenoy straightens up and rolls his shoulders.

"I could have. But this way was more fun." I snag the remaining hoverboard. "Will the lock keep her inside?"

The others are already aloft, Anti-Griz and the professor floating on either side of the equipment sled. The old man must be using Annabelle's hoverboard. He clears his throat. "Not for long. They're built to keep people out, not in."

"If Triana were here, she could hack it," Elodie says.

Leo snorts. "If Triana were here, we wouldn't need to lock up her alter ego."

"Good point."

"Let's get out of here." I lift off, hovering over Fortenoy's sled as he gets aboard. "How high can those creatures jump?"

Fortenoy flicks his controls, and his sled ascends. "Higher than you'd like to think. I suggest a five-meter flight path."

I initiate a call to my team, which now includes Anti-Griz. I still don't trust this version of him completely, but we have a common goal, so I'll loop him in. "You heard the man. Five meters. Elodie, link all of the hoverboards to mine. I'll follow the sled but maintain independence, in case we need to—" I break off. They'll get my meaning.

"But what about Triana?" Leo asks as they rise to match my altitude.

"We'll come up with a plan to get her back. It might involve kidnapping a top-lev. Are you up for that?" Who am I kidding? It will definitely involve kidnapping a top-lev. But I've abducted Annabelle Morgan before. The secret is to make it look like a protective detail.

"Why do we need her? I'm not going to risk my life and liberty for that woman." Anti-Griz's surly voice sends a shiver up my spine. He sounds so much like Griz and yet so different.

"You aren't going home without her." I cut the connection before he can answer.

TWENTY-EIGHT
TRIANA

R'GER STROLLS into the small cabin, and I back away. He might look like his counterpart in my universe, but his expression gives him away. His sharp eyes tick over the pile of equipment on the sled and O'Neill standing a few meters away, then to the closed door the professor just escaped through. "What are you up to, Annabelle?"

I gulp. How much does R'ger know? Is he connected to the professor's experiments? I decide to go on the offensive. "Hello, Father. *I'd* like to know what *you're* up to." I fold my arms and pretend to relax against the wall.

A ghost of a grin twitches over R'ger's lips, then they stretch into another wide, false smile. "The best defense is an attack. Just like Daddy taught you."

"Then you know I'm doing business, *Daddy*, just like you taught me. Making a trade. Earning my keep." Maybe if I stick to generalities, he'll give me a clue as to what's really going on.

"Trading what, Annabelle?"

So much for that idea. "The professor has some equipment we thought might be profitable." R'ger's eyes light up, and I panic. What if he tries to take the stuff? I force a sigh. "But it turned out to be less promising than we'd hoped. Not worth boosting to orbit, for sure."

He strolls across the room and looks down his nose at the jumble of electronics on the sled. "That's a good thing. Now you can pay me instead of wasting your credits on this junk." His finger slides across the top of a rectangular device. "Although this might be worth a bit." He jerks his head at one of the thugs standing by the door.

The man on the right hurries over and picks up the box, tucking it under one arm. The cable trailing from it gets caught on the jumble below. He tugs, but it doesn't come free. In response to his grunt, a second guard joins him, helping to detangle the wires snaking into the equipment beneath.

I glance at O'Neill, and he jerks his eyes at the two men bent over the sled. Instinctively, I surge forward, slapping the tranq ring against the first guy's neck. He stumbles and drops the metal box. I pull my stunner out of my pocket with my other hand and fire at the second guard as he straightens.

Yanking my ring away from the first victim, I spin to face R'ger, my stunner pointing at his chest. Behind him, the third guard lies on the carpet, as the fourth one crumples into a heap beside him.

Alarm crosses R'ger's face, then he banishes it, clapping slowly. "Nicely done, Annabelle. You got the drop on my security team. I'm so proud."

I ignore his condescending tone and flick into the cabin's surveillance to keep R'ger from calling out. With a few tweaks, and a slightly illegal—at least in my universe—line of code, I put a block over the cabin. "He can't call for help. Now what?"

"Surveillance shows no one else outside the cabin. There's a hover car on top of the canyon with two life signs nearby. I'm sure we can take them out. The question is, do we take R'ger with us, or leave him here?"

"I don't know yet." I give R'ger the once over. "Hands on your head."

R'ger makes a show of shaking out his cuffs, then complies. O'Neill moves in behind to yank his arms down and secure his wrists behind his back. Then he pushes the older man into a seat.

I move to the side so O'Neill can slip tie R'ger's leg to the chair without stepping into my line of fire. I keep the weapon trained on Altabelle's father while O'Neill secures the four security personnel and relieves them of their weapons. He borrows one man's belt and slides a blaster into the holster. "You want one?"

Do I? Normally I don't like weapons, but my body seems pretty comfortable with them in this universe. Muscle memory is a weird and wonderful thing. "Those dudes are all pretty big. Will any of their belts fit me?"

"This should work." He pulls one from the smallest of the unconscious men and moves behind me to buckle it around my waist.

I take a moment to enjoy the feel of my husband's arms around me while he settles the belt low on my hips. When he steps away, I squelch the little swell of abandonment. He's literally four steps away.

With a growl, I wave the stunner under R'ger's nose. "What does Annabelle owe you?"

Confusion chases across R'ger's face. "What game is this? You know exactly how much you owe me."

"I want to make sure we're on the same page. You've been known to change the rules without consulting me." I have no idea if this is true, but it seems like a good guess.

He gazes at me for a few seconds, clearly trying to figure out what angle I'm working. Then he shrugs. "Three point eight million, give or take a few thousand. If I'd realized when you asked for it how long it would take for you to repay me, I might have reconsidered. Although, let's face it, I'll never pass up a chance to stick it to your mother. But it's been almost four years, and I want my investment back."

"Are you working with Fortenoy?"

R'ger's brows draw down in a scowl. "You know I can't stand that sleazy artichoke. It's one of the reasons I'm trying to cut you loose. I don't trust him to pay me back. Ever."

O'Neill steps into R'ger's blind spot and pulls up the surveillance data while I question the old man.

"What if I get rid of him?"

Both R'ger's and O'Neill's heads come up in surprise.

"What?" I frown at the men. "I agree with R'ger. He's a sleazy artichoke. Altabelle doesn't deserve to be stuck with him. Even if she's the one who gave him control in the first place."

"Why do you keep referring to yourself in the third person?" R'ger twists his shoulders, probably trying to get comfortable with his arms behind his back. Or maybe trying to escape. I'm not worried—O'Neill is a pro.

"Doesn't matter." I back across the room, keeping an eye on R'ger, and pound on the internal door. "Professor, get out here. We're leaving."

O'Neill slides up to me, keeping his eyes on both R'ger and the internal door. "Exactly what do you mean by 'get rid of him'? It sounds... ominous."

I swallow a chuckle, but I'm sure he can hear it in my voice. "Don't worry, I'm not going to off anyone. But I'm betting we can gather enough evidence to hand him over to Valti and let her deal with him. That way, she's not out of a job when we—" I glance at R'ger, who's listening intently while pretending to examine the decor. "When we go home."

O'Neill nods once, then slips behind me. "I'll see what the professor is up to." He knocks on the door again, but no one answers. "I hope the old man is just hard of hearing." He turns the knob, then throws the door inward, crouching and aiming his stunner around the jamb.

Nothing happens. I flip through the cabin's control system and turn on a light.

"Zark." O'Neill steps into the room but returns within moments. "He's gone."

"Is his equipment here? Maybe we can trigger the return without him."

"Nope, it's gone too."

TWENTY-NINE
VANTI

WE REACH the end of the canyon where the shuttle waits. With my night vision lenses activated, I can see when a pack of the terrifying three-eyed creatures appears, prowling around the ship. I fire my blaster, setting a small bush ablaze near the passenger hatch. The creatures howl—a cross between an angry toddler's shriek and metal shearing—and scatter.

Elodie yelps, her hands clutched to her head. "What was that?"

"Didn't you see them?" Leo points toward the hills where the creatures escaped. He's visible in the glow from the smoldering remains of the bush as we land nearby.

"How did you see them?" I ask.

"I might have a couple of augmentations I haven't mentioned." He points at his eyes.

Interesting.

The shuttle hatch pops, and we crowd into the airlock, holding our hoverboards.

"Open the cargo hold," Fortenoy calls as he and the professor pilot their sleds to the rear of the ship.

I flip a salute at him and pull the outer passenger hatch shut. Elodie releases the inner one, and we troop inside. She pauses long enough to swipe her holo-ring, releasing the cargo hatch, then scoops up the cat and drops into one of the passenger seats. "I hope someone else can fly this thing. My head is killing me."

"Did you get hurt?" I stop beside her seat on my way to the rear.

"No, but these headaches have been getting worse over the last few days." She rubs her temples. The cat purrs and rubs his head against her arm.

"Do you normally get migraines? Can't the med pod fix them?" Leo drops into the seat beside her.

"Didn't work." She leans back and closes her eyes. "I might need to see an actual medical person."

We all shudder in sympathy.

"We're all packed up." Fortenoy strides into the small passenger area. "The equipment is packed, and the sleds are tethered to the back."

"Won't they burn up as we go through the atmosphere?" Anti-Griz asks.

Fortenoy gives him a "what a stupid question" look and shakes his head. "No, this ship has a force bubble to protect us from friction, space debris, etcetera. It forms around anything attached to the hull."

Griz would have known that. The sooner we can get him back, the better. I turn to the others. "We need a plan."

"The plan is to return to the ship and jump, hopefully sending Ser O'Neill back where he belongs. And my drone with him. Any of you want to go with him?" Fortenoy flashes his corporate grin. "I can make it worth your while."

"We aren't sending him back until we have Annabelle, too. Griz will kill me if we leave her behind." I fold my arms. "Besides, I'm not letting that Annabelle Morgan loose in my galaxy. There are enough self-serving top-levs here already."

"Good luck with that." Fortenoy ducks to step through the hatch into the cockpit area. "I'm headed back to the ship."

He gets one leg through the hatch before I get him in another arm lock. I must be tired—I'm moving slowly. "I don't think so. Sit." I swing him around by the throat and push him toward one of the plush chairs. "We aren't going anywhere."

Fortenoy drops into the seat, rubbing his throat. "You know I could press charges against you for abuse."

I look at the others. "I haven't hurt you, and you'd need witnesses. Did you all see anything untoward?"

Leo, Anti-Griz, and Elodie all chorus, "No."

A second later, the professor shakes his head. I need to keep an eye on him—he's not one hundred percent on Team Griz-iana.

"But I have drones, remember?" Fortenoy waves at the air above his head.

"You think I left those running?" I pull out my drone-killer and wave it, chuckling as his face falls.

"You mean we didn't get Sera Morgan on vid?" He rubs his throat again.

"That was a bluff. I don't like to leave any evidence."

"But my system is supposed to report when the drones are disabled." He flicks his holo-ring and brings up a control panel. "Son of a beach! How'd you do that?"

"Triana built this for me ages ago. It disables and spoofs. You can see why I might want her back."

He flicks the control panel shut. "Does she take on work-for-hire? I can—"

"She's the heir to the Morgan empire. I don't think she needs to work for a living." I turn to the others. "What's the plan?"

Anti-Griz raises a hand. "Annabelle's going to have to wait for daylight to leave the professor's cabin. We took her hoverboard and the professor's sled."

I pivot to van Lieugen. "Did you have any other transportation?"

The old man shakes his shaggy head. "Just the sled. But she can call a bubble. It'll take a while, but they'll come out if she pays a premium."

"And we know she's got the credits for that." I turn to Anti-Griz. "Can you—never mind."

"What?"

"I was going to ask if you could disable her access to the Morgan accounts, but you can't. Griz could—his board sec agent credentials gave him access—"

Anti-Griz blinks, then a little smirk crosses his face. "As far as the tech here is concerned, I *am* him." He flicks his holo-ring and swipes up a file. "I might need your help to get to the right place in the interface. I'm not familiar with board security systems."

Zark. Telling a disgraced security agent he can now access the most secure files of the organization that fired him was probably not a good move. Although, from what he's let drop, the disgrace may have been a cover story. Either way, I now have another potential threat to track. "Actually, I'm not sure you can do it."

The smirk grows, and he points at me. "False. You think you're so clever at hiding your thoughts and emotions, but I have a lot of experience reading Lindsay Fioravanti. You're lying. Don't worry. I won't do too much damage. Here."

Double zark. One thing at a time, Vanti. Focus on getting Annabelle under control. "Let's figure out the plan before we tip her off."

"Fair enough." He pushes the files aside.

I look away, hoping he won't read my zing of triumph. Griz would never be distracted so easily. "What if we let her call a bubble, then intercept it?"

"Can you do that?" Leo asks. "Doesn't Triana usually do all the fancy stuff?"

"She does the fancy coding stuff, but I'm the expert at physical security." I turn to Fortenoy. "You're going to use the ship's surveillance to watch for a bubble. It will come past here, correct?" I turn to the professor.

He nods. "The only place that'll send a vehicle to my cabin is Rent-a-Bubble in Samag. They'll go right by us on the way."

I swing back to Anti-Griz. "Monitor her financials—I wouldn't put it past her to hire a private car from much farther away. Triana can afford it."

Anti-Griz pulls the files up again, stretching them across the space in front of the seats. "Let's see. I'm logged in, and here's the security interface."

I try hard not to roll my eyes—it's not his fault he's unfamiliar with the system, and frankly, I want to keep it that way. "Let me help." Grabbing his wrist, I use his hand—because the system won't respond to mine—to swipe through the screens as fast as I can. In a couple of places, the system balks, sensing my manipulation. I step back and let it read his eyes, vital signs, and movements, confirming he's not under duress. Then I take over again.

"Zark. Griz has the tolerances set tight." I hide my approval under the grumble. I let him reinitialize yet again, then get to Triana's financials. "Not a moment to spare."

"What?" Leo asks.

"She hired a private bubble in Collinsville to come in from the other side." I mime dropping over the top of the steep box canyon. "We're lucky that property doesn't have room for a shuttle to land or she'd have gone directly to space, and we'd never see her again."

We hash out a plan. Leo disappears into the tiny galley to feed Apawllo and grab food and water for the team. I turn to Fortenoy but point at van Lieugen. "He's coming with me. Without him, you can't trigger the translation, so I'm trusting you to wait patiently until we get back."

Fortenoy rocks his head back and forth, as if he's considering his options. "We'll see. I've got his equipment. Maybe I'll fly back and take my chances." He pushes out of his seat, moving toward the cockpit.

Elodie chuckles but doesn't open her eyes. "Not to worry. He can't go anywhere without me. He can't fly."

Fortenoy's eyes dart to Elodie. "You think I don't have a shuttle license? I'm a pilot, remember?"

Her eyes open, and she looks him up and down. "Sure, I remember—you were flying the *Solar Reveler*. But this shuttle is assigned to me. And I locked it."

"I'm the CEO of *CelebVid*. I own this shuttle. You *can't* lock me out." He struts to the hatch, swiping his holo-ring. "Ooh, look, you locked the system." He spins around so we can see the hologram in his palm. "Look at this! I have the override codes." He pulls his ring to his face and whispers, then draws it away again. The formerly red telltales are green. "And I'm in. Now what do you say, Elodie-Oh?"

"I say, 'Get him, Apawllo!'" She flings out a hand to point at the cat as he stalks out of the galley, licking his chops.

The cat strolls across the deck and leaps into the chair Fortenoy just vacated.

The pilot's gaze darts from the cat to Elodie and back. "What's he supposed to be doing?"

"I dunno. Looks like he's cleaning himself."

We all look at the cat, who now has one back leg high in the air. He looks up, glares at us, then goes back to his business.

The clang of a slamming hatch rings through the shuttle. Fortenoy swings around, but the doorway to the cockpit is closed. "Who's in there?" He presses his hand against the access panel, which lights red and stays that way.

Elodie smiles and picks up the cat. "Leo. He's a pilot, too. And he's blocked the hatch with a wooden spoon. No one's getting in there until I tell him to open it. Sometimes, low tech is best." She takes Apawllo's face in her hands and presses her nose to his. "You's a good distraction. Mommy wuvs you."

THIRTY
TRIANA

WE DECIDE to leave R'ger's guards in the cabin, after administering the tranq pin to the three who were simply stunned. That should keep them out of trouble for the rest of the night and into tomorrow, based on what Valti said. I set the surveillance system to record inside—so the professor will have evidence if they destroy anything. Of course, that will only help him if he's brave enough to use it, but that's not my problem.

Yikes. I'm starting to *think* like Altabelle. The sooner we can get home, the better.

While we're stealing equipment from R'ger's guys, we borrow a couple of grav belts, too. O'Neill tethers R'ger's belt to his, putting him a meter in front of us. I try to pretend I'm not disturbed by the idea of a human shield, but it makes me squirm. Then O'Neill activates R'ger's shield—like the one Valti had. Turns out I'm okay with it if he's protected.

"Wait." I leave O'Neill and R'ger by the back door and dart across the room to our captives.

"What are you doing?" O'Neill asks through the audio implant.

"Subterfuge." I unlatch the two remaining grav belts, my nose wrinkling when I have to manhandle the unconscious men to get their belts free. This whole life of crime is sort of icky. I slave the two empty belts to my own, so they float across the room behind me. "These grav belts send out signals—I'm hoping bringing them with us might confuse whoever's waiting up top. If I'm correct, we'll register as R'ger and his four friends."

"Until they try for a verbal confirmation." O'Neill hits an icon, and he and R'ger start to rise.

I match my lift to theirs, with the empty belts keeping pace. "You think they'll expect a call? I can keep R'ger from contacting them, but I can't fake his voice on this short notice."

"Then we'll have to hope their operating procedures aren't as careful as ours. Where are our bogeys?"

"One is inside the vehicle. The other is waiting beside it." I peer through the gloom but can barely see the canyon wall as it slides past us.

A familiar voice breaks into our conversation. "What's taking you guys so long?"

I accept the connection. "Vanti?"

A faint growl answers me. "Linds. The professor and I have been waiting."

I glance at O'Neill. He *almost* rolls his eyes as he responds. "You've secured the vehicle?"

"Of course. Just waiting for you to get here so we can get on with this."

"You could have given us a hand."

As we come over the top of the canyon, a holo-ring flares, illuminating Valti's pale face and copper updo. She stands beside the bubble, tapping the fingers of her right hand against her left arm. "I figured you could handle it. Bear could."

O'Neill and R'ger touch down a few meters from her. Valti whips out a weapon and trains it on the older man. "You didn't say you were bringing a hostage."

I land beside the vehicle. "Hostage? No, he's…" I shudder and turn to O'Neill. "Is he a hostage?"

He gives me a blank stare. "More or less. We thought Linds and the professor were his minions, so we needed leverage."

"But what do we do with him now?"

"We can tranq him and leave him here." Valti swipes her ring, and the door of the bubble pops open. "Or we can tranq him and throw him in the car. Or I suppose we can do either of those things without the tranq, but that means he can cause us grief."

"We aren't leaving him here! He might be a jerk, but he's still Altabelle's dad. You said those creepy alien animal things would eat people!"

"I'm not sure I said 'eat' but close enough." Valti climbs into the bubble. "Whatever you decide, get on with it."

"Put him in." I jerk my head at the bubble. "He can sit next to her."

O'Neill's lips twitch as he pushes R'ger toward the car.

But the old man holds his ground. "You aren't her."

I freeze. "What do you mean?"

"You aren't my daughter." As he speaks, a faint air of wonder drifts over his face, followed almost immediately by calculation. "Did the crazy man actually make his system work?"

"What system?" I pretend disinterest and climb into the vehicle, taking a seat in the middle row.

R'ger gets in and sits beside me instead of Valti. "His alternate universe thing."

"You know about that?"

"Do you really think I would show up on anyone's doorstep without research?"

"So you know which of your schemes they'll fall for?"

R'ger smiles gently, looking more like the man I know. It's a genuine smile, as if he's proud of me. A little flutter of satisfaction warms my heart. I wonder if Altabelle is as desperate for her father's approval as I seem to be.

"Whose vehicle is this?" O'Neill sits sideways in the front row of seats so he can watch our captive.

"It's mine, of course." R'ger leans back in the seat, as if he hasn't a care in the world. "It's set to return to my home."

"That place near the beach in Everet?" O'Neill sweeps a hand through the control holo, but it doesn't respond.

R'ger's head swings back and forth slowly, as if he's disappointed in O'Neill's question. "You don't really think that's my home, do you?" He shivers dramatically. "It's simply a convenient meeting place."

"But you left all the boxes there." The words burst out of me. I've got to know what that's all about.

"The boxes?" R'ger chuckles. "That really bugs you, doesn't it? Why do you think I leave them? My Annabelle hates it, too. They're empty, of course. I don't leave money laying around."

"Your Annabelle?" I ask, as casually as I can.

"You obviously are not my daughter." He waves at me. "Physically, perhaps, but I believe the professor's experiment was successful and you are the Annabelle from another reality."

"Universe!" van Lieugen hollers from the back of the vehicle. "Why can you people not understand the difference between—"

"Can it, Doc." Valti claps a hand on his arm. "No one cares but you, so why get so bothered about it?"

"Precision of speech is important!" He breaks off with a little yelp when Valti squeezes his arm.

I turn back to R'ger. "Yes, O'Neill and I are from another real—universe. We want to go home and send your Annabelle and O'Neill back."

R'ger wrinkles his nose. "I think I prefer you."

"That's a terrible thing to say about your own daughter!"

"But you *are* my daughter. Or you're the daughter I might have had."

"You're the one who said you wanted to 'stick it to' my mother. Maybe that attitude is part of why Altabelle isn't the sweet little thing you're looking for." I glare at him.

He laughs dryly. "I only meant you would be easier to get my credits from. I can use a soft touch, as it were."

I trigger the audio implant and call O'Neill again. "We need to get Altabelle free of this guy."

O'Neill's gaze flicks to me, then back to the older man before he replies on the audio. "How do you propose we do that? We can't exactly transfer credits from our universe. And you wanted to get rid of Fortenoy, too. How are you going to do all of that?"

"I don't know, but there's got to be something." I turn away from R'ger, making it clear I have no intention of speaking with him further.

R'ger doesn't bother being offended. He transfers his attention to

O'Neill. "If you free my hands, I can direct the bubble to take you wherever you'd like to go."

"I don't think releasing you would be a good idea. Besides, I'd like to see where you live."

"But I don't want *her* to see where I live." R'ger jerks his head back at Valti.

Valti smirks. "Shoulda thought of that before you preprogrammed your bubble to go home. Arrogance will get you in the end, old man."

R'ger grinds his teeth, and I try not to smile. Okay, that's not true. I try not to let him see me smile, though.

THIRTY-ONE
VANTI

WITH LEO LOCKED in the cockpit, Elodie mostly useless thanks to her migraine, and Fortenoy refusing to help, we're down to the professor, Anti-Griz, and me. I don't trust the old man farther than I can throw him, so I leave him with the others. Anti-Griz and I gear up and head back to the cabin.

Not that I trust Anti-Griz much more than van Lieugen.

I pull up the professor's surveillance system, but Annabelle isn't logged in. Does she not know how to do it? Or has she got other means of watching us?

"I think she paid off Fortenoy." Crouching beside me in the shadow of the cabin, Anti-Griz pulls up Triana's financials again. There's a huge pending payment to an anonymous account.

"That is so not happening." I grab Anti-Griz's hand and swipe a fraud alert onto the payment. "That should hold her for a while."

A little smile hovers on his lips as he shakes his head at me. "You're so much like her, but so different."

"Like who?" I push his hand through a sequence of icons, taking care to go at a steady pace. The system doesn't trigger the duress alert —success!

"My Linds. Just when I think you're a totally different person, you do something that's one hundred percent her."

I drop his wrist like it's on fire and shift away. "I'm not her."

"I know." His face goes cold, and he turns away to slide up and peer through the nearby window. "This is the lab. No activity."

We creep around the back of the cabin. The sky has lightened as dawn approaches, and the professor's untidy back yard is a shadowy mess. We stay close to the wall, where the drainage system—absolutely necessary in the rainy season, but an empty gravel ditch the rest of the year—provides a clutter-free path.

The first window is dark, but light glows from the kitchen. I give hand commands, and Anti-Griz lifts over the dark window and slides back down on the opposite side of the door. He rolls his shoulders away to peer through the second, lighted window and holds up one finger.

"She's alone. Pacing across the living room." His voice comes through my audio implant, soft and familiar. On a mission like this, I can almost imagine this is the real Griz. "What does that other me see in her?"

Almost.

"Triana is different." The words pop out before I can censor them, but my training holds, and they're subvocal. I grit my teeth. "No chatter—we're on a mission."

I can't see his face, but I imagine him raising one eyebrow.

Focus, Vanti.

A ping to my surveillance net alerts me to a bogey approaching. The system identifies it as an unoccupied bubble from Collinsville Travel Luxe. Seconds later, a large shadow appears overhead. The first rays of sunlight glint on a long, bulky vehicle until it descends below the lip of the canyon.

"Where's it going to land?" Anti-Griz asks.

"There's a cleared space on the far side of the cabin. But we'll grab her when she exits the building."

I ease closer to the door, my hoverboard floating a few centimeters above the gravel.

The lock clicks, loud in the early morning silence, then the door opens a few centimeters. Annabelle peers out, and I flatten myself against the wall, grateful for my customary black clothing. Triana might tweak me about wearing it all the time, but my habitual combat gear has saved my bacon more than once. With the stealth filter engaged, my shirt and pants shift to a mottled black and gray camouflage that blends into the early dawn. A thin hood covers my red hair, and the built in tech hides my pale face.

The door opens wider, and Annabelle steps out. She strides along the little path to the landing pad as if she owns it.

I launch.

And slam into an immoveable, invisible wall. Ow! Forking zark that hurts!

As I nurse my throbbing nose, Annabelle pauses and turns. Her gaze runs over me, and she lifts her chin in a faint but obvious gloat. Without a word, she stalks away.

Anti-Griz fires his stunner, but it flares against the same invisible barrier. He ducks to avoid the non-existent splash back. "She has a force shield."

Annabelle saunters away, swinging her hips a little.

"I can see that." I wipe a hand under my nose, checking for blood, then flick my holo-ring in one smooth movement. The glow of the holo reveals clean fingers as I pull up my tech suite. "I'm going to try to disable the field. See if you can cancel the bubble rental."

"On it." Anti-Griz pokes at his holo as he crouches beside the door, his head bobbing up every few seconds to track Annabelle's movements.

She pauses at the corner of the little house, making a show of checking around the building, as if she fears someone is waiting. Then she presses a hand to her chest with a dramatic sigh. "You should have brought a bigger army, Agent O'Neill. Your little deck hand friend appears to be less competent than you believed." She turns to blow a kiss at us, then strolls to the waiting vehicle.

My teeth grind together, and I force my jaw to relax. I don't need this smug top-lev getting into my head. I focus on the tools at my command. I flip a signal disrupter at the rental.

Nothing happens. Annabelle steps into the rear of the luxury vehicle, and the door closes behind her. The engines hum, and a voice commands bystanders to step away from the vehicle.

If Triana were here, she could have customized the signal disrupter since she coded the original. It's not a vehicle disabler, but I'm sure she could have changed it. The original version distracts drones tracking a vehicle—much like the professor's anti-paparazzi system.

OOH, there's a thought. I flip into the cabin's security, using the back door I installed earlier. Luckily, Annabelle doesn't have Triana's skills, and she left it open. I fire the anti-paparazzi pulse.

The bubble thuds to the ground, silent and dark.

"Nice!" Anti-Griz pumps a fist in the air. "Let's get her!"

With one hand outstretched to save my throbbing nose from any residual force shields—the pulse should have taken them out, but I'm not taking any chances—I race across the small yard. Anti-Griz beats me to the vehicle, slapping his palm against the door. "Come on out, Annabelle. There's nowhere to run, and I've cancelled the payment on this car."

I frown at him. "I thought *I* disabled the vehicle."

He shrugs. "You did. But she won't get another one with a black mark on her credit rating."

"I'm betting the Morgan name will overcome the black mark."

"I suppose." He slaps the car again. "Come on out."

The door opens, and a voice says, "Payment revoked. Please exit the vehicle. A lien has been placed against your credit account. Payment for vehicle delivery is required."

Annabelle glares at us from the plush comfort of the back seat. "I'm not getting out." She waves a blaster at us.

"Fine." I fire the stunner from inside my pocket, and she topples over.

"Nice," Anti-Griz says again. "Why didn't you do that back inside the cabin? You could have saved us a lot of time."

I raise an eyebrow. "She was watching too closely then. But she's been awake almost twenty-four hours, so she's tired. I could tell she wasn't as alert." I wave at the door. "After you, Griz."

His grin wavers at the nickname, but he climbs in and taps his holo-ring. "I might need some coaching to get the payment reinitialized."

"No problem." I settle next to him on the rear-facing seat and swipe the door closed. Grabbing his hand, I flick through the settings and adjust the destination. Then I reinitiate the payment. A green accepted icon appears, and the vehicle lifts off.

As we skim toward the shuttle, Annabelle moans, then sits up. "I'm not going back."

"I'm afraid you are." I pull out my stunner and point it at her, so she doesn't do anything stupid. "I'm sorry if your universe isn't as nice as this one, but that's your own fault, isn't it? Go make nice with your mama, and maybe she'll welcome you back into the Morgan empire."

I've met the Ice Dame, and I sincerely doubt this will happen, but I'm not going to say that.

Annabelle shakes her head as if I'm an idiot and turns away to gaze out the window. Her shoulders slump. If she's trying for sympathy from me, she's picked the wrong target.

I glance at Anti-Griz. He might be more susceptible. He catches my eye and rolls his own. I stand corrected. I guess I shouldn't be surprised he's impervious to Annabelle—he has someone waiting for him in his own universe. Me.

But not me. I take this quiet moment to check in with my heart. Griz and I have been friends a long time, and I might have had a tiny crush on him in the beginning. But our first undercover assignment revealed he and I are not meant for each other. I poke at my feelings. Sure, I want my friend back, but I have no romantic inclinations in that direction. But I'm glad this Ty O'Neill has someone waiting for him, too.

The bubble descends, and the voice tells us to collect our belongings and exit the vehicle. I back out, keeping an eye on Annabelle, then use the stunner to wave her out. Annabelle heaves a sigh and climbs out. Anti-Griz follows.

Inside the shuttle, van Lieugen and Elodie doze in reclined passenger seats. The cat opens one eye and glares at me from his position stretched across the back of another seat. Fortenoy lounges nearby, reading something on his holo-ring. He sits up as we enter. "Finally. Can we leave now?"

I motion Annabelle in and tell her to latch her harness. She complies, and the cat leaps to her lap. Fortenoy pounds on the hatch to the cockpit.

I flick my comm system and connect to Leo. "We're back and have Annabelle. You can let Fortenoy in."

"Aye, aye." Something bangs against the hatch—the wooden spoon being removed?—and it swings open.

"About time." Fortenoy pushes past Leo and stomps into the cockpit. "Strap in, people. We lift off as soon as I get through the checklist. I've got things to do."

I take a seat near the airlock to keep Annabelle from trying anything stupid, but she appears to have given up. She leans back in the seat, eyes closed, hand stroking Apawllo's scruffy fur. Everyone else appears to be asleep. Even Anti-Griz has relaxed.

Amateurs. I'm not closing my eyes until we get Griz and Triana back.

A SOFT THUD and clunk startle me awake. Glad I didn't announce to the group my intention to stay alert, I peel my eyes open and complete a quick status check. Everyone else is still sacked out in their comfortable seats. I rub my eyes and take a few deep breaths, flexing my arms and legs in an effort to get my brain back online.

Ugh. Groggy. I slip a stimpatch from my pocket and stick it to my neck. I don't like them, but you use the tools you have to get the job done. The stimulant trickles into my system, and my mind seems to come back to life. Unlike coffee, it's a gentle dial up of energy rather than a jittery jolt.

"We've docked in the *Solar Reveler*." Fortenoy's voice comes through the speakers and my audio implant. "System checks complete. The hatches are unlocked. Let's get this thing done. Oh, and Vanti, you have a visitor in the forward lounge."

Anti-Griz's eyes meet mine as the lights come up, his brows rising. I shrug and rise. "You wanna take charge of Sera Morgan?"

"My pleasure." He pulls a stunner from his pocket and turns to Annabelle. "Sera? Please accompany me to your cabin."

I signal Leo to keep an eye on them, then make my way to the lounge. When the door slides open, I stride in to find a red-haired man waiting for me. Arun Kinduja.

He jumps to his feet and bows in the same archaic way R'ger does. "Agent Fioravanti, it's a pleasure to finally meet you. When I arrived on station, Captain Chowdhury said you'd be returning to the ship soon. Is my cousin with you?" He leans to the side to look around me, even though the door has closed behind me.

"Sera Morgan is, uh, indisposed at the moment." I gesture toward the seat he just vacated. "And unfortunately, we must return to Kaku immediately, so you won't be able to visit with her this trip."

Arun remains standing, his handsome face still and watchful. "If I didn't know better, I'd think you were trying to keep me from seeing her."

"Not at all." I gesture to the chairs again and take a seat. "I'm surprised you didn't attend the wedding, if you're so anxious to meet her."

He slowly drops into the chair, his brow furrowing at my suspicious tone. "I had a previous engagement. I run a small trading business and can't drop everything to visit family. They didn't exactly give us a lot of advanced notice on the wedding."

"They've been planning it forever. I know for a fact that invitations went out months ago."

"I schedule cargo eighteen months out. As I said, I can't always drop what I'm doing." He smiles that charming top-lev smile, and my brain seems to turn off.

"Of course." I look around the room, trying to figure out where to go with this conversation—how to prolong it. Because something about this man makes me want to spend as much time as possible with him. "Can I offer you a beverage or snack?"

He waves at the small table beside his chair at a half-empty glass and a crumb-laden plate. "Already done. Your captain was quite hospitable." He steeples his fingers together and gazes at me. "I don't suppose you can tell me what's really going on? R'ger can vouch for my discretion."

"What do you mean?"

He smiles a little sadly. “I’ve heard a lot about you, Lindsay Fioravanti, most of it extremely positive. But I have to say pretending ignorance is not working for you. You said two of your crew members experienced dysphoria after the jump, and you wanted to discuss it with me. Now you’re jumping back to Kaku, and my cousin is indisposed. I have to assume she is one of the ‘crew members’ who was affected.” He smiles blandly at me.

I stare him down, trying to order my thoughts. Do I tell him what happened or try to get rid of him? My gut instinct—which I almost always listen to—is to trust him. But this isn’t my secret.

But maybe it shouldn’t be a secret. Especially from someone who might be able to help us—or at a minimum, make sure van Lieugen and Fortenoy aren’t double crossing us.

“Let me explain.”

THIRTY-TWO
TRIANA

R'GER'S fancy bubble speeds through the night, leaving the desert behind. As the sun begins to rise, we pull up in front of a vast, walled compound on the outskirts of Collinsville. The vehicle stops, but the front gate doesn't open.

"I'm afraid this is the end of the line, my friends." R'ger stretches his legs out in front of him, leaning back against the seat. If his hands were free, he'd probably lace them behind his head. "My security team knows I'm under duress."

Valti peers out the window. "Really? Because I don't see any activity. And according to my research, your entire security team was back at the professor's cabin."

I twist around to frown at Valti. "Really? His team is only four guys?"

She flicks a disdainful hand at the estate. "That doesn't belong to him."

R'ger jerks but doesn't say anything.

"How do you know?" I ask.

"The old guy isn't the only one who can research." She flips through data so fast I can't read any of it. "When I was assigned to this mission, our research team didn't think he was enough of a threat to worry about. Turns out they were right. He's much less of a tough guy than he wants you to believe."

"He's not a mob boss?"

"Hardly. He doesn't even work for one. That's all show—he's trying to impress Annabelle."

I turn to look at R'ger. "Why?"

He twists away for a moment, then turns back to me. "When she left Imogen, Annabelle asked me for a loan. We haven't had much interaction, so I figured it was a way to build a connection. I was wrong. She's all business, just like her mother."

"You thought pretending to be a ruthless gang leader would bring you closer to your daughter?"

"When you put it that way, it sounds stupid." R'ger looks out the window again, his shoulders stiff. "Imogen is this big deal. And I've always been a bit of a screwup. I left the Kinduja family decades ago, to try to make my own fortune, but I never succeeded. And they named my brother the heir while I was gone. Now I'm the sad old uncle who doesn't do anything right. I didn't want her to know."

"But you loaned her four million credits!"

"Yeah. But I had to borrow it from him." He nods out the window.

While we were talking, the gate slid open. I hadn't noticed, but I'm sure Valti and O'Neill did. They appear unsurprised to see Arun Kinduja striding toward the car, the early sunlight glinting off his auburn hair. A small drone hovers over his shoulder—probably security.

The vehicle's door pops open, and Arun sticks his head inside. His brows pop up when he spots me, and he makes an aborted move to back out.

R'ger raises a hand, and their eyes meet. Arun gives the older man a quick once-over. "You didn't tell me you were bringing Annabelle to visit."

I stare at Arun, my mouth open. "What are you doing here? You're out there." I wave a hand and wrap my knuckles on the ceiling. "Ow!"

Arun's gaze ticks over the professor, Valti, O'Neill, and back to me. "I guess you'd better come up to the house." He climbs into the vehicle, settling on the back seat beside van Lieugen, then flicks a command on his ring. The car slides up the drive, and the gate closes behind us.

"Would someone please explain—"

Arun cuts me off. "Sorry, cousin. In a moment." He looks at the others again. "And maybe this should be a family discussion?"

The bubble stops, and we climb out in front of a large house with a vast stone façade, all tall columns and wide windows. The door opens as we approach, and Arun leads us to a long, narrow room on the right. Stone benches stretch along the inner wall, and floor-to-ceiling windows offer a view of a massive, manicured lawn with angular hedges around a vast rectangular pool.

"If you'll wait here…" Arun urges Valti, the professor, and O'Neill into the cold room.

O'Neill stops, hands on hips—his right hand very close to the blaster in his holster. "She's not going anywhere without me."

Arun's eyes narrow as he assesses O'Neill's stance. "We're family. She's quite safe with us."

"That is not the impression Ser Kinduja has worked very hard to project." O'Neill gives Arun his own once-over. His eyes linger on a bulge under Arun's jacket.

Moving slowly, Arun uses two fingers to grip the open edge of his coat. He pulls it aside to reveal a flat, black box strapped to his waist. "It's not a weapon."

O'Neill frowns. "What is it?"

Using his forefinger and thumb, Arun pulls the box from his belt and holds it out. O'Neill nods at me, and I reach out to take it without coming between the two men. A stasis box.

"I know what this is!" Ignoring O'Neill's cry of warning, I pop it open. "Cookies!" I take a deep breath of the fragrant, buttery scent. They smell exactly like the cookies Dav makes in my reality. "How'd you get Dav's cookies?" I reach for one, then freeze.

"What?" O'Neill's hand drops to his blaster. I shake my head at him and turn to Arun.

"She's behind all of it, isn't she?"

Arun's face softens, the pity obvious. His eyes flicker to Valti, the professor, and O'Neill. "You want to discuss this in front of them?"

I point at my husband. "He can come. Those two can stay here."

Without waiting to see if they comply, I swing around and stride across the wide hall toward a door on the opposite side. Arun closes in beside me, his fingers flicking through his holo-interface. The door swings open, and the four of us enter. It swings shut, cutting off a muttered argument between Valti and the professor.

This room is smaller and much more comfortable. Thick carpet covers the floor, with many smaller rugs layered on top. An expensive couch and matching chairs stand grouped in front of a river rock fireplace with carved wood mantel. Crystal decanters hold beverages in several shades of amber beside cut glasses.

R'ger makes his way toward the bar. "Anyone want a drink?"

Arun frowns at his uncle. "I'll order coffee. Annabelle?"

"That isn't Annabelle. At least, she's not our Annabelle." R'ger pours a couple centimeters of liquor into a short, wide glass and offers it to me. When I refuse, he turns to O'Neill who also declines.

"Was the professor's experiment successful, then?" Arun takes a seat in one of the armchairs and flicks his holo-ring to order the coffee.

"Does everyone in this reality know about the professor's experiment?" I demand.

"Universe," O'Neill mutters under his breath, and I smack his arm. "Ow."

"R'ger forwarded the information to me when he borrowed the car." Arun closes his holo and settles back into his chair.

"The Ice Dame funded Altabelle's escape, didn't she?" I sit back, arms crossed. "Just like back home, but on a different timeline. She paid for the ship by sending the credits to R'ger."

"The Ice Dame?" R'ger chuckles. "That name fits."

Arun snorts. "Dame Morgan made arrangements with me to fund you through R'ger." A low door opens, and a bot rolls into the room. It settles beside Arun, and the top unfolds to reveal a steaming pot of coffee, cream, sugar, and four mugs. He moves the tray to a low table, and the bot folds up and trundles away.

I set the box of cookies beside the coffee, then change my mind and take one. After adding plenty of sugar and cream to my mug, I let Arun fill it with coffee and scoot back into the corner of the couch while the others fix their own beverages.

"But Fortenoy was an unexpected problem." Arun stirs his coffee, then places his spoon on a plate next to his own cookie. "We've been trying to get rid of him for months. I had hoped the demand for quockoas would do the trick, but the man is determined to stick with Annabelle."

"Is that why you wanted the rodents?" I snicker.

My cousin gives me a conspiratorial grin, then turns a questioning eye on O'Neill. "I take it you two are together in your universe?"

O'Neill nods.

"Do you think we can nudge that along here?" Arun suggests.

I shake my head. "No'Neill and Valti are a couple here." In response to his unasked question, I explain. "The O'Neill in this universe and Agent Fioravanti are contracted. They're both undercover, investigating Fortenoy—" I swing around to O'Neill. "Is that a real CCIA investigation or did the Ice Dame put her up to it?"

Arun and R'ger exchange a surprised look.

"Oops, you didn't know she's CCIA?" I dart a look at the closed door. I hope Valti won't take my mistake out on Altabelle. "She and No'Neill are investigating Fortenoy. But it could be a fabrication—my mother is good at meddling in her daughter's life."

"I'm pretty sure it's a real CCIA investigation." O'Neill puts a hand on my arm. "I hesitate to suggest this, but maybe we should let Altabelle live her own life."

I glare at him, but he's right—I'm turning out exactly like my mother. Trying to "fix" someone else's life from behind the scenes.

On the other hand, maybe that's what Altabelle needs—someone to put her life to rights. The last of the grudge I've been holding against my mother evaporates. She might have controlled a large portion of my life from behind the scenes, but she did it for me. And if she hadn't, who knows where I'd be now. Making bad decisions with my universe's version of Fortenoy?

I give my husband a brilliant smile. "All of the Ice Dame's meddling led me to you, so I forgive her. Let's fix Altabelle's life and get out of here."

Fixing Altabelle's life turns out to be ridiculously easy. Valti and Arun compare their information. Combined with images of the address book I found on the ship, there's more than enough evidence to send Fortenoy to Attica Prison for at least a decade. Thanks to the influence of Dame Morgan and Arun Kinduja, Altabelle and her crew will get off with an unofficial warning.

Being a top-lev definitely has perks.

"You'll have to come clean to Annabelle," Arun tells R'ger as we get into his shuttle. "If you don't tell her, I will. Once we get her out of Fortenoy's control, I'm done playing your games."

R'ger heaves a sigh and waves us off. "Have her call me when she gets back." He turns to me, his arms spread wide. "It's been a pleasure meeting you, my dear."

I step back, holding out a hand to fend him off as he comes in for a hug. "I wish I could say the same. Maybe you should tone down the phony if you want a relationship with your daughter."

A spurt of annoyance crosses R'ger's face, then disappears into his usual insincere smile. "I'll keep that in mind."

I don't think he's learned anything. But based on what the others have told me about Altabelle, maybe they'll get along great.

We strap in, and Arun launches the shuttle. After a short, uneventful flight, he docks in a berth beside the *Solar Reveler*. The ship slides in so smoothly we don't feel a thing. Like the jump that brought us here. I suppress a shiver and follow the others into Station Aldrin.

THIRTY-THREE
VANTI

ARUN KINDUJA LEANS BACK in his chair, his fingers steepled together as he stares across the crew lounge. The door opens, startling him, and Elodie plods in. Her face is lined and haggard.

I make the introductions.

Arun stands and bows. "I've seen your vid content. You're quite amusing."

Elodie smiles, but her usual sparkle is dimmed. "Thanks. I just do my thing. People seem to like it." She turns to me. "Do you want me to talk in front of him?"

"He knows everything I know."

Arun smiles at me, and warmth fills my chest. What the heck is wrong with me? *Focus, Vanti.*

Elodie drops into a chair, her head shaking side to side. "This is going to sound, well, I guess compared to what we've been dealing with, maybe it won't be so weird—"

"Spill it, Elodie."

"I can see the other side."

I stare at her, my mind a blank. "The other side of what?"

She waves an arm erratically. "The other universe! I can see it. Like the professor."

My brows try to pinch down, but I don't let my expression change. Years of practice have perfected my poker face. "Like the professor *said*. His advertisements claimed he could see the other side, but he never once mentioned it when we actually spoke with him." I flick my comm interface and link to van Lieugen. "Professor, please come to the lounge."

He replies almost immediately. "I'm busy here!"

I flick my holo-ring and flip a vid to the lounge projector. The lower half of van Lieugen's body protrudes from an equipment case. Wires and cables fall from the open door, making it look like the professor is being swallowed by a boxy space squid. Or maybe Cthulhu.

"Professor, can you really see the other universes?" I ask.

Van Lieugen jerks away from the cabinet, his white hair crackling with static electricity. He gazes around the room, trying to locate the cams. Finally, he stills, facing the wrong direction. "I can detect them."

The cams rotate the view so he faces me. I make a rolling motion with my hands, which he can't see, then flick the command to activate the holo on his end. I try the hand motion again. "Detect them how? And what can you see there?"

He launches into a technical dissertation that meanders through my brain without making a single impression. After a few minutes, I fling up a hand. "Can you put that in words of less than three syllables?"

Elodie runs a hand through her hair, making it stand up much like the professor's. "He's saying his equipment can locate signals from the other dimensions and show how closely they match our own." She leans toward me and lowers her voice. "Although based on our experience, I'm not sure how accurate that match is."

"I heard that, young lady!" The professor's hair quivers with indignation.

Elodie swings around to face the hologram. "I meant you to, old man." She turns back to me. "Look how far off Annabelle is from Triana. And him." She points at Arun.

He straightens in his chair. "Am I in the other universe?"

"Of course."

"But they've met me? The alternate Annabelle and Ty?"

I wave the professor's hologram closed. "You're apparently a black-market trader. Anti-Griz told me Annabelle had a cargo of quockoas for you."

He chuckles—at the nickname, I assume—then his eyes narrow, as if he's calculating something. Return on quockoa sales perhaps. He shakes his head with a rueful grin. "Anti-Arun is a much braver—and more foolhardy—trader than I'll ever be. The penalties for trading quockoas without a license are astronomical. And licensure requires a custom environment with several levels of inspections—" He breaks off and turns to Elodie. "Sorry, beside the point. Tell us what you can see."

I give myself a mental headshake. Focus on the mission—getting Griz and Triana home—not the handsome man. I turn to Elodie. "The migraines?"

She nods, dropping into a chair. "They started after the jump—I've never had them before. I did a med-pod scan before we hit Aldrin, and it turned up nothing. But the pain kept returning. Then I started hallucinating." She raises her brows, as if she expects us to argue with her.

When we don't, she goes on. "First, I was seeing the ship, but the corridors didn't look right. It was like an overlay of reality, but as if someone had moved some of the walls. I mean bulkheads. Then I saw trees in here." She swings an arm to indicate the compartment. "And little creatures—"

"Quockoas?" Arun scoots forward in his seat, his face alive with curiosity.

"I guess? Little furry guy about so big." She holds her hands about a half-meter apart. "Huge eyes, cute button nose, throws eggs at people."

Arun nods, his eyes sparkling. "That's them! You saw the cargo?"

"I suppose. I tried not to. When we went to the planet, the pain lessened, but I still saw those weird overlays. This time, it was people. At the professor's cabin. Triana's dad was there. With these big ugly guys I didn't recognize. And Tom, but he was mean. I don't think I was there."

"What do you mean?" I ask.

She waggles her head side to side in indecision. "I caught glimpses of the ship, too, but at a distance. Not much happening, but I was in the engine room?"

"Yes! O'Neill said you're the engineer on the *Solar Reveler* in the other universe." I look around the compartment. "What do you see here?"

"Empty cargo hold." She points at the deck and sways in her seat, grabbing the arm of the chair. "There's no floor. Just empty space, and a few bots loading crates down there." She closes her eyes and leans back.

"Maybe we should take her to engineering." Arun jumps to his feet. "If the other Elodie is there, maybe we can communicate with her!"

The speaker pings. "This is your captain." Chowdhury's smooth, deep tones ring through the room. "We'll be departing Aldrin Station in thirty minutes. Ser Kinduja, if you wish to return to your ship, I suggest you go now."

Arun flicks his holo-ring and murmurs into it. My audio alert fires, and his voice curls in my ear, warm and inviting. "I'd like to stay aboard, if you don't mind, Agent Fioravanti."

"I thought you were scheduled out eighteen months, Ser Kinduja. Don't you have work to do?" I take Elodie's arm and lead her toward the door.

Arun grins as we pass, then falls in behind us. "I might be too busy for a cousin's wedding, but there's no way I'm missing this! Plus, my first mate can handle the cargo transfer. And our next stop is actually Kaku, so it works out perfectly."

Coincidence? Or the multi-verse lining things up? We may never know.

"Fine with me. I hope Fortenoy doesn't charge you for a cabin."

He laughs. "Tom owes me, so I think I'm good."

I swing around and raise a brow at him.

He smirks. "That's a story for another time."

We get to the engine compartment, and I use my security credentials to open it. Or I try to access it, but the door refuses to move. Elodie pulls out of my grasp and waves her own hand at the access panel, which lights up green. "I guess Tom hasn't locked me out yet."

"Why would he lock you out?" I step over the lip of the hatch and to the side, back against the wall. It's an old habit—one that has kept me alive on occasion. I scan the compartment, but it's empty except for rows of white equipment boxes.

"When we were on the planet, he threatened to throw me out if I don't start producing content. I refused to give him anything with you or Ty or

Tri—Annabelle." She puts out a hand to touch the closest white cabinet. "I'm here."

Arun and I exchange a confused look.

"And?" he prompts.

"I mean, the other Elodie is here. I can see her engine room. Cute pillows!"

"Pillows?" Arun mouths at me.

THIRTY-FOUR
TRIANA

We exit the shuttle and step into a small waiting area. Four other hatches provide access to the other ships docked at this node. Fortenoy paces in front of the hatch leading to the *Solar Reveler*. When he sees me and O'Neill approach, he lunges forward and grabs my wrist. "Where have you been? And what's he doing with you, again?"

"None of your business." I wrench my arm away, but his fingers bite, squeezing the bones together. "Ow!"

O'Neill pulls his stunner. "Let her go."

Fortenoy looks at the weapon, and a smirk tips the corners of his mouth up. "You aren't a station employee here, punk. Use that thing, and security will be all over you. In fact, there they are now."

A quartet of agents dressed in Aldrin Security uniforms converges on us. Valti slips between two of them, stopping in front of Fortenoy. She flicks her holo-ring and flips a couple of files at him. "Thomas Fortenoy, you're under arrest. Here's a list of charges filed against you by the CCIA. We've accessed your records, which indicate you are literate and capable of understanding these charges. Anything you say from this point forward will be recorded as evidence. Do you have any questions?"

"You're CCIA?" Fortenoy's face goes from smug to terrified to cunning in the blink of an eye. He releases my arm and flings up his hands, palms out. "It's her ship. I'm only an employee! I'd be happy to testify against her."

"Sera Morgan is cooperating with our investigation. These agents will escort you to the Station Detention Center where you'll be held until we can transport you to Sally Ride for trial." Valti takes a step back, and the agents surge forward.

"You can't do this! I have connections at the highest levels!" He points at me. "Call R'ger! He'll help us."

"Us?" I cross my arms and stare at him. "You tried to throw me under the shuttle, and now you expect me to help you?"

Arun steps out from behind the largest security guard, taking a place at my shoulder.

"Kinduja is in on this too!" Fortenoy's eyes widen as he realizes what Arun's appearance beside me means. "It's all a top-lev plot!" He clamps his mouth shut, glaring daggers at me as they drag him away.

"Don't you have to go with them?" I ask Valti as she urges us toward the *Solar Reveler*.

"I'm not missing this. I haven't seen my partner in days, and I want to be there when he comes home." She glares at O'Neill.

"Fair enough." We clatter into the airlock and make our way to the crew level. "Where's the professor?"

"He's taking his equipment to cargo." O'Neill steers me down the hallway past the crew quarters to the door at the rear marked Engineering. "You need to talk to the ship's engineer—to make sure she lets the professor do his thing."

The four of us clomp through the door and down the ladder. Using Altabelle's access controls, I flick the unlock codes, and the door slides open.

Soft light greets us, reflecting off white bulkheads and decks. A sparkly pink curtain hangs across the short passageway, hiding the rest of the compartment. Behind us, the door whooshes shut, closing out the rumbling engine noises.

That makes no sense. Why would the engine noise be outside the engine room? Tinkling music and the scent of eucalyptus and vanilla reach me. We push through the curtain and stop, staring.

The small space between the rows of white equipment blocks what looks like a cozy parlor. The bulkheads are painted a pale pink, and flower-patterned tile covers the deck. A shaggy throw rug in pastel hues hides part of the tile. A pink hammock swings gently at the far end, above a matching couch with overstuffed cushions and yellow and green throw pillows. Elodie sits on the couch.

"Come in, dear!" Elodie sings. "I've been waiting for you!" As I cross the colorful floor, she leans forward to pour tea into a cylindrical ceramic cup. "Sugar? Cream?"

"Sure, I guess. Thanks." I sink into a huge, pale blue poufy thing. The sides and back come up around me, forming a comfortable chair. I take the cup she offers and raise my brows at O'Neill, then tap my ear to indicate the audio implant.

Elodie raises her cup in a toast. "It's safe to speak here. I have auditory scramblers installed and running. And no one comes down here. I've cultivated the image of the cranky, half-crazy engine chief. But you're always welcome, Triana."

My brows go up, and my mouth drops open.

"I know." Elodie giggles. "She told me."

"She who?"

"The Elodie in your universe, of course."

Valti drops onto the opposite end of the couch from Elodie. "You can talk to their universe?"

Elodie pours more tea and hands cups to Valti, O'Neill, and Arun. "Talk is not the right word. With the current alignment of the universes, I am able to communicate with my alter ego. It's not perfect—I'm not sure she really believed I was real. But I learned about you two from her." She points at me, then O'Neill. "And apparently there's some physicist trying to fix it?" She looks around the room. "Where is he?"

"He's in the cargo hold, installing additional equipment." Arun leans against one of the large boxy white cabinets and sips his tea.

"You mean that ridiculous thing he put in a few weeks ago? Is that what caused all this trouble?" She picks up a plate and offers it to Valti. "Cookie?"

Valti takes one and nods her thanks. She nibbles the cookie, then catches me staring. "What?"

"Vanti doesn't eat sweets."

"I keep telling you I'm not Vanti." She takes a bigger bite. "Mm, chocolate chip."

"You knew about the equipment?" O'Neill asks Elodie.

She shrugs. "Of course I knew about it! It's connected to my Plexorics. But—"

"You have Plexorics?" Arun pops away from the cabinet as if pulled by strings. "The DW-5s or the PK-49s?"

Elodie smiles smugly as she rises from the couch. "DW-7s."

"No way! This ship is too old to have DW-7s."

Elodie leads us toward a hatch hidden behind the couch and hammock. Pausing beside the door, she hands out chunky bracelets. "These will shield us from the radiation."

"Radiation?" I slide the circle over my hand and squeeze gently. It irises down small enough that it won't slip off.

"The DW-7s are actually safer than most engines." Arun clamps his bracelet on, practically bouncing with excitement. "But this is standard safety protocol."

"How do you know about the DW-7s?" Elodie waves her holo-ring at the access panel, and the hatch slides open.

"Starship engines are a hobby of mine. I wanted to get a pair of Plexorics for my ship, but they said they weren't retrofitting. At all." He gives her a pointed look.

Elodie nods. "They aren't supposed to. I'm not sure how Annabelle and Fortenoy got these, but they were installed a few months ago. I wonder if that had something to do with the translation?" As she walks, she uses her finger to write calculations in the air. They hover around her, like a cloud of gnats, moving with her. "Yeah, I don't think it would have worked with the original engines. Retrofitted DW-7s operating at 84% in a jump flux could create quantum niches. They don't happen in ships built around the DW-7s, of course."

"Are you saying this ship is the only one in which this experiment would work?" I ask.

She nods at me, smiling fondly as if she's a teacher and I'm a particularly smart student. "Exactly. What are the odds of those factors coming together? Makes you wonder about the universe's sense of humor, doesn't it?"

Inside the engine compartment, a meter-high block with a rounded top is bolted to the deck. Its dark casing seems to reflect light, making it hard to see despite the glare of the seven purple lasers that stretch away into the distance. The bright beams of light rotate along a single axis, slow enough to count.

Arun runs his hands over the dark metal, then glances at Elodie. "May I?"

She nods, and he pops open a hidden panel to ooh and ah over the interior.

"Where's the professor's stuff?" O'Neill asks. "Are we ready to go?"

"It's connected down here." Elodie leads us along a narrow walkway beside the spinning beams. "Don't touch anything."

I lift both hands to shoulder level, palms out. "Not touching anything." I rub behind my ear. "They're so quiet, but I can feel them. Hey, that reminds me—why did I hear engine noise *outside* the engine room, but not inside?"

Elodie throws a grin over her shoulder. "That keeps people away. I like my privacy, and most people don't like noisy, stinky machinery." She stops beside the blocky housing at the far end of the purple lasers. A tangle of cables snakes away from the bottom, through a hole in the bulkhead. "That's where it's connected. I checked it out when they first installed it, of course, but I thought it was just monitoring equipment. I must have missed the triggering array." She shakes her head in dismay. She leads us back to the outer room where she drops onto the couch. "I want to see the new stuff. But first, I need to talk to my other half."

THIRTY-FIVE
VANTI

My eyes meet Arun's quizzical expression. I pull a confused face in reply. The exaggerated expression feels good but wrong. When Arun grins in response, the wrongness goes away and warmth spreads through my chest.

This guy is bad news for my super-controlled secret agenty-ness.

Elodie seems to freeze for a few seconds, then jerks and shakes herself. "That was—wow." She turns to face us, her fingers trailing lovingly along the white cabinets. "We're on the right track. Fire up the Plexorics and make sure Annabelle and O'Neill are alone in their cabin when we jump to Kaku. I'll double check the professor's work, but if he did what he said he was going to do, we're golden."

Perfect.

"Hey, as long as we're down here, can I get a peek at the Plexorics?" His grin reminds me of one of Griz's nephews when Griz's brother Yuri gave him a play drone shaped like a dinosaur.

Elodie jerks her head toward the back of the compartment. "She says it's back here."

I trail along behind. "Shouldn't you be checking van Lieugen's set-up?"

Elodie waves a hand over her shoulder at me. "We've got two days before we can jump."

"Actually, if you've really got the DW-7s, we can get to jump velocity a lot faster. They've got thrust like you won't believe." Arun hurries ahead. "Let me show you."

The engine compartment opens off the rear of this one. We have to don protective wrist devices that emit a programmable fluctuating force shield. Or so Elodie and Arun say. I put on the bracelet and follow them to the back.

She opens the hatch, and a brilliant purple glow dazzles my eyes for a second, until an invisible visor—courtesy of the wrist device—dims the display to a bearable level. We step through the hatch.

A meter-high device, blocky with a rounded top, stands a few steps from the hatch. Its dark casing seems to defy vision—my eyes can't get a lock on it. Or maybe that's the magic visor. Or the seven dazzling beams of purple light that stretch away into the distance. They rotate along their central axis, slow enough to count the individual rays.

Arun sucks in an awed breath. "Fantastic! I can't believe they were able to install them in this ship."

"The *Solar Reveler* is longer than the other ships of this design, and the deck of the engine room was specially reinforced to accommodate racing engines. That was long before the DW-7s were invented, of course." Elodie's voice picks up its usual enthusiasm as she natters on about the engines.

I let them chatter, wandering around the engine—how can this thing possibly make a ship go? It's just lazily spinning. The glow of the purple beams illuminates the small room. It's quiet here—either the protective shield blocks the engine noise or there isn't any. At the far end, the rotating rays disappear into another rounded block. A series of cables trail off the back of the block and disappear through a hole in the side bulkhead. "Is this supposed to be here?" I call.

The others look up, then hurry toward me. They crouch to examine the bundle of wire, conferring quietly in a language I don't understand—like the discussion between the professor and Elodie at the cabin. Who knew she was so smart?

Elodie straightens, her face bleak. "That's the professor's link. If I'd come down here before we jumped, I would have seen it, and we could have avoided everything!"

"You can't possibly blame yourself for this." Arun rises and puts a hand on her shoulder. "You are a passenger, not the engineer. I don't see how you can possibly understand everything we've been discussing given your advertised educational background, but you clearly do! Have you earned a couple of doctorates in physics and astromechanics that you don't put on your social media profile?"

Elodie's dismay melts away, and she smirks. "Nope. I'm just good at this stuff. It all makes sense."

"Maybe she's linking to the Elodie in the alternate universe who runs this ship for a living?" I suggest.

They both turn to stare at me. Arun's mouth opens and closes a couple of times before he gets any words out. "That's... wow."

"Maybe that's how you know about quockoa, too." I turn and head for the hatch.

After a moment, he takes a few long strides to catch up. "No. I did a report about quockoas in grade school. And I can't see the other side like Elodie. I don't think." He stops and turns, taking in the engine room. "Nope, nothing."

"If the universes are really diverging, like the professor says, I wonder if Elodie will keep her engineering genius?"

We both look back at the woman still examining the engine mounting. "Now that I've shown her how to amp up the output, I guess we'll find out. In a few hours."

THE SHIP EASES AWAY from Aldrin Station, and we head for the jump belt. Arun said we'll need about seven hours to reach jump velocity, so we settle into the crew lounge to wait. Elodie, Arun, and the professor kibitz for a while—at least I assume that's what all the tech talk is. I find a comfortable seat and relax.

Although I told myself I wouldn't sleep until we got Griz and Triana back, and I'd really like to spend more time with Arun, I can't keep my eyes open. My body knows I'm safe and decides it's time to shut down for a while. I lean back in my corner of the couch and let my eyes close.

SOMETHING WAKES ME. Thanks to years of practice, I wake fast—completely alert within seconds. I lie still, eyes closed, letting my other senses take in data. My eyelids lift a fraction, and I peer into the dim light without moving my head.

"You can move, Vanti." Standing by the door, Leo chuckles. "No big bad waiting to attack."

I sit upright in one swift movement, flipping aside the blanket over my body. "Where'd this come from?"

"Arun. He figured you could use the sleep, so he moved your legs onto the couch and covered you. It was touching. He's a keeper."

I glare at him as I get to my feet, but my heart throbs before settling back into its usual, slow rate. "I can't believe I slept through someone moving me."

Leo grins wider. "You were so cute. You nearly strangled him when he lifted your feet, but we talked you down."

"Really?"

"No. You were out cold. You're not as scary as you'd like everyone to think."

I pad across the compartment, coming right up to him until my face is centimeters from his chest, and give him my best death glare. "You have no idea how scared you should be."

His eyes go wide for a second, then he laughs and pats my head. "You're so cute!"

I restrain myself from choking him out by shoving hard against his chest. He stumbles back into the corridor, landing against the far bulkhead.

I check my chrono—we've been underway for twenty hours. "Twenty hours! We were supposed to jump at seven. Did I miss it?"

"That's what I came to tell you—we'll reach jump velocity in a few minutes. Arun said we could have done it hours ago, but the other Elodie insisted we wait. Something about the location in the space time continuum. I think she's full of zark."

I head down the passageway. "Annabelle and O'Neill are in their compartment?"

Leo stretches his long legs to catch up. "They will be shortly. That's why I woke you—so you could say goodbye."

"Uh, thanks? I don't care about them. I want Griz and Triana back." I hurry up the ladder and stop outside the forward guest suite.

The door slides open. Arun, Elodie, and the professor chat in a corner. Fortenoy and Anti-Griz stand side by side, not speaking. Annabelle sits on the sofa petting Apawllo. I clear my throat, and they all turn.

"There she is." Arun smiles warmly at me, then turns to the others. "I guess it's time to get this show on the road. Shall we proceed?"

Annabelle gives the cat one last stroke, then hands him to Elodie with a sigh. Anti-Griz drops to the far end of the couch, leaving as much room between him and Annabelle as possible. He's been giving me soulful looks the whole time, but I'm ignoring him. The sooner he gets back to his version of me, the better.

We parade out, and the door swooshes shut behind us.

"I suggest you lock that, if you don't want Annabelle to sneak away." I point at the hatch.

Fortenoy gives me a sour look. "Already done. I'm going to the bridge. Jump in five minutes. Get yourselves secured." He stomps away.

"I'm not going anywhere." I lean against the bulkhead next to the door of the opposite suite. "I don't trust that woman."

"I'll stay here with you." Arun takes up a position on the other side of the door. "She might be my cousin in an alternate world, but I don't—"

"Universe!" Professor van Lieugen stomps his foot like a toddler. "How many times to I need to tell—"

I lean close to his face, and he breaks off, much more intimidated than Leo. I've still got it. "We don't care, professor. Let's get on with it."

Elodie and the professor disappear down the ladder to the crew section. Leo's eyes bounce from me to Arun and back, then he follows them with a wink and a smirk. I make a note to take him down a peg later.

Arun watches him go, then looks at me. "You do this kind of thing often, Agent Fioravanti?"

I snort. "Guard people so they can get translated back to an alternate universe? Sure, all the time."

His face goes the tiniest bit pink, but he grins. "I meant that more generally. You're a security agent. In my experience, that means protecting top-levs, but your life seems a bit more adventurous."

"I've been lucky." I roll my right shoulder away from the bulkhead so I'm facing him more directly. "My new job is watching over Elodie, which looks likely to be a bit more precarious than the usual top-lev life. Assuming *she* still has a job after this."

"She works for Fortenoy?"

"In a manner of speaking. *CelebVid* provided the ship, and she's supposed to travel around getting into trouble and broadcasting her adventures. But since she refused to film Annabelle and O'Neill, she might be..." I draw one finger across my throat.

"You—she could travel with me." He turns away so he faces the opposite hatch again, not looking at me. "I have an empty cabin in my ship. As long as you—I mean *she* is content to follow my schedule..."

A little spark of happiness flickers in my core. "Would you have room for both of us? She's hired me to provide security."

"Of course, if you don't mind sharing a cabin. It's pretty big. Or if you prefer, I have a couple of empty crew berths. I was thinking about converting them to additional cargo, but..." He stares at the opposite door for a while. "Is Leo part of the deal?"

"Not really. He came because we had room on the ship. I don't know how long he was planning to stay. The cat is non-negotiable, though." He glances at me, and I look away before he catches me staring. "You should talk to her."

Before he responds, Fortenoy's voice comes over the speakers and our audio implants. "Jump in thirty seconds."

"You know space travel protocol requires passengers to strap in for jump." Arun doesn't move from his post.

"I know. But we aren't technically passengers. And the jump here was the smoothest I've ever experienced. Maybe van Lieugen's equipment did that."

"Or maybe it was a coincidence. Still, protocol aside, I've never had a problem." He settles both shoulders more firmly against the bulkhead. "I'm willing to risk it."

I smile, enjoying the warm happiness in my chest. "Me, too."

THIRTY-SIX
TRIANA

As we approach the jump point, I swing by the bridge. Carina LaSalva sits in the left chair, and the right is empty, as before. She glances up as I enter, glares at me, and turns away.

"What's wrong?" I drop into the empty seat.

She flicks through her screens, ignoring me.

"Carina, what's the matter? I thought you'd be happy I got rid of Fortenoy?"

She swipes a few holos a little more violently than necessary, accidentally flinging one to the observation screen at the back of the little cockpit. The station lights up, requesting a login.

"You went to the planet."

"Yeah, I'm sorry I slipped out like that. I know we had a spa day plan—"

"Oh, get over yourself. I'm used to you sneaking out on spa day. But you went to the planet." Her deep voice drops lower and softer. "With him."

I get up to silence the annoying voice demanding a username and password, then return to the co-pilot's station. "You're mad because I went with O'Neill?"

If she glares any harder, she's going to give herself a stroke. "I called dibs!"

I sigh. "I told you he's contracted. That deck hand—Linds? They're a couple."

"And he went to the planet with you?" The focus of her anger shifts. "That slimy, two-timing cheater!"

I'm glad she's forgotten that Altabelle was also in a relationship at that point. "Nothing happened! We were working."

"But why did you need to work with him?" she wails. "Why couldn't it be that Leon guy?"

"Leo? He didn't have the skill set."

"Oh, is that what we're calling it now? A skill set?" She bursts out of her chair, stomping across the tiny cockpit and back. She stops beside me, cocking a hip and batting her eyelashes. "Do I have the right… skillset?"

"Carina!" I jump up. The space between the seats is too small, and she falls back. I grab her arms to keep her from crashing against her chair. "It was business. There's nothing between me and that guy. He's with Linds." I'm not sure why it's so important to me that Carina believes this. I barely know this woman, but I sense that she's a good friend to my alter ego, and I don't want to leave her completely alone now that we've gotten rid of Fortenoy. "Look, maybe when we get to Kaku, we can go out together? We haven't had a girls' night in a long time." I hope that's true.

Carina drops into the seat, hope spreading across her face. "Really? That would be awesome!"

I hesitate. "Yeah. Remind me when we get there, okay? I've got a lot on my mind right now."

She puts a hand on my arm. "Breakups are never easy—even when the guy is a jerk. I'm here for you."

I squeeze her fingers then let go. "Thanks. You're a good friend." I hope Altabelle is worthy. "I've got some things to take care of. I'll see you after the jump."

"Don't wallow. He's not worth it." She frowns and turns back to her holos. "We'll both find someone better."

I leave her in the cockpit and return to Altabelle's utilitarian cabin. O'Neill isn't here. I pace the deck, waiting for him to arrive. We can't jump until he's here, too.

O'Neill, van Lieugen, Elodie, Valti, and I decided to keep the true nature of our jump between the five of us. I made an announcement before we departed Aldrin, explaining that the professor had hired us to transport the equipment to Kaku. Apparently, Fortenoy and Altabelle hadn't scheduled a pickup at Aldrin—they didn't seem to have a very good business plan.

After taking us to Aldrin, Arun returned to his own ship. They'll follow the *Solar Reveler* back to Kaku. Unlike the Arun in my own universe, this one doesn't run a regular shipping company. The contracts with Altabelle had been engineered solely to get rid of Fortenoy. Most of the time, Arun is too busy running the Kinduja empire to fly his own ship.

The countdown on my cabin display drops closer to zero. As the captain, I will give the final command for jump, but Carina and the others will be suspicious if we don't go on schedule. I toggle my audio implant and call O'Neill. "Where are you?"

"Right here." The door slides open, and he strides in. He wears a new coverall, and his face is clean shaven.

I wait until the door slides shut, then throw myself into his arms. After a long, delicious kiss, I pull back. "What happened to evil O'Neill's goatee?" I slide a hand up his smooth cheek.

He does a dramatic shudder. "It was itchy. He'll have to grow his own." He lowers his face to mine, stopping before our lips touch again. "You ready to go home?"

I pull him the last two centimeters and press my lips against his. I am *so* ready.

Carina's voice comes over the speakers. "We've reached jump velocity. Captain, go or no go?"

I pull away from O'Neill and tap the screen by the hatch. "Elodie, are we ready?"

"The professor's equipment is up and running. My contact in the other reality—"

"Universe!" van Lieugen yells in the background.

Elodie ignores him. "—says all systems go."

"Roger." I flip to the bridge connection. "Carina, we're go for jump."

"Gotcha." The system clicks twice—Carina switching to the all-call channel—then her voice echoes through the ship. "We are go for jump. Crew, take your assigned stations. Jump in thirty seconds."

The chrono on my display flips through the countdown. At ten seconds, Carina starts counting aloud. "Ten, nine, eight, seven, six, five, four—"

Elodie yells over Carina's count, "Wait! There's a loose cable! Professor, get that—"

—and we jump.

I grab O'Neill's hand. He swings me around until his arms are around me, my back pressed against his front, and he grips my other hand. His chin touches my shoulder and his breath whispers against my ear. "Whatever happens, we're together."

"Did you feel anything?" I ask.

His head shakes, his cheek tapping against mine. "We didn't last time either, remember?"

My audio implant pings, and Carina's voice comes through. "Jump complete."

I close my eyes with a groan. "We didn't make it!"

"No, we did." O'Neill's body moves, turning me with him. "Look. We're in our cabin!"

"Really?" I open my eyes and look around the cabin. We're facing the external bulkhead now, and the windows give us a view of deep space. Stars twinkle in the velvety black, then fade away into the glow of a sun beneath us.

The sun is beneath us—we've jumped! Ships always exit jump at the "northern" pole of the star, which means the sun is exactly where it should be.

And we have windows! Altabelle's cabin had no external bulkheads. I turn within O'Neill's arms and squeeze him tightly. "I hope this isn't some *other* alternate universe! That's what always happens on *Ancient TēVē*. We'll keep jumping for the rest of our lives!"

The speaker pings and someone pounds on the cabin door. O'Neill pats down his pockets and pulls out a stunner. "At least No'Neill left me a weapon." He pushes me to the side of the door, standing between me and the hatch, then hits the release.

The door swooshes open. A sleek red head peeks through. "Triana? Griz? Is that you?"

"Vanti!" O'Neill grabs his former partner in a fierce bear hug, then lets go almost as quickly. "It is you, right? Not Linds?"

She smiles and punches his arm. "It's me. Don't even *think* about calling me Linds."

Arun crowds in behind her, a broad smile on his face. "I guess the jump was successful." He looks exactly the same as the Arun in the alternate universe, except he's wearing less fashionable clothing.

"You came with us?" I step around O'Neill and hold out a fist. "Hi. I'm Triana."

He knocks his knuckles against mine. "Arun. Nice to finally meet you, cousin."

The audio pings again and a low female voice speaks. "All secure from jump. We will arrive at Station Kelly-Kornienko in forty-three hours."

"That was Carina!" I grab O'Neill's arm. "How is that possible? Did they jump instead of us?" I wave at Vanti and Arun.

"No, we're in our universe." O'Neill gestures to the luxurious cabin. "This is definitely not Altabelle's ship."

"Where's Elodie? And Leo?" I swing to Vanti. "Is the professor with you?"

"Chill, they're all here. I already checked in." Vanti taps her jaw below her ear. "What are you all wound up about?"

"That voice—that was Carina LaSalva. From the other reality."

"Universe." Arun and Vanti speak in unison, then laugh.

Vanti is laughing. I lean closer to O'Neill. "We're definitely in the wrong universe."

"She laughs once in a while. But usually at someone else's expense." He frowns in mock concern and raises a brow at Vanti. "You're not trying to date me, are you?"

Vanti's face goes blank, like a curtain falling over a stage play. "Date you? No. Are you sure you're Griz? That other O'Neill wanted—" She breaks off, shuddering dramatically.

"Just checking. But I didn't realize I was so repulsive."

"I know No'Neill's dating life is extremely important, but can we talk about how Carina LaSalva ended up in this reality?"

"I don't know what you're talking about." Vanti raises a brow at Arun, and he shrugs.

I push past them.

O'Neill hurries to catch up with me as I run up the passageway. "It did sound like her."

I reach the bridge, but the hatch doesn't respond to my holo-ring. "Let me in!" I pound on the door.

It slides aside, and Fortenoy glares out.

I jump back with a cry, slamming into O'Neill. "What's he doing here?"

"He owns the ship." Vanti comes up behind me. "He's the CEO of *CelebVid*."

I take a deep breath, trying to get my galloping heart rate under control. Like Vanti and Arun, the Fortenoy in the other universe is not the same as this one. "Sorry." I suck in another deep breath. "Why is Carina LaSalva here?"

"Who?" Fortenoy crosses his arms. "There's no LaSalva here."

"Actually, there is." Carina comes up behind Fortenoy, but she's different, too. Her hair is braided tightly to her scalp, and she wears an attractive white uniform. "I'm Carina Chowdhury Nowak LaSalva, but I don't use that name anymore. How'd you find out?"

Fortenoy shakes his head slightly. He doesn't want me explaining anything to the woman. I give him a narrow-eyed look that's supposed to say, "We'll talk about this later," and turn back to the woman. "Sorry, I knew a Carina LaSalva once, and when I saw your name…"

She stares me down. "I thought I'd removed that name from all my records, but I guess you can't scrub the net completely." With a curt nod, she returns to the cockpit.

"Anything else?" Fortenoy asks but doesn't wait for an answer before shutting the hatch.

"I guess that's the last piece of the puzzle." I head down the passageway toward our cabin. The others fall in behind me. "Carina LaSalva was here the whole time, too. Everyone is accounted for."

"Altabelle's ship had half a dozen deck hands we didn't know." O'Neill puts a hand on my lower back as we return to our cabin.

"But did she? I saw the names, but I never saw anyone else on the ship. Did you?"

"Actually, now that you mention it, no." He waves the door open and waits for me and Vanti to precede him into the cabin. "Leo, Linds, and I did all the unloading. Fortenoy watched."

"Those others might have been a way of laundering credits." Arun drops onto the sofa, and Vanti sits beside him.

I dart my eyes at O'Neill then at Vanti and back to him. Vanti doesn't sit next to anyone. Even when she was dating O'Neill's brother, she never looked so relaxed.

O'Neill raises a brow and gives a faint shrug. "Laundering?"

"You assign fictional names to unnecessary positions, then pay those people. The credits go into accounts you control, of course, but it's a way of hiding money. Not a very successful way, I might add." Arun turns to Vanti.

She shakes her head. "Doesn't fool anyone. But people still try it." She shrugs. "Amateurs."

THIRTY-SEVEN
TRIANA

We gather for one last meal before docking at SK2 later tonight. Leo uses the AutoKich'n to whip up an amazing meal and serves it in the crew lounge. Fortenoy and Chowdhury stay on the bridge—this close to the station, one of them has to be on duty, and I think Fortenoy is anxious to distance himself from us.

"He's cancelled my contract." Elodie scoops a little meat into a small dish and puts it on the floor for Apawllo. The cat turns up his nose, then snags the biggest chunk with a claw as he turns away and ducks under the couch.

"Are you going home, then?" I pour bubbly for everyone to celebrate our safe return.

"Zark, no." Elodie grins fiercely. "Arun has offered to let me travel with him. I can help with the engines in exchange for transport, and he'll get a cut of my new sponsorships. I'm going to go super viral. Fortenoy will rue the day he fired me."

I cut my eyes to Vanti. "Are you going with her?"

Her poker face firmly in place, she nods. "Our arrangement was separate from her deal with *CelebVid*. And my..." She glances at the professor, but he's completely focused on his food. "I have my own *sponsor,* so I don't need to get paid. Although I'm getting a cut of anything Elodie makes, too."

Does Arun know Vanti is a CCIA agent? I shoot him a look. He's watching Vanti with a pleased smile. I'd better ask him later. He's family, after all, and while I'm pretty sure his business is on the up and up, I'm not going to let him get blindsided.

I turn to van Lieugen. "What about you?"

The professor keeps shoveling food into his mouth, his eyes trained on a tiny holo-screen hidden under the edge of the table.

"Professor?" I tap his arm.

"What?" His head snaps up, eyes wide. "I was paying attention!"

We all laugh.

"What are your plans, professor? More multiverse studies?" I ask.

He waves a hand, as if the multiverse is so last week. "I've proven it's there. I'm writing my paper, but I fully expect my peers—ha! Idiots, more like! My peers will ignore or ridicule my work. But I don't care because the data we gathered suggests something even bigger!"

"What's that?"

He doesn't reply, and I tap his arm again. "What's the even bigger thing?"

The professor's face takes on a crafty smirk. "I'm not telling you! You'll have to wait until I publish. I'm not letting any of you steal my research." He shoves a roll into his mouth, as if to keep himself from saying anything else, and flicks his holo-vid back to life.

"That just leaves you, Leo." Arun lifts his glass toward the chef. "This meal was fantastic—I'm sure you could get a job at any restaurant or estate you wished. Are you staying with Elodie or moving on to something else?"

Leo blinks. "Do you have room for me on your ship?"

"If you'll feed us this well, I could be convinced to let you stay."

"I'll think about it." Leo rubs his chin. "Although, I got an offer from a place on Armstrong while we were there. I was also thinking about a visit to Lewei."

"I would highly recommend against that." Vanti leans across the table.

"I wouldn't suggest anyone visit Lewei, but especially not you. Your family connections make you extremely vulnerable."

Elodie frowns. "I was hoping to go there."

Vanti raises one brow. "Why?"

"I've never been. It looks so exotic! Especially Luna City."

"I won't by flying there any time soon." Arun shakes his head as he picks up a roll and pulls it apart. "You'll have to find a ride with someone else."

At his words, Vanti leans back, the tension draining from her body. "Listen to your new captain. He's a wise man."

"Speaking of wise..." I take a scoop of mashed potatoes and dump a big pat of butter on top. "Do you still understand all of that astrophysics stuff? I don't remember you ever talking about that when I used to visit on Kaku."

Elodie shrugs. "Most people find quantum physics boring. It's always been a hobby of mine."

Arun nods. "I can confirm—'norms' don't like astromechanics. Or philosophical mechanics and basic engine construction, for that matter." He waits until Elodie looks away, then mouths at me, "She doesn't have a clue."

I guess the farther we've gotten from the other universe, the less Elodie remembers. Or maybe my cousin thinks he's funny. "You never explained how you figured out all of the alternate reality stuff. Did Altabelle and No'Neill tell you they were from another reality?" I watch the professor from the corner of my eye, but he's too engaged with his calculations to notice my deliberate provocation.

Leo starts laughing and points at Vanti. "She made me watch *Ancient TēVē*. Every multi-universe and alternate reality show out there. And it told us nothing."

Vanti drops her head into her hands. "That is fifteen hours of my life I will never get back."

"Which one was the best?" I can't resist asking.

She groans again.

"I liked the cruise ship one." Leo downs the last swig of his drink and rises to start clearing the table. "I wish there were more."

I laugh. "*Galaxy Cruise: The Movie*? That's one of my favorites!"

"It was completely unrealistic," Vanti complains.

"Well, duh. It's supposed to be funny, not real. Anyway, the book was better."

"There's a book?!" Vanti thuds her forehead against the table.

"A whole series." I wink at Leo. "I'll send you a link."

Before they can answer, the audio pings, and Fortenoy's voice echoes through the cabin. "We've docked at SK2. Welcome home. Now get off my ship."

If you enjoyed this story, and would like more Space Janitor, you can get a free story on my website, https://juliahuni.com. I'll keep you up to date on my next Space Janitor novel, and you can find out more about my other books.

AUTHOR'S NOTE

February 2023

Hi Reader,

Thanks for reading! I grabbed the template for this note from the last Space Janitor book, and was astounded to realize it's been a year since I published Triana and Ty's last adventure! My publishing schedule hasn't actually slowed down, but I put out five books in other series last year, so it might have seemed like that.

If you liked this book, please consider leaving a review on your retailer, Bookbub, or Goodreads. Reviews help other readers find stories they'll like. They also tell me what you like, so I can write more.

Speaking of which, did you like getting Vanti's point of view in this story? I've had a few readers request she get her own books, so this one is a possible jumping-off point. What do you think? Should I write a series with Vanti, Arun, Elodie, Leo and Apawllo? Shoot me a note at Julia@juli ahuni.com, and let me know what you think.

If you haven't joined my newsletter list yet, you can sign up on my website, and I'll let you know when my next book is coming. You can also download free prequels and find out about sales. I promise not to SPAM you, but I will keep you updated on what I've been up to.

If you're curious about the other projects I've been working on, I published a series of romantic comedies under the (super secret!) pen name Lia Huni. If you like closed-door, small-town romantic comedy, then you might enjoy those stories, too. I'm currently finishing up the first draft of the fourth book under that name.

After that, I'll be back to my *Colonial Explorer Corps* series or maybe the new Vanti series.

And if you're looking for *Galaxy Cruise: The Movie*, there isn't one, yet. But there definitely is a book series, although it isn't mine.

As always, I need to thank a few people. Thanks to my sprint team who keep me writing when I really don't want to: A.M. Scott, Hillary Avis, Paula Lester, Kate Pickford, Lou Cadle, and your *Old Pal, Marcus* Alexander Hart. We lost Tony James Slater—don't worry, he's still alive, but with a toddler on the loose, he can't write from midnight to four am (Down Under) anymore.

Paula at Polaris Editing polished my manuscript to perfection, for which I thank her profusely. Any mistakes you find, I undoubtedly added after she was done! My deepest appreciation goes to my alpha reader and sister, Anne Marie, and my beta readers: Anne Kavcic, Barb Collishaw, Jenny Avery, Larry Searing, and Paul Godtland. They caught all of the plot holes and inconsistencies that a multi-verse story is bound to create!

My grateful thanks go to my faithful readers who keep asking for more Space Janitor. It goes without saying (but I'll say it anyway): I write these for you!

Thanks to my husband, David, who manages my business, and to Les at GermanCreative for the beautiful cover.

And of course, thanks to the Big Guy for making all things possible.

ALSO BY JULIA HUNI

Colonial Explorer Corps Series:

The Earth Concurrence

The Grissom Contention

The Saha Declination

Colonial Explorer Corps: The Academy Years (books 1-3)

The Darenti Paradox

Recycled World Series:

Recycled World

Reduced World

Space Janitor Series:

The Vacuum of Space

The Dust of Kaku

The Trouble with Tinsel

Orbital Operations

Glitter in the Stars

Sweeping S'Ride

Triana Moore, Space Janitor (the complete series)

Tales of a Former Space Janitor

The Rings of Grissom

Planetary Spin Cycle

Waxing the Moon of Lewei

Former Space Janitor (books 1-3)

Changing the Speed of Light Bulbs

The Phoenix and Katie Li

Luna City Limited

Krimson Empire (with Craig Martelle):

Krimson Run

Krimson Spark

Krimson Surge

Krimson Flare

Krimson Empire (the complete series)

ROMANTIC COMEDY (AS LIA HUNI)

Stolen Kisses

Stolen Love Song

Stolen Heart Strings

FOR MORE INFORMATION

Use this QR code to join my newsletter and stay up-to-date on all my publishing:

Printed in Great Britain
by Amazon

22693976R00138